X MARKS THE PAST

X MARKS THE PAST

REG RAWLINS, PSYCHIC INVESTIGATOR
BOOK TWENTY-TWO

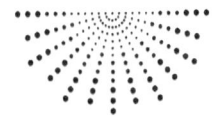

P.D. WORKMAN

PD WORKMAN

ISBN: 9781774687444 (KDP Paperback)
ISBN: 9781774687451 (KDP Hardcover)
ISBN: 9781774687475 (Lulu Paperback)
ISBN: 9781774687468 (Large Print)
ISBN: 9781774687482 (Digital)
ISBN: 9781774687499 (Auto-narrated audiobook)

ALSO BY P.D. WORKMAN

FIND MORE BOOKS AT PDWORKMAN.COM

MYSTERY/SUSPENSE:

Reg Rawlins, Psychic Detective
Paranormal Mystery & Adventure

What the Cat Knew

A Psychic with Catitude

A Catastrophic Theft

Night of Nine Tails

The Immortal's Key

Yule's Sinister Spell

Fairy Blade Unmade

Web of Nightmares

A Whisker's Breadth

Skunk Man Swamp

Magic Ain't A Game

Without Foresight

Careful of Thy Wishes

Time to Your Elf

Undiscovered Tomb

Missing Powers

Thrice Spared

Cloaked Campaign

Sleepwalker's Sanctuary

Cat Tales in the Swamp (Short Story)

Tainted Truffle Treachery

A Fowl Play on Christmas Day (Christmas crossover story)

Lunar Lies

X Marks the Past

Spellbound Statues (Coming Soon)

Fur and Fury (Coming Soon)

Kenzie Kirsch Medical Thrillers

Unlawful Harvest

Doctored Death

Dosed to Death

Gentle Angel

Rushin' Death

Posed for Death

Death of a Corpse

Endowed with Death

Shattered to Death

Captured in Death

Currying Death (Coming Soon)

Healed to Death (Coming Soon)

Death's Charm (Coming Soon)

A Bleeding Hearts Valley Thriller

An Abrupt Departure (Coming Soon)

AND MORE AT PDWORKMAN.COM

To forever friends

* * *

CHAPTER ONE

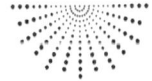

*R*eg was surprised to find the door to Marian's business, Psychic Beginnings, locked. As far as she knew, Marian kept regular hours, and was always at her storefront during the afternoon and evening, prime time for a psychic consultant. Reg preferred working at night, often staying up until dawn conducting seances and other psychic consultations. Midnight, the witching hour, was the best time to reach through the veil and contact those on the other side.

Also the time of day that people were the most vulnerable to suggestion, especially where it concerned ghostly and mystical happenings. It was a time-honored tradition to tell ghost stories and to invoke the spooky, scary, and macabre after dark.

A very profitable time of day for someone in Reg's business.

But most of Marian's business, in the small storefront on Main Street, took place in the late afternoon and early evening. By the time midnight rolled around, she was probably asleep in her bed.

Reg gave the knob another twist, as if she might have been mistaken the first time and the mechanism was just sticking. But no, it was locked. In the middle of the day when Marian should have been there.

Maybe she was sick or had needed to go out of town to visit a sick relative or attend a funeral, something that was last-minute, so she hadn't had time to tell everyone.

Not that Marian was obligated to tell Reg what she was up to. While Reg had not gotten along with Marian when they had first met, wary of her rival in the psychic consultations business, she had come to respect Marian during her stay in Black Sands, and they had gradually fallen into a fledgling friendship.

And Marian had once helped Reg with a particularly stubborn problem involving spectral spiders.

Which was why Reg had hoped to meet with Marian today. A little problem that she figured fell within Marian's psychic wheelhouse.

The doorknob was unusually warm in Reg's hand. It must have been in the sun all afternoon and had absorbed a lot of heat. Reg let go and studied it.

She had never particularly noticed the doorknob before. A quick twist and she was into Marian's space. Only this time, finding herself locked out, did she stop to look at it. It seemed to be made of old brass, tarnished and darkened around hand-carved ornamentation. Two curved swords or sabers crossed to form an X, surrounded by stars, curlicues, and symbols she didn't recognize. Something that might have made sense to someone three hundred years ago. Or to the more modern witches of Black Sands.

Reg gathered her red box braids in both hands to push them back behind her shoulders while she leaned forward to scrutinize the carvings.

It was an old lock. Not hard to pick or, with her recently discovered telekinetic abilities, to manipulate mentally. But she didn't want to break into Marian's business. She wanted to talk to Marian. Getting inside her storefront while Marian was out wouldn't do Reg a lick of good.

Sighing, she turned away from Marian's storefront and headed toward The Crystal Bowl.

The restaurant Reg had first gone to the day she arrived in Black Sands was still her go-to place to eat. It was within walking distance of the guest cottage she rented from Sarah and welcoming to most of the very diverse races found within the small town.

Though they *had* barred Reg from service there at one point. Corvin had said they would get over it and forget about her heritage quickly enough, and he had been right. Within a few weeks, Reg had once again been able to patronize her favorite eatery without any opposition.

When she opened the door and walked into the warm restaurant, the aroma of roasted garlic and herbs washed over her and made her stomach growl. Reg headed straight for the bar. She boosted herself up on the stool and arranged her brightly colored skirt. Bill, a ghostly pale bartender, was on duty. He nodded and smiled at her. "What'll it be?"

Reg was not normally opposed to a couple of drinks with dinner, but she'd felt like she was in a fog all day, and she worried that any amount of alcohol would send her into a stupor for the evening when she needed to be focused on her clients. She might be able to convince a client that her drifting off at the seance table was a trance but, to give her clients the best possible experience, she needed to be awake and alert.

"Start me with a Coke," she suggested.

"*Just* Coke?"

Reg nodded. "Need to be clear-headed tonight."

He raised his brows in disbelief but didn't say anything. He went about pulling a chilled glass of Coke for her.

"Meeting someone tonight?"

"Well, I had planned to, but I don't know now."

He placed the glass in front of her. "Your favorite warlock?" he suggested.

Reg felt a flush of warmth spreading across her back and neck and knew that her least favorite warlock had just entered the room. Her mortal enemy and the only one who could get her heart pumping like that just by being close.

She turned her head and found Corvin there, as she had expected. Tall, dark, and handsome, with a long black cape around his shoulder. His small beard was impeccably trimmed, and he might have walked right off a movie set, cast for the role of the villainous warlock.

Corvin smiled at Reg, raising goosebumps all along her arms and neck. She gave a shiver and took a few swallows of the Coke, which did not give her the fortification she needed.

Corvin walked over to the bar and joined Reg uninvited, signaling to Bill for a tumbler of Jack Daniels.

"Regina," he purred in greeting.

"I'm not in the mood today," Reg warned.

"The mood for what?" Corvin countered, giving her an innocent look.

"This," she made a gesture to take in the two of them together, "the whole flirtation and seduction thing. I just want to get something to eat. I have clients to deal with tonight. I don't have time for a bunch of nonsense."

"I see," he murmured. "Well, that does present difficulties, doesn't it?" He leaned closer, and she could smell the heady scent of roses as his pheromones washed over her.

"Corvin..." she growled a warning.

Bill placed a glass in front of Corvin, casting a solicitous glance at Reg. "You okay, Reg?"

She was fighting her attraction to Corvin, dizzy with his charms. It was obvious that she was tired. She would normally have been faster, able to raise a psychic shield against the effect of the pheromones and to reflect the heat he exuded back at him. She touched her temple, trying to concentrate and to raise the energy she needed to fight him off.

"Don't let him..." she said vaguely. She couldn't put her concern into words. Corvin would do everything within his power to get her out of the restaurant to somewhere private he could convince her to yield her powers.

It had happened once, before she had known anything about the curse he carried enabling or requiring him to consume the powers of others. When someone with Corvin's affliction stripped the powers from a victim, he did not return them. But circumstances had required him to do just that in order to save Reg's life, and he had.

Making him not only her enemy, but also her savior. Then and the many times since he had stepped in and assisted Reg in fighting another foe or giving her the energy boost she needed to protect or rescue others. Most recently, a pack of werewolves.

Of course, Reg had helped Corvin a handful of times as well. Having held the same powers and been in each other's minds several times, Reg could not close the psychic connection between them fully. However much she wished to separate from Corvin and block him from reading any of her thoughts or feelings, it was impossible.

"Release her," Bill ordered Corvin.

Corvin looked at Bill, his eyes cold. "You have no authority over me."

"If you want to eat or drink in this restaurant, I do. Or you will be kicked out. Banned, if it continues."

"I'm just having a drink with my friend. Reg does not object, do you, Reg?"

He held her gaze, smiling, wrapping the tendrils of his mind around her, tightening his grip, sneaking into the deeper crevices of her brain.

"You're tired," he observed. "What's been going on? You're not sleeping?"

Reg made an effort to push him out, with little effect.

"Release her," Bill ordered again. "We will not tolerate this kind of dark power being used in this establishment."

Corvin stared at Bill and, for a moment, Bill's expression

slackened as Corvin was able to use his influence on the bartender as well. With his attention briefly distracted from Reg, she was able to rally and raise a psychic shield against his intrusion, throwing him out of her mind as forcefully as possible.

Corvin gripped the bar for a moment as if he had lost his balance and might fall. He steadied himself and looked back at Reg, smiling. "Cat still has some claws."

Reg covered a yawn. "Even when I'm tired," she told him. She looked back at Bill. "Thanks."

Bill studied Corvin for a moment longer, blinking slowly, then nodded and turned to serve someone else down the bar.

"Take care," he warned Reg. "Do not let down your guard."

CHAPTER TWO

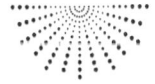

S hall we…?" Corvin suggested, nodding to the tables.

Reg *was* there to eat and so was Corvin. They might as well eat together, as long as Reg didn't have any alcohol and stayed on top of her game. She wouldn't give him another chance to sneak past her defenses.

"I suppose," Reg agreed with a shrug.

Corvin shook his head, eyes glittering. "Such enthusiasm. Has our relationship become such a bore?"

It was not even close to being boring, but Reg enjoyed pulling Corvin's chain. She covered a fake yawn. "Well… we have known each other for a couple of years now… maybe the magic has gone out of our relationship." The fake yawn turned into a real one, which Reg tried unsuccessfully to repress. "Oh. I am tired," she admitted.

"Why aren't you sleeping?"

Reg made a motion to brush off this question. She did not want to discuss sleep or why she wasn't sleeping. Dinner with Corvin would keep her awake and alert. A few cups of coffee would help. She was sure she would be fine once she got through her afternoon slump. Her evening clients would have no idea she wasn't sleeping well.

A waitress came over and asked what they were drinking so she could keep them supplied. Neither Reg nor Corvin needed to look at the menus. They had been going to The Crystal Bowl for long enough to know what was on offer and what they liked. They placed their orders, and the waitress retreated to pass them on to the kitchen.

Reg let her eyes wander around the restaurant. She kept her shield up against intrusion from Corvin so he would not be able to enthrall her, but otherwise ignored him.

A woman came out of the ladies room to return to her table. An older woman with a green turban, glittering jewelry, pouchy eyes, and a drooping face. Marian. Reg had not been able to find her at work, but had been drawn to the restaurant to find her. Marian sat alone, scrolling on her phone.

Reg wondered if she should invite Marian to join them. She and Corvin were not there for a romantic date. Marian wouldn't exactly be a third wheel. Corvin turned his head to see who Reg was looking at. He gave her a sour look.

"I don't think we need to invite the old maid to join us."

"She's by herself. And don't call her an old maid. She's not that old."

"Old enough to be your mother."

"Well… maybe. But she's not exactly *ancient*."

"I would have thought that by now you would have figured out that in our world, chronological age has very little to do with anything," Corvin pointed out.

Corvin, Sarah, and other magical practitioners Reg knew claimed to be centuries old. And then there were the immortals, who might be thousands of years old.

"So, how old is Marian?" Reg asked, "And who cares whether she is married or not? *You're* not married."

Though Corvin had been married several times, mostly to nonmagical partners who had therefore predeceased him long ago. And to a witch named Verity who had made herself into a powerful sorceress. But she was now gone as well.

"The point isn't whether Marian is married or not. She has never been married, therefore making her an old maid. And worse than that, she *acts* like an old maid, and I don't need to be around someone like that."

"Are you afraid that she'll try to snare you in matrimony? Or just be a downer?"

Corvin raised a brow. "I find neither one particularly palatable. I'm here to enjoy my meal, not *endure* it."

While Marian's face was naturally unhappy, Reg wasn't sure that indicated her actual outlook. She seemed friendly enough when Reg would visit with her and didn't spend her time bemoaning what a terrible life she had. She had recently adopted a new cat, which seemed to have lifted her spirits.

That sounded like something one might say about an old maid.

Reg picked up her glass and had a few swallows of Coke, then returned it to the ring of condensation on the table. She was marshaling arguments for why they should invite Marian to join them, even though she didn't particularly want to. It just seemed cruel to sit there with Corvin while Marian languished in the corner by herself.

While she was thinking of why it was the right thing to do, another familiar figure entered the dining area.

He was even more handsome than Corvin, with close-cropped hair, a carefully trimmed goatee, and sparkling green eyes. October Phoenix. A man with a lupine nature. Reg smiled upon seeing him.

But October didn't have eyes for her. Not even noticing Reg or Corvin, he headed straight across the dining room to Marian's table.

Reg could feel Corvin laughing, though, when she looked at him, his face was smooth, with no hint of a smile.

"Well, then. Maybe our Maid Marian isn't such a prude after all," he told her.

"We don't know anything about them or their relationship." Reg watched October greet Marian and sit across the table from her. They did not kiss or hold hands. But they didn't look like just casual friends, either. Was it possible they were related? Mother and son? Brother and sister? Distant cousins? Marian was not any kind of skin changer; maybe they were old friends. Or maybe October was simply there to consult with Marian. Perhaps he just wanted to put her skills as a psychic to work.

But if October wanted a psychic, why hadn't he come to Reg? She knew that her skills were head and shoulders above Marian's and was sure that October must have recognized that fact. He knew how she could communicate with the wolves telepathically. That she'd had the power it took to break the magical bonds that had held them prisoner. He had to know Reg's psychic gifts were significantly stronger than Marian's.

"You look like you swallowed a lemon." Corvin looked at her over the top of his glass as he considered his drink and took another sip. "I thought you felt sorry for Marian."

"I... I don't feel anything for her."

Certainly not jealousy.

Reg immediately scolded herself for thinking that. Who had said anything about jealousy? She had no reason to be jealous of Marian or the fact that October had joined her for dinner. Reg already had a dinner partner nearly as handsome as October.

"Nearly as handsome?" Corvin demanded.

Reg smirked and reestablished the psychic shield, trying to keep him from accessing any of her thoughts. "I thought you didn't care about looks."

"When did I ever say that? I put a lot of time into ensuring I am... presentable. If one is to go fishing, one must bait the hook."

The thought of Corvin trawling for innocent young women who would have no idea how he could take their powers from them was repugnant, something that always made Reg feel physically sick. She grimaced and shook her head.

"So you *like* October?" Corvin asked. "How much do you know about him?"

"I know enough," Reg asserted. "And it's not like we're dating. I just know him… from the business with Jake and the wolves. We're… acquaintances. Maybe friends."

"So he can date who he likes."

Reg darted a look back at October and Marian. "You don't think they're really dating, do you?" Reg asked. "I mean…. Marian looks so much older than October."

"And now we're back at age again. I thought you were not concerned with age. You don't know anything about either of their backgrounds. For all you know, October could be a hundred years older than Marian. What then? Then you wouldn't mind them getting together?"

Reg shook her head, frowning. "I didn't say that I wanted them to get together. Or not get together. I don't care. I just think… it looks strange, that's all."

The waitress brought them their dinners and hovered for a moment to make sure that everything was in order and they didn't need anything else. Corvin nodded and smiled before waving her off. Drunk with Corvin's charms, the waitress stumbled away with stars in her eyes.

But there was no reason for concern if she didn't have any powers. Corvin would not be interested in her.

Reg and Corvin were silent for a few minutes, digging in and appreciating their dinners. Reg looked over at October and Marian again.

"What do you think they're talking about? Are they old friends? Or is it business?"

Corvin didn't look at them. "You're the psychic. And I thought you didn't care."

"I don't. I'm just curious. They're… an unusual match. I think it must be a business consultation."

She knew it was bad form to read someone's thoughts without their knowledge and permission, but she pushed her thoughts a little closer to Marian's and October's, hoping to get an idea of what they were thinking and feeling without intruding too much. October's head went up and he looked around warily. He noticed Reg for the first time and acknowledged her with a smile and a nod. Then he returned to his conversation with Marian.

"That was reckless," Corvin told her.

"I was just… wondering. I wasn't pushing."

"Yes. Of course. And how would your friends react if they knew you were trying to read them?"

"I wasn't trying to read their minds. Just their… expressions and body language. Like I always have. I'm good at reading nonverbal cues."

"That's what the nonmagical world told you, but that isn't necessarily the truth."

"Well…" Reg tried to think of another argument or explanation for why she had been trying to read them. "I just don't want anyone getting hurt."

"From a business consultation?"

"I… what business is it of yours what I think or do? You're not my partner or my boss. You don't have any more right to know what I'm thinking than…"

"Than you do of knowing what Marian and October are discussing?"

"Just eat your fish," Reg snapped.

She sipped her Coke and watched October in her peripheral vision for a few minutes. Everything seemed friendly between October and Marian.

She could almost convince herself of it. That they were just friends or business associates. But deep down in a hidden place inside her, she couldn't help the green worm of jealousy that turned and twisted inside her.

CHAPTER THREE

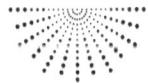

October and Marian were heading out before Corvin and Reg finished their after-dinner coffees. The two of them stopped by Reg's side, smiling pleasantly.

"Of, I didn't see you here," Marian said, though it rang false to Reg's ears. Marian had probably seen them. Or October had told her they were there. "How are you, Reg?"

She said nothing to Corvin, shunning him like much of the magical community of Black Sands.

"I'm fine. Actually, I was hoping to see you. Maybe I could set up an appointment? To consult with you on a matter."

"Oh, of course. Give me a call, and I will be happy to set up a date and time for you."

"Do you have your calendar with you now?" Reg reached for her phone to open her digital calendar, though she never actually used it. All her appointments were written down in the paper planner on her kitchen island, where she and Sarah had access to it.

"Oh, no." Marian made a motion for her to put it back away. "I don't keep it electronically." She shook her head slightly. "I'm surprised you do."

"Well…" Reg put her phone into her pocket. "I really don't. But why would it surprise you?"

"Oh, you know. Psychics and electronics. And any time-keeping system, really."

"What about psychics and electronic calendars?"

"Because psychics have such difficulty in writing down their schedules. And electronics just make things worse. Recording a psychic's schedule in an electronic calendar is almost impossible. I don't know anyone who has been able to do it, honestly. A real psychic, I mean. Not those shams."

Reg thought about all her many failed attempts to record her plans in her electronic calendar. Friends said that it would be easy. She just had to tap in the appointments as they were made, and they would be right there in front of her. And if she forgot something, an alarm would go, reminding her. But every attempt, started with the certainty that she would be successful this time, ended in utter failure. Confusion reigned. She couldn't find the entries she had already input, even with the search function. It didn't remind her when it was supposed to. She ended up with double bookings.

"I… had no idea," she said lamely. "No one ever told me."

"That's why my paper calendar is at my shop, and you can only get on there if you call me while I am there. Give me a ring, and I'll find a time to meet."

"Okay, I will."

"Or you can always drop by," Marian said, smiling.

"Well… that's what I tried to do today, but you were here."

"Oh. So I am!" Marian laughed. "Well, put your psychic skills to work next time and come when I'm there."

"Uh, okay." Reg's eyes went to October. "So… you guys know each other?"

"Sure, Marian and I are old friends," October informed her. Something about his green eyes made her think that he might be lying to her. But why lie about something that didn't make any difference to anyone? Maybe he was just distracted.

Or maybe he didn't want Reg to know that he had been consulting a psychic. When he could have come to see her. Reg had thought they were close enough that he would come to her if he needed help. Even though they hadn't known each other very long, they had worked closely to save the wolf pack, and Reg was officially a friend of the pack. Didn't that make her October's friend too?

"Maybe we could all get together one day," Reg suggested.

Marian looked at Corvin with disdain and said nothing. October's lip curled in a snarl, but he spoke calmly and politely. "Perhaps it befits a practitioner of your caliber to be friendly with one of the cursed, but I will have nothing to do with them personally."

Reg's face burned. October and Corvin had both been part of the council formed to deal with Jake and his experiments. October as a member of the pack and Corvin as the leader of the warlock coven. The circle had also included Letticia, the leader of Sarah's coven, and others Reg didn't know. Reg had assumed that since they had worked together, October would not object to doing something with Corvin.

It had been a stupid, impulsive thing to say. As if they were teenagers going to school together and going on a double date or group date would be less awkward and stressful than a single date. But they were not all going to be friends. If Reg wanted to do something with October or get closer to him, she needed to do that alone. Corvin could not be part of the equation.

She could only blame the stupidity of her suggestion on the brain fog she was suffering from her sleepless night and the befuddling power of Corvin's pheromones.

"I meant... you and me and Marian," she amended. "We could ask Sarah along, or someone else... just do something as a group. Aren't there any community events coming up...? Spring equinox is coming up, isn't it?"

"Perhaps we could work something out," October said stiffly. "We'll see."

He and Marian left together. Reg watched them go, October touching Marian's elbow. Reg's face was still burning as she turned her attention back to Corvin. The hum of conversation around them resumed. She had been unaware it had stopped.

Corvin gazed back at her, unperturbed. "It comes as no surprise to me how other people feel about my affliction. I have lived with these prejudices for a long time. Much longer than you have been alive."

It always surprised her to remember that the handsome, distinguished-looking warlock was not in his forties but centuries old.

Reg took a long sip of her coffee. "I didn't mean to make everyone uncomfortable. I just didn't think."

"Few people are as open-minded as you, Reg."

And her feelings about Corvin were just as negative as anyone else's. Maybe more so, since no one else had been through what she had with Corvin, having her powers stolen away, and dealing with many subsequent attacks and close calls. She had to be crazy to keep being pulled in by Corvin. But his charms were just so… charming. She was resigned to the fact that their lives were intertwined and she couldn't do anything about it. And Corvin was so persistent. Even when she was determined, she found herself unable to resist him for long.

At Corvin's signal, the waitress brought over the bill and a credit card folder for Corvin. He glanced at the strip of curled paper and signed it with an X, returning it to the waitress with a black, unmarked credit card.

CHAPTER FOUR

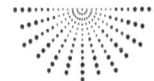

*I*n the shaky reality of Reg's dream, the sleek cat, all black but for a white patch on her chest, roamed the green forest, watching for intruders, slinking through the undergrowth, her nose twitching, seeking out the smells of other animals or, worse, humans tramping through her sacred lands.

Humans could not be trusted near the sacred. They were too immature to understand how to deal with these things. They were like kittens who didn't know where to put their paws and would not listen to their wise old dam who had lifetimes of experience.

Humans had to be kept away at all costs, and that was her job.

She came across the rank canine smell of a wolf and parted her lips to snuffle it deeper, to taste and smell the identity of the intruder. Male. A fully mature adult.

She was familiar with the wildness of him. Not just wolf, but man too. He used his man form rarely. Nose-blind, defenseless creatures without a pack, fangs, or claws. The cat followed the scent trail just above the ground, following it as the wolf crept through the forest, watching it, guarding it, just as she guarded her territory.

They were not enemies, as different as they were. Their territories overlapped and they were both charged with keeping the sacred spaces safe: keeping a careful watch, weaving protective spells, howling a warning or, when necessary, using tooth and nail to drive a persistent intruder away.

She came within sight of the wolf and, for a few minutes, just crouched there, eyes and ears trained on him, motionless.

The wind shifted and he caught her scent. He turned around, seeking the source of the smell. He approached, keeping low to the ground, non-threatening, ears pointing forward. They knew each other well, their paths crossing many times. The wolf touched his nose to hers, then backed off.

She asked for news. He shared his discoveries of the past few days, which she memorized. She returned the favor, recalling any encounters or important pieces of information he might need to know.

There were an increasing number of infringements upon their land by humans. The creatures were multiplying and spreading out, not satisfied to stay in their own allotted territory. Their kits did not believe the ancient stories, did not accept the ancient wisdom of staying away from these sacred spaces, respecting the rites that had kept the forests safe for hundreds of years.

They would cut down trees, start fires, hunt the wild animals, and pollute the water, air, and land. The guardians needed to do everything within their power to prevent that from happening.

* * *

Reg awoke from her restless sleep and dreams. Try as she might, she could not find sleep again, even though she'd only had an hour or two of disrupted sleep. The hot sun shone through the windows, and she was too uncomfortable with the light and heat to fall asleep again.

Eventually, she crawled out of bed. Starlight meowed and wound his way around her ankles.

Reg bent down to scratch the tuxedo cat's ears and chin, smiling affectionately at his mismatched green and blue eyes. With her thumb, she stroked the splash of white fur in the third eye position that gave him his name.

"Yes, good morning to you, too! Already starving this early in the morning?"

He wasn't used to her being up that early, so he couldn't have been too hungry.

"Do you know, I dreamt I was a cat?" she told him, scratching his ears and stroking his fur while he meowed piteously, clearly wanting breakfast, not chatter. "A black cat," she went on, thinking back to the dream where, as a cat, she had groomed her fur, "a black cat, with a white mark here." She touched his white chest. "But not as big as your shirt."

He snapped at her hand to remind her that he didn't like to be poked in the chest, then immediately bumped her hand with his forehead in apology, still begging for food, and tried to lead her to the kitchen.

She did not need his meows or for him to physically lead her to the kitchen to know what he wanted. She could sense his feelings and thoughts, but not in words, like a human; it was something less defined than that.

But he still felt like he needed to take her in hand and walk her through the process to hurry things along. He *was* hungry and didn't have all day to wait for her.

"Okay, okay. I will get you your food," Reg assured him. She followed Starlight to the fridge and opened the door to see what she had on hand. Sarah had brought a tuna fish casserole over from the main house. Reg's landlady often brought over leftovers or cooked for Reg, seeming to believe that Reg could not fend for herself, even if her fridge were filled to bursting. Maybe Sarah was used to cooking for more people than just herself and couldn't help but make too much.

Reg appreciated the friendly gesture, but rarely ate Sarah's food. She fed what she could to Starlight and hid the rest in the garbage. If Sarah could pretend not to see the rest of the food in Reg's crowded fridge, she could pretend not to see it in the trash, either. Sarah was not supposed to be snooping around the guest cottage anyway. In some circles, landlords actually respected their tenants' privacy and didn't let themselves in at random intervals to clean, cook, decorate, or add clients to the calendar.

Not that Reg didn't appreciate all these efforts. Sarah was more of a mother to her than many of the foster mothers she had lived with as a child. At least Sarah understood Reg's unusual gifts—better than Reg did. Her foster families, social workers, and doctors had all thought that there was something wrong with her head and had done what they could to quash her unusual behaviors and to make her behave more normally.

Normal was overrated.

Reg was much happier living as a psychic, and whatever else she was, in Black Sands.

Minus any encounters with evil beings.

She could do without those.

Reg dished out some of the tuna casserole for Starlight as he purred, rubbed against her legs, and reached his paws up to the counter and her elbows, trying to encourage her to get his breakfast ready faster.

"It's coming, it's coming," she promised him.

He gave one more loud meow as she put the bowl on the floor and started gobbling it down, making annoying chuffing sounds.

"Slow down, or you're just going to throw it up again."

Reg suspected that if left to his own devices, Starlight could get his own breakfast. He had very strong gifts of his own, probably stronger than Reg's. But they enjoyed the owner/pet relationship. Or maybe it was a feeder/pet or feeder/master relationship; neither of them was under the illusion that Reg actually owned Starlight or was *his* master.

CHAPTER FIVE

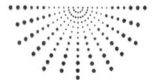

o being owns another," Harrison agreed, startling Reg so that she let out a little shriek.

She put her hand over her pounding heart. Harrison, an immortal who had protected her when she was a child, was standing a few feet away in the living room.

The tall, lanky man wore what looked like green silk pajamas embroidered with dragons, cowboy boots, and a wide, poofy hat that drooped down the sides of his head. His thin handlebar mustache stood straight out on either side.

"Sheesh. How long have you been standing there?" Reg demanded. "I've asked you before not to sneak up on me."

"I did not sneak." Harrison demonstrated a few mincing tiptoes, exaggerated like a cartoon character.

"Well, give me some kind of warning you are there."

"Reg," he said seriously, looking into her eyes, "I am here."

Reg rolled her eyes and shook her head. "Before you startle me," she reminded him. But she knew it was no use. As someone who could move forward or backward in time, Harrison really didn't understand the point of positioning his actions in a certain order.

"You're going to make coffee?" Harrison asked.

Reg nodded. "Yes. I definitely need my caffeine this morning."

"Can I press the button?"

"You can press the button."

Harrison joined her beside the coffee machine and pressed the big Brew button. The machine started to gurgle and hiss, sending Harrison into a fit of giggles. He watched the machine, his face two inches away from it, as it brewed and started to stream fresh, hot coffee into the carafe.

Reg opened the fridge to look at the offerings jammed into it, knowing Harrison would want something to eat, and it might as well be something she already had rather than his making food materialize out of thin air.

"Leftover pizza?" she suggested. "Pepperoni?"

"Yes," Harrison approved, still staring at the coffee machine. "And ice cream?"

Reg pulled a random pint of ice cream out of the freezer, hoping he wasn't going to put it on top of the pizza.

"Cold or warm?"

"Ice cream is cold."

"Yes. Do you want to eat the pizza cold, or do you want it heated up in the microwave?"

"Oh, in the microwave!" He sounded like an excited child offered a trip to Disneyland.

Reg put a couple of pieces of pizza on each of two plates and put the first in the microwave.

By the time both plates of pizza were heated, the coffee had finished brewing. Harrison carefully poured it into a mug and presented it to Reg, smiling proudly.

"Thank you," Reg told him politely.

He himself did not drink coffee, but he had a blast making it. He accepted the pizza from Reg and rifled through the drawers.

"You don't need a fork," Reg told him. "Just use your fingers."

He nevertheless got out a two-pronged BBQ fork and a steak knife. He cut off neat triangles of pizza and somehow ate them off the fork without poking himself in the mouth or eye. Reg shook her head.

"So what are you doing here? Did you just come for a visit, or did you want to tell me something?"

Sometimes, he had a warning for her, aware of something that was going to happen in the near future. He might be concerned about her association with Corvin, who held a large portion of the powers of another immortal, Samyr Destine, also known as the witch doctor. Or Harrison might show up with Weston in tow. Weston, who he claimed was Reg's father. Reg didn't know if she actually had the blood of the immortals in her veins or if immortals reproduced through non-standard means, like the gods in Greek mythology, who conceived offspring through a wide variety of methods.

"Reg is happy here?" Harrison asked tentatively. "In this life?"

"Well, yes, I am. Black Sands is a good place for me." Reg looked around the guest cottage, neat and homey, certainly the nicest place she'd ever lived in since aging out of foster care. "It is comfortable. I have Starlight. I have friends."

"And coffee and pizza."

"Yes."

"And you miss nothing?"

Miss. What did Harrison mean by that?

"I don't want for anything," she said uncertainly. "I am making enough money to support myself and pay for the things I need. It's a good life."

"Without a mate?"

"Oh. Well." Reg's cheeks warmed. With her pale redhead complexion, her face was probably bright pink. "There is still time for me to find a mate if it's in the cards. And if not, I am happy without a mate."

"In the cards?" Harrison looked around.

"I don't know if I'm meant to find a mate or just live on my own. I'm okay being single."

She thought about Jake, the man she had once thought would be her mate for life, but who had turned out to be very different from what she had thought. He had not treated her well and had bound her to him without her knowledge. Looking back at the rotten way he had treated her while she'd been under his spell, she couldn't believe that she had thought it normal and wanted to stay with him.

If that was what it was like to have a mate, she was better off without one.

Harrison was walking around the living room with a piece of pizza in his hand, apparently having abandoned the use of the big fork. He looked carefully through Reg's shelves, and brought a package over to her. He laid it down in front of her on the island.

"What is in the cards?"

"Oh." Reg hadn't actually meant that she was going to read the tarot cards. She picked up the box and slid the deck from it. The cards were warm in her hands, vibrating with energy.

She normally didn't feel her gifts quite so strongly in the morning or when she was tired. Evening and night were when the world came alive for her. First thing in the morning was quite a different story; she normally didn't like to do much of anything.

Maybe it was because Harrison was there. Reg glanced at him, again smiling at his flamboyant outfit. Warlocks like Corvin and Davyn wore their sedate black cloaks, looking solemn and mysterious. Harrison's colorful and eccentric outfits, always slightly missing the mark, were much more fun. She wondered whether he was the only immortal who enjoyed human clothing so much, or whether most of them did.

How many immortals were even left in the world? Despite the name, the long-lived immortals could be killed by violence or magic if their opponents were strong enough, and Reg had only met Harrison, Weston, and the witch doctor personally. She didn't know if there were more immortals in the world or if any others visited the humans on her plane. The pantheons of gods that had once existed in various cultures around the world seemed to be dwindling to nothing.

Reg automatically started shuffling the cards, closing her eyes briefly to focus her energy on the deck, reaching out with all her senses to touch each one.

A card jumped the deck, landing on the island with a soft flap. Reg looked down at it. It had fallen face down. While she could pick it up without looking at it and shuffle it back into the deck, she knew better than that. A card that jumped the deck was probably significant.

She touched it on the back, waiting for a moment, then slid her thumbnail underneath and turned it over.

CHAPTER SIX

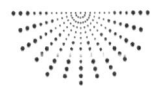

*I*t should have come as no surprise to Reg that the card that had jumped the deck was the Lovers. The card depicted a man and a woman in front of two trees; it represented deep connections, relationships, and choices. She and Harrison had just been talking about mates, so of course the Lovers card had shown up.

Did it represent a relationship she was already in? Someone who was out there waiting for her in the future? The fact that the card had jumped out of her hand suggested that it would quickly come into play. It signified something that was to happen soon.

She had planned to pick up the Lovers card, put it back in her deck, and then put away the deck. She had the answer that the querent had sought. *Was a mate in the cards for Reg? Apparently so.*

But when she grasped the card to pick it up and put it back in her deck, she experienced a chill, raising goosebumps all over her body. Reg closed her eyes and saw the cat and the wolf from her dream; suddenly, the wolf's eyes turned from yellow to green. The same color as October's eyes. Was *that* who the wolf in her dream was? It made sense that she would dream about him after seeing him at the restaurant.

She was drawn toward the handsome werewolf. But she didn't feel ready to start a romantic relationship so soon after what had happened with Jake. She had no desire to end up in that kind of situation again. Even setting aside the spell he'd bound her with, Jake had been arrogant and emotionally abusive, and she wasn't going to put up with that from any man again, no matter how attractive he was.

Reg let out her breath and opened her eyes again.

"I guess that answers your question," she told Harrison.

Starlight meowed. Reg looked at him and then looked around. Harrison was no longer in the room. Reg turned a full circle, checking whether he had just walked into another part of the cottage. Harrison did not have a clue about etiquette and how a guest should not just wander around the host's house without permission. Not that he had been an invited guest in the first place.

"Did he go?" she asked Starlight.

He meowed again. Of course Harrison had gone. And without even giving Starlight the usual pets and cuddles. The remainder of Harrison's pizza lay on the counter and the aroma of melted cheese and tomato sauce lingered in the air. The ice cream, when Reg looked around for it, was gone. That figured. Harrison had a sweet tooth and a definite taste for chocolate.

She slid the Lovers card back into the deck and smoothed the edges so she could no longer detect it with her fingertips. Yet she was still completely aware of where it was in the deck. She could still feel it there, in the center of her body. She reached for the box to put the deck back away, but the call of the deck in her hand was too strong. It did not *want* to be put back away.

"I don't have time for this," Reg said aloud. Although, of course, she had all the time in the world. She didn't have any psychic consultations until that evening. She had all morning and afternoon to do what she chose, and it certainly did not take hours to read tarot.

But she didn't want anything else to be revealed yet. She did not want more details about her future. Whether it involved October, Corvin, or any other potential mate. She just didn't want to know. With sheer determination, she put the deck of cards back into the box and closed the lid.

"There. That's that. I don't need any complications in my life right now. This is a good life, just like I told Harrison. Better than any situation I have been in before."

Ample food, shelter that was hers for as long as she needed it, friends, acceptance of her... quirks. Enough money that she didn't have to worry about her survival.

Jake was out of her life, and she was doing just fine without him or any other man.

Reg's phone vibrated. She had left it on the counter by the microwave, so she walked around the island to pick it up again. She looked at the caller ID.

October.

Reg looked around the room, expecting to see Harrison still standing somewhere, chuckling to himself about making October's name appear on her phone.

"Funny, Harrison," she told him, even though he was not visible. He could still be there, watching her and listening to her.

She waited for a few more rings before picking the phone up and sliding to answer the call.

"Hello?"

"Reg. Nice to hear from you."

"Uh... you called me,"

"Did I? It must have been a pocket dial. But I was thinking of you, so it is serendipitous."

"Or something," Reg muttered.

"What?"

"I just said… it's nice to hear from you, too. I was sorry we didn't get the chance to talk last night at the restaurant."

"Yes. Well, I was there to see Marian and, when I saw you, you were there with Corvin." October said his name with distaste.

"I thought that you and Corvin were friends," Reg said. "I thought he had told you about me, and that was how you knew what I was when we first met. And he helped with freeing the wolves…"

"As he is the leader of the coven, there are times that I need to talk with him or coordinate something with him. But a friend… no. I could not be a friend with one like him."

"Because of the curse. Because he is… a Hunter."

"There are predators, and there are predators," October said obliquely.

She supposed he was referring to himself, an apex predator when he took his wolf form, and Corvin, who preyed on weaker and uninformed practitioners, stealing the essence of who they were. She considered what Corvin did to be reprehensible. But she wasn't sure how much control he had over what he did when driven by his hunger. And certainly, he couldn't help the fact that he had been born with the curse. No more than Reg was responsible for the gifts she had been born with, or the upbringing that had shaped who she would become.

"So… maybe we could have dinner sometime," she suggested to October. "Not with Corvin or Marian or anyone else. Just you and me. To… catch up. Tell me what you've been doing since we freed the pack."

And what he had been talking to Marian about. She had the niggling need to know why he had been seeing Marian. Reg was sure that they were not connected romantically. That meant that he had gone to Marian for professional advice. Why Marian instead of Reg?

October hesitated. Reg reached out to him mentally, trying to coax him into agreeing with her.

Just to meet for supper. That wasn't a big commitment. People did it all the time without ulterior motives. Just two friends meeting briefly to catch up on each other's lives and enjoy each other's company.

"Yes... I guess we could get together," he agreed. "But not at The Crystal Bowl. There are too many eyes and ears there. Too much interest in what we might have to say to each other."

Reg's cheeks burned, realizing she had been one of those who had shown too much interest in October's affairs at The Crystal Bowl.

"Okay," she agreed. "Where do you want to meet?"

Reg's mind raced as she tried to think of a suitable place to meet. Somewhere private, but not too lonely. While she felt a strange pull toward October, she knew little about him and didn't want to put herself into a vulnerable position again. Not after Jake.

"How about the Moonlit Grotto?" she suggested. "It's pretty decent."

It was quiet, but not isolated. Off the beaten path and not patronized by as many practitioners as The Crystal Bowl, an established witch's hangout.

October considered, then agreed. "Okay. How about tonight at eight?"

"I have appointments later in the evening. Clients," Reg explained. "I don't suppose you could meet at... like... four or five? I would say yes to eight, but I have paying clients..." She was sure he was going to turn her down. Who wanted to eat supper that early?

"Fine," October agreed. "Five?"

"Okay. Good. Five o'clock."

"I'll see you then."

Reg hung up with a mixture of anticipation and dread.

She didn't have any romantic interest in October. Was she sending him the wrong signals? Was he expecting an intimate meal?

Not at five o'clock, surely.

Her heart was racing as she turned around to find Starlight sitting on the kitchen island, staring at her with his mismatched blue and green eyes.

"Well," she said to him. "I guess I'm seeing October tonight."

Reg took a deep breath and tried to calm herself. She had plenty to do before the dinner appointment rolled around. She just needed to focus.

She glanced at the tarot deck on the counter again, but she had already decided she didn't want to know anything more.

Instead, she would focus on preparing for her readings that evening. She would need to be able to focus on them and give them her full attention.

And not to think about October's green eyes and the strange pull she felt towards him.

CHAPTER SEVEN

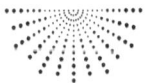

$\mathcal{I}$t seemed like the day was gone in the blink of an eye. It was time to get ready for dinner. Reg looked at herself in the mirror. She hadn't planned to change out of her standard "work uniform," the voluminous, brightly colored skirt, blouse, and a headscarf around her braids. It wasn't a date. It was just two acquaintances. Maybe friends. Getting together for a meal. But she found herself doubting her decision. Should she try something more mainstream? Change her flashy jewelry for something sedate? Maybe even some of her real gems?

As she gazed at herself in the mirror, Reg couldn't help but think about Harrison's question: "And you miss nothing?"

Was something missing from her life?

And if so, could October fill that hole?

She shook off the feeling. She had told Harrison that she was happy, and that was the truth. She had everything she wanted in her life. Things got a little rocky from time to time, and she always had to be on guard against Corvin and other possibly dangerous practitioners, but where in the world did anyone live without any danger? Someone walking across the street in suburbia could be mowed down by a drunk or elderly driver.

She was fine as she was. She didn't need to dress up for October. He already knew who she was and how she presented herself. Glamming herself up would just make him wonder what she was trying to hide. She didn't want him to think she was ashamed of who or what she was.

She fed Starlight, even though he'd probably already had enough food for the day. He was putting on a little weight. But Reg didn't think it was fair for her to go out for dinner and Starlight to go on a diet.

"I won't be late," she promised. "I'll be back in plenty of time for my first appointment."

Starlight ignored her, loudly chawing his food.

* * *

The Moonlit Grotto had just opened for evening business, so it was not full. A few early birds like Reg and October, mostly retirees who were probably going home to bed. The savory smells of garlic bread and cooking meat wafted from the kitchen.

Reg was just starting to wake up.

October had made it to the Grotto ahead of her. He was watching the door from the bar and, when he saw her come in, he slid down from his stool and joined her.

"Reg, good to see you." He stood there, awkward. Reg reached out a hand to him, since greeting him with a hug or kiss didn't seem appropriate. October looked relieved and took her hand. "Thanks." He gave her hand a squeeze and a brisk pump, then let it go.

Reg wondered briefly how werewolves generally greeted each other. Thinking about domestic dogs and their butt-sniffing when they met each other, she had to choke back a laugh. Not a socially appropriate greeting for a restaurant.

October frowned briefly, then motioned to a booth. "We're over here. Can I get you a drink? I don't know what you like."

Reg looked at the glass in October's hand. While it could have been any clear liquor, it looked like plain water. No ice or twist of lemon, just water. She remembered from dining out with him before that he only drank water. Knowing now that he was a werewolf, this preference made more sense. As did his disdain for sweets. His choice of meat and fish was not part of a low-carb or other trendy diet. It was his wolf nature. Just as Reg's siren nature had given her a definite preference for fresh seafood and water that had not been sitting in a bottle for weeks, absorbing all its chemical tastes.

But she still had plenty of human tastes as well. Coffee. Chocolate. Jack Daniels.

"A coffee," she suggested as they walked over to the table.

October flagged down a waitress and put in the request. They sat down.

"It doesn't keep you up all night?" October asked. "A lot of people won't drink coffee this late."

"I have clients until two or three in the morning. I don't want to go to sleep."

"Two or three? So you're a night owl."

"Seances work better at midnight or later. I've always been a night owl. Even as a kid, they could never get me to sleep before midnight, and then getting me up in the morning for school..." She shook her head. "As you can imagine, that did not work well when I'd only had a few hours of sleep. If they could get me up, I'd sleep through my morning classes. If I could."

"You must have been a joy to parent."

Reg shrugged. "I was not an easy child. I had a long stream of foster families from the time I was five. Maybe a few times before that, too. And none of them practitioners, so my behavior was a little... concerning to them."

October sipped his water. "I can well imagine. You're very skilled, which is surprising for someone whose abilities were suppressed as a child."

"So I'm told," Reg agreed. "I've had some good teachers and

35

friends helping out. A mentor helping to train me in... certain areas."

She wasn't sure she wanted to share anything about her fire-casting abilities with October. Though he acted like he knew everything about her, not many people knew about that particular gift.

"How about you?" Reg asked. "I guess you grew up knowing what you were."

"It would be pretty hard to suppress lycanthropy... though I suppose there might be cases where the person suppressed any memories of the shift, if the alternative was thinking that they were crazy or it was particularly traumatic. But yes, I grew up with the loup-garou. I knew what I was, had many relatives who were shifters. It was normal to me. It wasn't until I was older and took up traveling that I realized how different the culture I grew up in was from the mainstream. I'm glad that I went through my adolescence within that closed culture. I can't imagine trying to keep the changes secret while attending a mainstream school."

Reg smiled. "Have you ever seen *Teen Wolf?*"

"Funny movie. Not a lot of truth in it. But some of the problems of unintentional shifting are uncomfortably accurate."

They looked over the menus for a few minutes in silence. Reg was happy to see everything was printed, with no fancy cursive fonts, and there were plenty of pictures, allowing her to quickly identify what she wanted. She hated fancy restaurants with menus entirely written in cursive and French. She'd learned to ask about the daily special or request the catch of the day to prevent embarrassment over being unable to decode the menu.

Once she'd figured out what she wanted, she closed the menu and put it aside.

"Tell me if this is too personal, but... I don't know a lot about how it all works. Zora's babies, they were born as wolves, and then as they've gotten older, they've started to be able to shift partway or for a short period, and she says they'll get better as they get older. But when you talk about growing up, it doesn't sound like you were... a wolf. So... how does that work?"

"It depends on the mother. If she is not a shifter, or her preferred form is biped, she will remain in biped form throughout the pregnancy and bear a biped child. Or two or three. They will start to shift in their teens. Sometimes preteens, if they are precocious. But if the mother is like Zora, preferring canid form, then she will remain in that form throughout the gestation. She'll have a litter of pups, and they will develop the ability to shift at around a year old."

"That's amazing. Zora says her pups are already starting to show the ability to shift even though they're only a few months old."

"Who knows what all of the consequences of Jake's experiments will be."

Reg nodded soberly. It was something she didn't like to think about. What he had done and had planned to do. The horrors she had seen displayed on the shelves of the maternity room in his lab.

"So the mother chooses which form she wants to stay in for the pregnancy?"

"No... when we say we prefer one form... it isn't really a choice. It's innate. Likely, the form that we were born in will be our preference. But occasionally, you do see a... an odd case where the person's preferred form is *not* the form they were born in. It can sometimes come as a shock for the family."

CHAPTER EIGHT

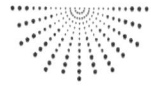

The waitress returned to the table for their orders. She topped off Reg's coffee and looked at her inquiringly. Reg put in her order for the cedar-planked salmon. October chuckled.

"What?" Reg asked.

"The same," October told the waitress.

He and Reg reached for the menus to hand back to the waitress at the same time and laughed. Reg motioned to October, "Go ahead."

He scooped up the menus and handed them over. "No veggies with the salmon," he told her. "Just the fish."

She nodded and noted it on her order form. Not big on vegetables herself, Reg wondered whether she should give the waitress the same instruction, but she decided it might give October the wrong idea. She didn't want him to think that she couldn't make decisions for herself. She knew her own mind and didn't need him to tell her what she wanted.

The waitress retreated. October looked at Reg. "The menu is fairly comprehensive," he commented, "and we didn't talk about the options we were considering. What are the odds we end up ordering the same thing?"

"I don't know. But it looks great." She shrugged. "Maybe it was just because it was the best thing on the menu."

"That must be it," October agreed with a smile.

"So, how is the pack?" Reg asked. "It's been a couple of weeks since I saw Zora and the cubs last, and I don't really see any of the others."

October considered his answer, taking a sip of his water. "Physically, they are well, and I think most are recovered from their confinement. Or have healed as much as they will."

Reg knew there were several injuries or long-lasting effects from Jake's experiments that the wolves would probably never fully recover from. Some injuries could not be cured.

"Mentally, I'm not sure. They are definitely better running wild than being confined. But many are... still feeling the effects of what was done to them. Wolves are a hardy bunch, but they are not the same as they were before the experiments."

Reg felt a wave of sadness for the wolf pack. She lamented her inability to figure out what was happening sooner and being unable to effect a rescue until the very last minute. She should have been quicker on the uptake. She should have gotten the wolves out of there sooner. She could give the excuse that she had been waiting for the council to help release them and take them somewhere safe, but what if she had confronted Jake? Maybe handcuffed him. Tied and gagged him so that they could rescue the pack sooner.

"It isn't your fault," October told her. "You know I tried to get them out of there sooner, and look at how that turned out." His tone was bitter.

The one wolf they had lost had died after October's rogue rescue attempt

"Faolan would not have lasted another day in a cage," Reg pointed out. "At least... he died free."

They were both silent for a while, considering what had happened. Reg searched for a way she could have helped them sooner. But she had been blinded and confused by her relationship with Jake and by his lies.

"I should have... I could have done something to him. To stop him."

"You couldn't. He bound you. You were in his thrall. You were very strong to overcome his influence and do what you did. I know of very few humans who could have done what you did." He paused for a few beats. "Make that none. I don't know how you were able to overcome the binding spell and to help with the rescue and release them from their bonds."

"I had help."

"Some. But there was little the rest of us could do. Without your help, the entire pack might have been wiped out."

There was a lump in Reg's throat. She swallowed hard. She looked away from October, unable to tolerate the gaze from those bright green eyes.

"The cubs are doing wonderfully," October told her, his voice picking up animation and amusement. "As you noticed, they are very bright and are precocious in their ability to transform."

Reg smiled. The pups frequently made her laugh. They were so enthusiastic and full of life and curiosity.

"Especially Fenris," October said, shaking his head. "The mischief that dog gets into!"

Reg laughed. Zora told her the stories sometimes. And she always enjoyed seeing them.

"Of course we all understand that the reason he gets into so much trouble is because he is so smart," October went on. "But he will not be disciplined. Wolves do not usually have so many problems keeping their cubs in line. But he pays little attention to the attempts of his mother and the pack to correct him and teach him to follow the rules. He sees things so clearly in his little mind... he is always certain of himself and doesn't see the dangers ahead. He doesn't understand how pack discipline is necessary."

"A lone wolf," Reg suggested.

"Yes. I fear he will be unable to work within the pack structure and will be forced to subsist on his own."

Was that Jake's fault, too? Reg supposed that, given Jake's experiments on Zora and her unborn puppies, any adverse effects or changes in how the cubs typically developed were his responsibility.

She sighed heavily.

The waitress brought their orders to the table and set them down with a flourish. "Anything else I can get you?"

"This looks great," Reg assured her, mouth watering at the fragrant smells and the sight of the glistening fish.

"It does indeed," October agreed.

They dug into the salmon, which was prepared to perfection. Since her siren instincts had been triggered, Reg had found she preferred her fish to be raw or rare, and most restaurants overcooked it, resulting in a dry, flavorless dish.

She glanced across the table and was overcome with a wave of deja vu so strong that she stopped eating and gripped the table, staring at October.

He looked at her, eyes widening slightly. "Reg? What's wrong?"

"Have we been here before?" Reg demanded. "Did I know you... a long time ago?" She shook her head. The waves of familiarity were nearly overwhelming. She *had* been there before. Eating fish with October. Smoked fish.

"I..." October trailed off. "I have had strong feelings of deja vu more than once around you." He smiled, his green eyes dancing. "Maybe we knew each other in a past life."

Reg thought about Starlight and what she knew about his previous lives, or one of them, anyway. She had accepted he had lived other lives in the past. He was a cat. Wasn't it commonly accepted that cats lived nine lives?

But Reg hadn't ever thought about whether she had lived other lives, other incarnations. It didn't seem possible. Especially with her parentage. How could she have been the same person in any other form?

"Don't say that. Do you really believe that? About other lives?"

He cocked an eyebrow. "Do you not?"

"I don't know. I've always thought the idea was a little 'out there,' but I can't prove it. I know this life isn't everything, because I'm a medium. I've seen and talked to ghosts. Spirits. Whatever you want to call them. But not all spirits stick around after the person dies. Because I'd be able to see them, wouldn't I? I don't know if it is like that old *Ghost Whisperer* show where they have to choose to go on, and then go into the light and get to heaven or whatever else is there."

October nodded, listening closely but making no comment.

"But I believe some beings are reincarnated..." Reg decided not to tell him specifically about Starlight.

She and Starlight kept his past life—the one she knew about —quiet. Reg respected his desire just to be a house cat despite his powers, whatever his reasons for the choice. Maybe he'd gotten burned out in a past life and needed some rest and recovery time. Other than the occasions where he had needed to step in to save Reg. Reg didn't want the fame and the scrutiny that would come from people knowing who Starlight had been in the past. Celebrities were stalked, targeted, kidnapped, and held for ransom. If someone wanted access to the powers he'd had in past lives, what would they do to get it?

October was still looking at her, waiting for her to finish her thought. "I know that some beings are reincarnated, but probably not all of them. Maybe it's just like with ghosts... some spirits stay here, and some move on. Some stay... in heaven or wherever... and others move on to another life. Do they have a choice of what destination they go to? Is this earth the only place? I just have... so many questions about how it works."

October took a couple more bites of his fish and chewed

slowly, thinking through his answer. He laid his fork down with a soft clink.

"I don't have the answers," he admitted. "Maybe I know even less about it than you do. If you know reincarnates, then you're way ahead of me. I believe such a thing is possible but have never met a reincarnated being. Not knowingly. Maybe you're one. Maybe I am. There is no way to know the answers."

"So you believe in reincarnation."

"I believe that… it is a possibility. Not something I'll ever know for sure."

"Until you die."

"And maybe not even then. Do the spirits know where they are going? After they are reborn, they don't have any memory of the previous life, do they?"

Reg grimaced. "Well, some of them do. You hear about people who remember. Past life regression and all that."

"But that is hypnosis. A hypnotist could plant whatever ideas they wanted to. Maybe not even realizing that they were. They have specialists to question young children so that they don't accidentally implant memories. And I've seen studies about how easy it is to invent memories and not even realize you've done it."

Reg wanted to say that she would know if she had made something up, but her past was such a tangle of fractured memories that she couldn't be sure. She had tried to keep everything straight in her mind, but often encountered holes she couldn't account for.

"So you *don't* believe in reincarnation. You think it's just made-up memories." Reg wanted to pin him down to one opinion or the other. She didn't know why it was so important. But she wanted to know. She needed to know his opinion.

Why? It wasn't like it affected her whether he believed or not. She didn't even know for sure what she believed, so why was it important that October did?

October laughed. "I didn't say that. I'm open, Reg. I don't know whether reincarnation is real or not. Or whether there is something else. I'll take your word for it that there is an afterlife. It seems consistent with what I have seen and heard. But living multiple lives… I'm not sure of that."

CHAPTER NINE

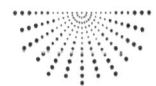

*T*he sense of deja vu was fading, and Reg could see they wouldn't get anywhere on settling their opinions on the reality of reincarnation. She cast about for another topic of conversation.

"So… how long have you known Marian?"

She was pleased that she had been able to keep her voice steady, giving away nothing about how she really felt about October seeing Marian, whether his purposes had been personal or for a psychic reading.

October scrutinized her intently. "Marian is actually the person who first mentioned you to me."

Reg was taken aback. "Marian told you about me? After we met in Bald Eagle Falls?"

"After we met the first time, yes. I could tell that you were a practitioner. You were from Black Sands, so I asked Marian if she knew you, and she gave me the scoop." He paused. "As much as she was able, of course. And she had heard about the happenings in the haunted theater so that I could offer my services in that regard."

"Well, I guess I should be glad of that. The production went off without a hitch, thanks to your… dehaunting services." She shook her head. "What exactly is it you do? I thought it had something to do with food testing. And then you helped with the theater. And then here... you're on some kind of council, deciding what to do with the pack..."

"No, I was the one who brought the problem to the council to enlist their help. I am not on the council myself. But you can't just ride into a town like Black Sands and expect to be able to do whatever you wish. Covens and town councils don't take kindly to violent action being taken against their citizenry. Even the likes of Jake Bosco."

"So... what *do* you do?" Reg persisted.

"I'm a... private consultant. I help with troubleshooting situations that could benefit from my particular gifts. As you've noticed, that covers a lot of ground. I like the variety. I don't like being tied down to one thing."

"And Marian? Is she a friend or a client?"

"Marian has been very helpful to me in the past. I don't know what you have against her, Reg. She is honorable and is good at what she does. She may not be flashy, but she knows what she is doing. I have been glad for her help in the past."

"I don't have anything against her," Reg protested, her face burning. She had thought she had managed to keep her inquiry casual, but he must have seen through her. "Marian is a friend. I just... she has never mentioned you, and you hadn't mentioned her before, so I was surprised to see the two of you together. I wondered whether... I don't know; I just wondered how you knew each other."

"I don't know what you're worried about, but I don't think she's going to steal your business. There is enough business in Black Sands for two psychics."

"Sure, of course. We refer people to each other, consult on more difficult cases and, if I need help with something of a more personal nature, she's always been great."

"But...?"

"Nothing. I didn't really like her when we first met, but so what? First impressions are not everything. I think Marian is great. I gave her a cat once, but it turned out they were not compatible…"

"That's surprising. Marian loved her old cat and she has a new one now that she seems to dote on just as much."

"Well, this cat… had some issues. Some behavioral problems. We eventually found him a home in Egypt."

"Behavioral problems?"

Reg raised her brows. "I would think you would understand about animals with behavioral problems. Animals experience trauma, too."

"Of course," October agreed immediately. "But most humans do not recognize traumatized behavior in animals."

"Well, he had been through a pretty bad situation." Reg thought about Horace and choked up a bit. "So it was understandable. He was… he had a hole that needed to be filled."

October nodded and put his hand over Reg's. It was warm and comforting. He opened his mouth to say something.

There was a flash, and Reg couldn't breathe for a moment. She was thrown back into a memory, a flashback more vivid than any she had experienced in years.

Reg addressed the warrior standing before her, dressed for battle in his loincloth and corselet. "I do not want to send you, El-Sayed," she said in a hoarse, whispery voice unlike her own. "But we cannot sit back and do nothing."

The warrior shook his head. "We must fight with all our strength. We cannot avoid the battle simply because we may lose. If we do not fight, we have already lost."

Reg nodded. "If the sorcerer is not defeated and becomes pharaoh of this people, many lives will be lost, maybe generations to come. We cannot allow this people to be conquered without a fight."

El-Sayed crossed his arm over his chest in a gesture of

submission and respect. "I and my men will fight with all our strength. We will not return defeated."

Reg swallowed. They would return in honor, having defeated the sorcerer and his ranks, or they would die on the battlefield. There was no room for retreat. They were the rearguard. The last defense. If the sorcerer's armies defeated them, it would mean the end of civilization as they knew it. They would be enslaved, they and their children, and their children's children.

El-Sayed's bright green eyes were undaunted. She knew he would fight until his last living breath, and his men would willingly follow him into death.

She began an incantation pleading for the gods to be with their army. As the warrior stood motionless before her, both arms crossed over his chest, she kissed a Wadjet Eye and hung the amulet around his neck. Her nearest attendant brought a box filled with small alabaster jars, each containing the herbs and unguents of her trade. She selected a jar of oil infused with frankincense and myrrh and wet her fingertips with the oil.

Still chanting, she touched his forehead in the third eye position to give him a clear mind, vision, and understanding. She touched his lips to give him clarity of speech as he commanded his men in battle. She put her hand over his heart and held it there for a moment, feeling his muscular chest taut beneath her touch, his heart pounding a slow, strong rhythm as he prepared to fight to the death. Swallowing a lump in her throat, she blessed his heart with courage and strength.

Hardly able to breathe, she dropped to her knees and prostrated herself before him. She anointed his feet. He and his men would need to be strong and fleet of foot. They would need to be agile, have a strong base, and be unmovable if pressed.

There could be no retreat.

There would not be.

She did not weep. She prayed to Horus and Sekhmet to

guide and bless the warriors as they defended their homes, their families, and her temple.

By the end of the day, they might be overrun. It might be the end of their world.

Reg stared into October's bright green eyes. For a few seconds, they both just stared, not daring to move. Eventually, October swallowed and withdrew his hand from Reg's.

"What was that?" he demanded hoarsely.

Reg had no idea how to answer. She drew a long breath, feeling as if she had not breathed for a thousand years. How many thousands of years had she gone back?

She'd had flashbacks before, but only to her own life. She'd never had a vision like that before.

"Did you see it too?" she asked tentatively. October must have experienced something, or he wouldn't be asking. Or was he just asking Reg where she had gone? What had it looked like to him? A trance? A seizure?

"Did I see it? What *was* that? You were just talking about Egypt; that must be why I saw what I did." He shook his head like a dog shaking off water. "Speaking of implanted memories..."

"What did you see?" Reg asked. She was having trouble catching her breath. He had obviously seen something in Egypt as well. But had he seen the same thing she had?

"I saw... myself going to war against an imposter. Someone trying to take over the rightful governance of the country. I must have been... I must have had an army under me. Some men, anyway. Some kind of commander or—"

"Overseer," Reg finished at the same time as October.

He frowned at this. "And you? I was talking to a woman, a sorceress or priestess..."

"Yes, that was me. You were going to fight and I was... blessing you. Doing some kind of rite to give you strength and speed in battle."

October sat back in his seat. "How did you do that? I knew you had psychic powers, but I didn't realize you could share a vision. That was... like a dream painter."

He was suggesting that Reg had projected the vision to him, like Damon did. Reg always had difficulty telling whether something Damon had put into her mind was real or not. She had asked him repeatedly not to do it, but he claimed that it was just part of his natural way of communicating and he couldn't help it.

Had she shared the vision with October? And if she had, where had it come from in the first place? Reg was sure she couldn't just have imagined it. There had been too much that she just wouldn't know. She had been to modern Egypt, and it had looked nothing like the building she had been inside during the dream. And the clothing! The short skirt and vest that the warrior had worn had not looked like any army uniform she had ever seen.

She could have pulled a lot of stuff from Hollywood, but the dream had certainly not had any of the feeling of a Hollywood movie. It had been gritty, real, and heartbreaking. She had felt the fear and dread of the approaching army, the reluctance to send the warrior and his army to make the last stand. It had all felt very real.

"I didn't do that," Reg said. "I didn't do anything intentionally. And I never had a vision like that before. If it was a memory—"

October shook his head. "If it was a memory of a past life, then why would this be the first time it's ever happened to you? Wouldn't you have had glimpses into the past before? The reason you saw that, or projected it to me, was because we were talking about past lives and Egypt. So, you concocted a vision of ancient Egypt. It doesn't mean you lived there in a past life. Or that I did. It's just your brain playing tricks."

"Why?"

October looked at Reg's face, at her coffee cup, at her plate.

He struggled to come up with something. "Maybe you're having a reaction to something. Something in your drink or dinner. Have you ever had anything like this happen before?"

"I... don't know. I've shared memories with someone else. But not... not like this. Things that I could remember. Things that had happened to me. Not just... random. An event thousands of years ago? It doesn't make any sense."

"That's the power of suggestion."

"Is that all it was?"

"It must be. You have a very vivid imagination. Maybe it was a fever dream. Are you feeling okay?"

"Yes. I'm fine. I'm not sick. No fever."

"Well... Maybe it was just a hiccup. One of those random brain zaps that never happens again."

"It was when you put your hand on mine."

October looked at Reg's hand, then shook his head. "I'm not doing it again."

Reg laughed. She wasn't sure why it was funny, but she was wound up and worried by this new development, and his reaction hit her funny bone. October smiled tolerantly, maybe recognizing the edge of hysteria in her voice.

"You need to get some rest," he suggested. "Take a day or two off and get caught up on your sleep."

How did he know that she wasn't sleeping? Were there bags under her eyes? Had she told him she wasn't sleeping well? She couldn't remember it coming up in the conversation, but it was one of those things that she might have said in passing. Small talk that she didn't even remember afterward.

"I have readings and a seance to do tonight. I'll catch up on my sleep after that. But this vision... this was not because I am overtired. It isn't just something I made up or imagined. It was real."

He looked at first like he might argue, but then he let out his breath slowly and gave her a warm smile. One of those smiles that sent a warm flush over her whole body and made her think of what it would be like to spend more time with him. *Lots* more time. Close, intimate time.

Then he looked for the waitress, making a writing gesture to signal that he wanted the bill. She brought him over a point-of-sale machine, along with a little tray holding two fortune cookies.

Reg looked at them in confusion. "This isn't a Chinese restaurant."

The waitress smiled. "And fortune cookies aren't Chinese. They are American, probably invented by Japanese immigrants." She shrugged. "But the owner likes them and decided we would start serving them after meals. So... you get some of the first fortune cookies offered by the Moonlit Grotto."

Reg looked at October. He shrugged. They each reached for the same cookie, then both switched and reached for the other. Then Reg switched back again, and October didn't, so they each picked up a different cookie. They cracked them open.

Reg looked at the little slip of paper that was supposed to contain her fortune. It was blank.

October was looking at his with a frown.

"Is yours blank too?" Reg asked, then said to the waitress, "I think there's a problem with the print run for these cookies."

"It's not blank," October said, and slid the little slip of paper across the table toward Reg. "It just has an X on it."

Reg looked at his, then back at hers, and realized hers also had an X that she'd been covering up by the way she was holding it. "Oh. Mine too. Yeah, something must have gone wrong at the printer. Maybe these were part of their test print to ensure the messages were properly centered or aligned."

"Maybe."

The waitress looked at the two "X" messages, laughing. "Well, I haven't seen any others like that! I'll grab you a couple more from the kitchen."

"Don't bother." Reg shook her head. She had a feeling that

any cookies they were given would have exactly the same message.

October paid the bill with the POS machine and the waitress thanked them, wished them a good night, and walked away. Reg stood up, but was still looking at the fortunes lying on the table. "What do you think it means?"

October shook his head slowly. "I wish I had some brilliant insight. Let's just say it was a misprint."

Reg knew there was more to it than that. But If it was significant, she was sure the universe would find a way to tell them what it was.

CHAPTER TEN

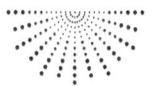

*R*eg's phone rang when she got back into her car. She pulled it out of her skirt pocket and put it in the dashboard mount.

Should she be surprised that it was Corvin?

Reg could have ignored the call, but chances were he would just keep calling her until she finally answered, and she didn't want him to call her during her appointments with clients.

She answered and switched to speaker so she could talk while she drove. "Hello."

"Regina," Corvin purred her name in his most alluring voice. "Are you stepping out on me?"

"Since we're not actually in a relationship… no."

"Oh, but you know how loyal I am to you," Corvin crooned. "Why do you want to chase after a dog like October when I am here waiting for you?"

"How do you even know where I am or who I am with? Are you spying on me?"

"I see things. Not always in the conventional way. Rest assured, I am not stalking you. Physically."

"Where are you?"

"Do you want to join me? Some after-dinner drinks,

perhaps? Some pleasant conversation. I'm unsure how much of a conversationalist a wolf can be…"

"We had some very interesting conversations. And I have clients tonight, so I'm not going out anywhere else. Even if I was interested, the answer would still be no."

"You don't think we are soulmates?" Corvin asked in a mock hurt voice.

"Ugh. I hope not," Reg responded with a laugh. "I'm not sure I believe in the idea of soulmates anyway. After Jake… I really thought once that we were made for each other. And… I couldn't have been much more wrong. I think it's a dangerous idea, the thought that we only have one true love."

Early the next afternoon, Reg decided that she would go see Marian. She had not been able to talk to her the first time about her little problem, but Marian had suggested that she stop by to see her during the day. Reg wanted to get there earlier so that if Marian closed up shop to go eat dinner or run an errand, Reg wouldn't miss her.

There was the possibility that Marian would be doing a reading or consultation for someone else but, if so, Reg could sit and wait, watching videos on her phone or something else similarly productive. Marian's business didn't seem that busy. She might have a few consultations a day, but there were large gaps between. Reg would be able to see her unless Marian's business had picked up significantly.

The day was hot and muggy. She had probably been unwise to pick the hottest time of the day to walk to Marian's storefront. She would be soaked in sweat by the time she got there. But it was what it was. She could shower and change when she returned home.

Reg rested her hand on the door for a moment before entering the shop. She looked down at the knob. It was plain and unornamented. She looked up to make sure she was at the right shop, not about to walk into some accounting firm or clothing store. It *was* Psychic Beginnings, Marian's storefront. Reg clearly remembered a different knob from the previous day. Had she gone to the wrong shop? Maybe that was why it had been locked so early. But no, it had been closed early because Marian had gone out to eat with October. She had been at The Crystal Bowl.

Reg must have dreamed the doorknob. She was mixing up dreams and reality. Understandable, with some of the dreams she had been having lately. It was very hard to push them to the side and carry on when she was awake as if nothing had happened. The dreams, when she could remember them, were so detailed and vivid.

Maybe October was right about memories. Maybe they were too changeable, too easily contaminated by dreams, suggestions, and subsequent events. They were fluid, changing each time they were accessed.

Reg turned the knob and pushed open the door. It wasn't going to get any easier standing there considering just how crazy she was. And she wasn't going to get any answers standing outside the shop.

An electronic bell chimed in the back as she opened the door, and Reg was greeted with the delicate scent of jasmine tea and the comfortable furnishings of Psychic Beginnings. Marian turned around to see who had come into the business.

"Oh, Reg, I'm glad you came."

Reg still wasn't sure of herself and her decision to consult with Marian, but she couldn't think of any other way to move forward and overcome her problem.

Marian looked back at the tea service in front of her. "I just made some tea. I didn't know who it was for, but I guess it was for you. Jasmine?"

"Sure." Reg often made tea for her clients so, although it

wasn't her favorite beverage, she found it tolerable. Once she'd added enough sugar and milk.

"Have a seat," Marian invited. Reg sat in one of the chairs positioned at the table in the center of the shop. Although it was padded and upholstered with a luxuriant green fabric that was warm to the touch, Reg was antsy and had a hard time finding a comfortable position and sitting still while she waited for Marian to finish preparing the tea service.

Marian brought a tray over to the table and set it down. She poured the hot tea into a delicate teacup and handed it to Reg. Reg inhaled the steam, feeling calmer and comforted. Her tense muscles relaxed. It was going to be okay. She was moving forward. Marian would be able to help with her pesky problem, and everything would be fine and go back to normal.

"Jasmine tea," Marian said, as she brought her cup to her lips and also paused for a moment to inhale, "is known to open one's mind to the unseen realms."

"Well, I don't seem to have any problems with that lately." Reg added several spoonfuls of sugar and a significant amount of milk to her tea.

"Perhaps you just need its calming powers. Or…" Marian gave Reg a small smile, "it is also associated with love magic. Perhaps there is a relationship in your life that needs attention."

Reg thought of October's startlingly green eyes. She had been seeing those eyes in more places lately.

But she didn't think October was romantically attracted to her. He was friendly enough and seemed to enjoy her company, but she was pretty sure he was not looking for a mate. Even if he was, how would Reg fit into the pack? It was helpful that she was able to communicate with the wolves psychically. But was she interested in dropping a litter of two or three lycanthropes? Raising them through the teenage years as they came into their transformative powers? She wasn't sure she was ready for that. Or that October would see her as the motherly type. Wolves mated for life, so when he selected a mate, it would not be for a casual fling.

"I don't have anyone right now," she told Marian. "No one special."

"I see." Marian took a long sip of the jasmine tea and closed her eyes, thinking and searching for an answer. "Well then, why don't you tell me why you are here today?"

She clearly knew that Reg wasn't just there for girl talk. They weren't that kind of friends.

"I don't know. It isn't really anything that complicated... I'm just having trouble sleeping. When I do sleep, I have vivid dreams and feel even more tired out. Like I had to live through what was in the dream and didn't actually get any rest at all."

"You look tired," Marian said with a nod. "Are you worrying about something? Going through any unusual stresses?"

"No... just that I can't sleep. That's the biggest thing bothering me right now. I really need to be able to get some rest."

Marian meditated on this for a few minutes. Reg let her do her thing and sipped the jasmine tea, wondering if it would really help her to open up and find out what was going on in her life.

"Why don't you tell me about the dreams," Marian suggested.

"I can't remember most of them. Or I just remember an impression or two when I wake up, but by the time I am up and around, it's gone."

"You said you don't remember *most* of them. So tell me about the ones that you do remember."

"Well, okay. Here is one that I had the other night."

CHAPTER ELEVEN

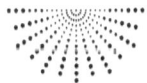

$\mathcal{R}$eg proceeded to tell Marian about the dream in which she had been a cat, prowling the sacred forests to keep them safe from humans, and had met a wolf who had a similar purpose in an overlapping territory.

She spread her hands questioningly. "So? What do you think?"

"Is it unusual for you to dream of being a cat?"

"Well, yes. Sometimes I dream about cats, but it is pretty unusual for me to dream that I am one."

"How has Starlight been? Do you have any concerns about him?"

Reg considered. "He's been normal. Sometimes, he behaves a little strangely but, considering his history and his psychic powers, I kind of expect that. He hasn't been sick or doing anything that concerns me."

"Have there been any other cats in your life recently? Horace?"

It had been a while since Reg had received a visit from the big black cat. He seemed to have settled well in his home in Egypt in Merneith's tomb. She hadn't been sure how he would fare there, but he seemed to be doing much better since joining with the ancient queen.

"No. I haven't seen much of him or any other cats."

"And the wolf that you met up with in this dream. Did he remind you of anyone?" Marian gave a faint smile.

Reg thought of the pack. She hadn't seen much of any of them, other than Zora and her pups and October. The wolf she had encountered in the sacred forest had been nothing like the rambunctious, precocious cubs. Not much like their quiet, thoughtful mother either.

But like October? Yes, the wolf in her dream had been much more like October. Wary, watchful, brave and strong. Protective.

"I suppose there were similarities to October," she admitted. "But he could have been any adult male wolf. I don't know that he was any more like October than any other adult male."

"Mmm-hmm." Marian sipped her tea and then stared into her cup, swirling the leaves remaining in the bottom. What did she see there? Anything that related to Reg? Anything that led her to the answers Reg sought? Reg looked down at her own tea. Cloudy with the milk, she could see little of the leaves in the bottom yet. She had another drink to empty the cup to study the remaining leaves. She was not trained in tasseography, but her psychic powers helped her to divine the meanings of the symbols in the tea leaves even without proper training.

The first symbol she saw was an X. Of course.

"I've been seeing the letter X a lot lately," she said. "Every-where I go. I even—"

"Let's do this properly," Marian interposed. She removed the cup gently from Reg's hands. She swirled the liquid that remained before swiftly inverting it onto the saucer. They waited for just a moment for any remaining liquid to drain. Marian then turned the cup back upright and peered inside.

"The X," she acknowledged. "As I'm sure you know, it could have a number of different meanings. You are facing significant challenges right now, and the X could represent a challenge blocking you or a crossroads at which you need to make a choice."

What kind of a choice? Reg wasn't facing any major life changes at the moment. She liked the way her life was and, after a lifetime of disruptive moves and changes, she just wanted to stay in one place and enjoy the stability and having a supportive community around her.

"What else?" she asked, "I guess the X is important or I wouldn't be seeing it everywhere, but I can't figure out what it means without something else."

Marian meditated upon the configuration of the leaves. "I see a long and winding path. A full circle, possibly indicating a repeating cycle, coming back to a place you have been before. And a key..."

Reg gave an involuntary shudder. She had dealt with keys before, discovering that they were not just a mechanical tool, an easy way to deal with a locked door, just as easily replaced with a set of picks if necessary. Keys could be dangerous, revealing hidden truths, giving the wrong person access to her home, or releasing a prisoner who should have been left confined.

"A key can symbolize the revelation of a secret or truth," Marian told Reg. "Perhaps there is a question in your life that you need an answer to. Now would be a good time to seek it."

Reg had questions, but she had found during her stay in Black Sands that not all questions needed to be answered. In fact, each revelation had deepened her belief that some things needed to be locked up forever. The answers did not always lead to peace and wisdom. They also led to heartache, rejection, and pain. Sometimes, it was better to remain ignorant.

Marian sat back in her chair, looking up from the leaves. "Tell me more about your dreams," she suggested. "The one about the cat and wolf is interesting, but I would like to know more."

"Most of the time, I can't remember what I dreamt after I

wake up," Reg reminded her. "Or, after a few minutes, I forget it all."

"You remembered one. And you remember some more. I won't push if you don't want to tell me, but I think that if you do, it could be enlightening. The more information I have, the more likely I am to be able to answer your questions and help you find your way through this winding path."

"I don't really see how it could help," Reg said. She thought back on the dreams she'd had lately, trying to pin down any details she had remembered the following day. There had been a lot of restless nights. A lot of dreams.

Yet only a few had stuck with her.

"Okay, then. There was one that I did remember pretty clearly…"

CHAPTER TWELVE

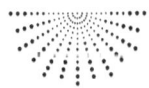

Reg waited near the gymnasium. The training center for the next group of contestants to compete in the games in Olympia was a busy place. The scent of sweat mingled with fresh earth filled Reg's nostrils as she watched the contestants train, enthralled by the beauty of their sun-kissed bodies and amazed by their feats of strength. She had written many verses about the perfection of their forms. Even the gods must be jealous of their beauty and achievements. Heracles could not have been much stronger and more skilled than the prospective Olympian champions.

She knew no one really believed anymore that the gods sat on the top of Olympus, watching the mortal contests and picking their champions. But sometimes she wondered…

She looked up the sheer face of the mountain and imagined it. What if there really were gods left in the world? What if they did pick their favorites in the contests? Honor the winners and consider admitting them to their exalted ranks?

She failed to notice the young man who had broken away from the group of contestants running through the sand and now veered toward where she was sitting until he was very close. She tore her eyes away from the mountain to smile at Petros.

"I am in awe of your abilities," she told him, admiring more than his abilities as she gazed at his oiled, glistening form just feet away from her. The magnificence of the human body was astounding. She could have written volumes about each hill and valley in his well-muscled body.

"My lady," he bowed his head to her. "Esteemed poet. Your words are my inspiration. They flow like sweet honey to the ear."

She smiled, turning her face away demurely. It wasn't long before she turned her gaze back toward him.

"Are you ready for the contest?" She asked. "You have worked so hard to get here."

"I will be ready when the time comes. So my trainer promises."

"You will surely win. I am certain you are the strongest and most skilled of all of the wrestlers."

"From your sweet lips to the ears of the gods," he said, with a respectful gesture toward the mountain top. "I cannot be so sure. Many of the other men here are equally skilled. It will be a close contest, and I would not dare wager the results."

"I have faith in you. Your strength, bravery, and fitness are known by all."

"And you? Is what I heard true? You will recite for the priestess of Hera?"

She dropped her eyes modestly and nodded. "It will be my great privilege to offer a few humble lines to the esteemed priestess."

"A great honor," he agreed. His green eyes traveled over her flowing white chiton and bared arms, while his entire form was open to her view. "I wish I could be there to hear you."

"I could recite some of my words to you. Another time, in another place," she told him delicately.

"That would be a very pleasant way to pass the time. I have

been utterly entranced by your words each time I have heard or read them."

She looked around. Others who had gathered to watch the contestants train were listening in on the conversation, their eyes no longer on the groups of men as they ran the other direction through the soft sand. Once they reached the other end of the track, they would be assigned their next exercise.

Petros realized he had been away from the other young men for too long. "Revered lady, I fear I must go, or I will be penalized."

"You know my residence," she whispered. "Please send me a message. Arrange for a place for us to meet."

A smile bowed his lips. "I will," he promised. "Fare thee well."

He ran to meet back up with his fellow contestants, putting on an admirable burst of speed, as light and fleet footed as a bird, that made the other observers whisper and murmur in approval.

He would win the wrestling contest, she was sure.

*M*arian's eyes were wide as she listened to Reg's account of the dream. Reg tried to tell it simply and without embellishment, but it had seemed so real to her, even after waking up, that it was hard not to go into great detail about the setting, the clothing, the young man's perfect body, and the courtly way they spoke to each other.

"So you were a poet," Marian said.

"The really funny thing about that," Reg told her, "is that I've never written a word of poetry in my life. I can't even stand to read the stuff. But when I was dreaming this… it was so real. I *felt* like a poet. I thought about how to write about what I was seeing. The contestants, the mountain, the air itself. Putting it all into words and phrases and making it all work in stanzas." She shook her head. "It was very strange."

"Like you really *were* the poetess," Marian said.

"Yes. But I wasn't. I mean, I woke up, and I was just me, and there was no… No Olympian in bed with me."

Marian cackled at that. "If only! There have been many times that I wished I could slide back into a dream and finish it." She sighed. "But that's just wishful thinking. However, I think there might be something more to these dreams."

She gazed into Reg's teacup once more.

"It is time for you to make some choices. To unlock the truth of the past."

"The truth of the past? But this was not something that ever happened to me."

Obviously, as she was not a poetess and had never known an Olympic contestant. Not to mention that the scene she had been a part of could only have happened thousands of years ago.

"Maybe it was Halloween," she suggested. "I went to… a toga party or a costume party, and I met…"

"A naked Olympian?" Marian finished. "You know that is not true. You never went to a toga party."

"No," Reg admitted. "It was just a dream. Just a silly dream. It must have been triggered by something that happened during the day. Just like at the restaurant yesterday when I had a vision of living in Egypt. At least I've *been* to Egypt. But not… thousands of years ago."

Marian's eyes glittered. "You had a vision of ancient Egypt at the restaurant?"

Reg shifted uncomfortably. "Well. It was just a flash… just a few seconds, I sort of glimpsed… I don't know. I was a priestess or something, blessing a warrior when he was about to take his men into battle. To protect us against… some evil usurper."

Marian nodded thoughtfully. "These experiences seem to be more than mere dreams or fleeting visions, Reg. They might be glimpses into past lives."

"Past lives?" Reg shook her head. "I don't think I have lived any other lives. I'm not even sure I *believe* in reincarnation."

"The soul is eternal and can carry memories from one life to another," Marian told her with certainty. "Sometimes these memories surface through dreams or visions, especially when something in your current life triggers them."

"You think I might have been a poetess in ancient Greece or lived in Egypt thousands of years ago?" She shook her head. "It's not possible."

"It is possible," Marian replied. "And there is a reason these memories are surfacing now."

"Why?" Reg demanded baldly, "And what am I supposed to do with them?"

"That's what you need to discover." Marian indicated the leaves in the teacup. "You have already noticed the recurring symbol of the X. These memories might be pointing you toward a crossroads—a decision you will be required to make."

Reg sighed. She tried to reject it, to push it all out of her mind. It was too much. They were dreams. Just the result of an overactive imagination, the same thing that a dozen doctors had told a dozen foster moms. Reg had an overactive imagination. They needed to be strict with her. Limit the amount of TV she watched. Give her chores to keep her busy. Ensure she knew the difference between what was real and what was not. Her imagination had been squelched for years as they tried to repress the colorful stories and visions Reg had related. Or learned not to tell anyone.

Marian touched Reg's hand tentatively. "Take it one step at a time. You need to rest. The lack of sleep makes it difficult to manage everything, doesn't it?"

Marian walked over to a shelf displaying various herbs and crystals. She picked up a small sachet filled with dried lavender. "Place this under your pillow tonight. Lavender is known for its calming properties and may help you sleep better." She selected a package of tea bags. "And valerian. Good for calming the overactive brain and helping you to relax before bed."

Reg accepted the offerings. She wasn't sure they would make

any difference. She had already tried everything she could think of to help her sleep. "Thank you, Marian."

"Keep a journal by your bed," Marian added as she escorted Reg to the door. "Write down any dreams or thoughts that come to you during the night or upon waking up."

"I will," Reg promised.

Though she wouldn't have a written journal. By the time she managed to get her pen out and scratch a few words, the dreams would be gone. The voice memo app on her phone would be a better plan.

She slid the lavender sachet and valerian tea into her pockets as she left, stepping from the cool air of Psychic Beginnings into the sauna outside.

Maybe after she saw her clients tonight, she would be able to sleep. Maybe she could put aside the silly worries and dreams and just sleep normally. Or whatever passed for normal in Black Sands.

She needed a good sleep without any disruption by Olympians, warriors, wolves, or warlocks.

CHAPTER THIRTEEN

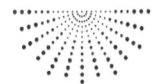

*R*eg did all of the things Marian had told her to do, adding in anything else she thought might help her to relax. Her readings had been a little difficult, evidence of her distraction, but the seance had gone well, with a bona fide visit from beyond the grave that had wowed her clients and was bound to get Reg some good referrals.

But after the seance, she had been hyped up. She was even more worried than usual about getting to sleep, making it more difficult to fall asleep. She had the valerian tea with lots of sugar. It gave her heartburn. She put the lavender sachet under her pillow. She coaxed Starlight into cuddling with her in bed while she watched a few videos on her phone to wind down. But she put down her phone before she was ready and closed her eyes, waiting for sleep to come. She knew the experts said that staring at your screens before bed was a bad thing to do, but she had been using night mode.

And still, sleep did not come.

It was a couple more hours before she finally managed to get to sleep. Even after initially falling asleep, she tossed and turned, waking and moving around restlessly, trying to find a comfortable position, that sweet spot that she could never find.

Then she finally fell into a dream.

She heard an uproar in the streets before the pounding on her door. She stared out at the dust on the horizon where the battle was taking place.

It had not been long enough. Their armies were well-matched; it would take hours before the battle was decided and their position was won or lost.

People were taking to the streets. Feet pounded up the stairs. A messenger boy coming to report on the outcome or a significant turn in the battle. She closed her eyes and started chanting.

Seconds later, one of her ladies knocked and approached her without leave. Reg watched the woman approach, face white and eyes wide. She kept her own face an impassive mask. She swallowed and lifted her chin.

"What news?"

Her lady bowed her head. "Mistress. My lady. Word from the battlefield."

"Yes. What is it?" she demanded impatiently.

The woman's eyes filled with tears. "They are lost, Mistress. Betrayed. Word of their movements reached the sorcerer before the battle began. A betrayal from within."

Her gut twisted, and she was filled with horror and grief. Her bright-eyed commander. The final rearguard. Her entire country. All lost.

"Who betrayed us?" she asked the maidservant.

The younger woman fell to her knees, terror written in her features. "I do not know." She crossed her arms over her chest. "Someone with the commander's ear."

Few would have known enough of their plans to give the sorcerer the information he needed to defeat them so quickly.

There was thunder in the streets. The sorcerer's advance guard was arriving in the city. They would burn and pillage. They would take the temples and palace first.

They were coming for her.

"Bring me the Chest of Anubis. And any of the sacred household who wish to enter his embrace with me."

The woman stared at her, frozen in place.

"We have not time," Reg said sharply. "If you wish to escape enslavement, we take our journey now."

The maid just knelt there. Reg strode to her and shoved her over. "Now, you silly woman. Don't delay." The thunder of feet in the streets rang in her ears. It would take the warriors time to break through the barred door, but it would not hold forever. She intended to be gone long before that.

Being knocked to the floor seemed to have broken the woman's trance. She scrambled to her feet and hurried from the room, returning only minutes later with the polished box filled with vials, each of which would escort one person to the embrace of Anubis and her ancestors. The lady knelt to present it to her. Reg set it on the table next to her and waited as the faithful members of the sect who had served with her filed in and lined up, arms crossed over their chests, to await their release.

Reg awoke with tears in her eyes and a lump in her throat. She looked around the room, trying to orient herself in time and space.

"Starlight? Star, where are you?" Her voice was cracking. "I need you."

For once, the cat did not take his own sweet time deciding whether to answer her call. She heard him jump down from whatever window ledge or furniture he had been asleep on in the living room, and he came into the bedroom meowing, looking at her in concern.

"Come here." Reg patted the bed beside her, and Starlight jumped up. Reg put her arms around the cat and buried her face in his fur. She knew he wouldn't like it, especially if she wet his fur with her tears and snot, but she needed to hold another living creature.

"Ohh," she moaned. "Oh, no, no."

It was silly to be crying over a dream. But was it any sillier than waking up afraid and having to turn on the light or check the house for burglars? Her heart was heavy in her chest, a lead weight that pressed down on her, crushing her. The grief she felt was real, even if the dream was not. Losing El-Sayed, her lover and faithful follower, the army, the final point of defense and therefore her country. Knowing there was only one way to escape the pillaging and enslavement that was surely coming.

The phone rang, and Reg knew it would be Corvin, sensing her emotions over their psychic link and alarmed by the sudden plunge into mourning.

But she didn't want to talk to Corvin.

There was only one person she could talk to. Only one who would understand what she was talking about.

She picked up the phone and rejected Corvin's call. She tapped her contacts list and searched for October's name. She touched the number, biting her lip. She glanced at the time to make sure it wasn't too early to be calling someone. She normally slept late in the morning, but she knew she hadn't been asleep for very long. She didn't think October would still be asleep, but he could conceivably be.

October answered within two rings, which suggested he hadn't been fast asleep.

"Reg?" his voice was thick with sleep or emotion. "Reg, are you okay?"

Reg sniffled and was unable to find her voice at first. She coughed and tried again. "I'm... I had a dream."

"I know," he said somewhat impatiently. "I did, too."

"It was horrible. I don't know... did he die? Did you see it? Or did you see her?"

"He was killed before the battle even began. Betrayed." His voice was tight with fury. "And her?" His voice cracked.

"She... when she heard the news, she..." Reg gulped and could not go on.

"She wasn't taken?" October pressed.

"No. She had a box. Filled with vials of poison."

October was silent. Reg swallowed, unsure what to say.

CHAPTER FOURTEEN

*W*hy is this happening?" October demanded.

He sounded like he was angry with her, but Reg held back her reaction to his tone as much as she could. He was probably just reacting emotionally to the dream the same way as she was. Her tears over the loss of everything in the dream were illogical. It wasn't her life. It was something that had happened thousands of years ago to someone else. Or else it was something she had just imagined. Either way, her tears and grief over what had happened did not make logical sense, so she could forgive October his anger.

"I don't know," she told him. It was probably because of her. For some reason, she had started having problems sleeping every night and, each time she did manage to get to sleep, she was having disruptive, disturbing dreams. "I guess… I must have triggered something at the restaurant. When I had that vision… it made you a part of it. Then you started dreaming about it too."

"Is this real?"

"What is real?" It was a question Reg couldn't answer herself. "Did it really happen, back in ancient Egypt? I don't know. You could look in the history books, I guess. See if you can find an event that matches up."

"There is a lot about that time that we only have vague allusions to. There is plenty that we have no idea about. There is no guarantee that we would be able to find any record of it if it did happen. But if we are both seeing and dreaming the same thing..." He trailed off, clearly having difficulty putting his thoughts into words. "Does that mean we both have actual memories of it? Or is it just a vision you had that you... shared with me, and now I'm dreaming about it too? Does it mean..."

"That we knew each other in a previous life?" Reg finished. "That we... shared something..."

She thought of the warrior in his shendyt and vest, prepared to go into battle with barely any protection. A tiny faction trying to protect their land from the usurper.

Her feelings for this warrior ran deep. Not just priestess and warrior, but a soul connection much more intimate than that; she must know a lot more about him.

"El-Sayed." The name rose to her lips and she whispered it across the airwaves to him.

"Mery," October murmured. *Beloved.*

They breathed, overcome by emotion.

"It must be a past life," Reg said. "Or a memory of someone who lived back then. I don't remember ever reading anything about this or learning it in school or anything. I don't know where else it would have come from."

"We need to talk," October said hoarsely after what seemed like a long period of silence.

Reg cleared her throat and thought about her day ahead. Of course she would meet with October as he requested. She wasn't sure they were going to figure out anything more, but she wouldn't turn him down. He was too important to her, and this ancient pain was now too close to the surface to deny.

"I have to see someone today. I have... a mentor. I am training." She thought about the dream of the athlete training in

Olympia. What would he think if she told him about that now? "But after that, maybe. This afternoon… three o'clock?"

He cleared his throat with a growl. "We can't get together before then?"

"I… can't. I have commitments. Would it be okay?"

"Three o'clock, then."

* * *

Reg forced herself to get out of bed and prepare for her day. It was still much too early. She wasn't normally up and around until nearly noon. But there was no way she could sleep any longer. She didn't want to dream any more, even if she could force herself to go back to sleep. And she was too worked up by her emotions and the discussion with October to settle down to go back to sleep.

Starlight followed her around the cottage, meowing to remind her that she needed to feed him as soon as she got up, even if it was earlier in the day than usual. She needed to go to the fridge, find him food, and fill his dish.

Reg looked at him, pushing aside the insistent thoughts about making sure he had plenty to eat.

"I would think that with your Egyptian roots, this would be important to you," she pointed out.

Starlight stopped rubbing against her yowling, and sat. He drew himself up very tall, like a statue of Bastet, and stared at her with his mismatched green and blue eyes. He seemed to be waiting for more information. Waiting for her to explain why this should be important to him.

"Don't you care about what happened in Egypt? The battles for land and power? If that was your land, and you were one of the gods over it, then didn't you care about all of the people who were affected? About the betrayal and injustice? I died because of what happened, if that was really me. And October died. And his men and the women who served me. All of them died because of that betrayal."

Starlight studied her through slitted eyes.

And what was he supposed to do about it?

It had happened thousands of years ago. How could he do anything about it now? What impact did it have on him, in this life?

In this life, he was not Bastet. He was Starlight, and Reg was responsible for seeing that his needs were met. He needed food, whether hundreds of people had died thousands of years ago or not. Everyone from that time was dead and gone now. Their bones turned to dust. Their souls part of eternity.

Reg sighed. "Was I one of them? Did I really live in that time? And die like I dreamed?"

He stared at her.

Why did it matter now?

Reg blew out her breath and shook her head in frustration. "I don't know why it matters now. But it must, or why would I be dreaming about it? There must be a reason that I started to see it now."

He blinked at her with one eye and then the other.

If Starlight had the answer, he wasn't giving it to her.

CHAPTER FIFTEEN

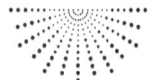

*R*eg felt like she was in a fog on her way to Davyn's house, located outside the town limits, where there was plenty of room to train. She should probably not even be driving. Maybe she should have used another method of transportation to get herself there. It had been several nights since she'd had a good sleep.

She turned the radio on loud and rolled down the windows to get plenty of air. It wasn't like she had to drive for hours. She could make it safely that far. After her training session, if she were too tired, Davyn would graciously offer his couch or spare bed for her to take a nap on to ensure she was safe to drive back home.

Should she have canceled the session? Agreed to meet with October earlier? She didn't like to miss her sessions with Davyn, and he had other work that he had taken time off from in order to work with her. It would be pretty rude not to take the time slot when he had specifically taken time off to train her.

Besides, she loved firecaster training with her mentor. She hated to miss it, even if she felt tired and a little foggy. She would probably feel much better after the opportunity to "play with fire."

Her control had greatly improved since she first started working with Davyn. She had come a long way since he had identified her as a firecaster and taken her under his wing. There were not many firecasters around. They needed to stick together. And it was rare that a firecaster got to be Reg's age before being identified as a firecaster or dying in a fire she had accidentally set.

It was something that she kept a secret from everyone but her closest friends, even among those who were practitioners. Firecasters were often ostracized, seen as dangerous and uncontrollable. But under Davyn's tutelage, she had been able to keep her powers under control and not accidentally light things on fire.

Most of the time.

She had lost control with the arrival of Ember. Apparently it was not unusual for a firecaster to be triggered by a firedrake in close proximity. It was probably good that the dragon was living with Davyn rather than Reg. He had better control than she did, and had more room for Ember to roam around.

The young dragon was getting big now, and Reg wondered what was in his future. Sooner or later, he would want to roam farther afield, and neither of them would be able to stop him.

Reg saw the turn-off for Davyn's house up ahead and was surprised she had arrived so quickly. She looked down at her speedometer and slowed way down for the turn.

Once on the gravel road, she kept her eyes open for Ember. He could have met her anywhere along the way but, usually, he waited until she was on the gravel road.

Sure enough, she was about halfway down the gravel road when something large and dark seemed to fall right out of the sky, coming to a stop in front of her car, hovering inches above the ground. Reg mashed the brake and managed to stop before hitting him. She sat there looking at him.

"You're going to get yourself hit one day. How would you like that?"

Ember's tongue hung out in a dragon grin. In her head, Reg saw a picture of the front end of her car all mashed in and Ember unharmed in front of it.

He was probably right. Dragons were pretty tough creatures. "Well, Wilf would not be happy with you if you wrecked my car. And how would I drive out here if I didn't have a car?"

He transmitted a picture of her flying through the air in dragon form. He had been overjoyed when she had first taken on her dragon form. He wanted her to do it again. He wanted her to stay in dragon form forever to keep him company. There were no other dragons in the vicinity, and he enjoyed the companionship.

"Well, I'm not here to fly today. I'm here to play with fire."

Ember took a deep breath and belched out a billowing cloud of fire. Reg shielded herself from it and sent a fireball hurtling back at Ember. He opened his mouth and snapped it out of the air, swallowing it, and looking at her with satisfaction.

"Come on. I have to get to my lesson. I'm not supposed to do this without supervision."

Ember rose in the air to let her pass. He swam lazily through the air in front of her, leading her on to the house. Reg followed, grinning to herself.

Ember was like a puppy. A very large, fire-breathing puppy.

Davyn was waiting on the front porch when Reg arrived. He sipped from his coffee mug, smiling at Ember's antics.

"He gets so excited when he knows you are coming over."

"I enjoy it too. I love to see him every time I am over. I miss the days when he was just a hatchling and I could carry him around in my purse."

He hovered over Reg as she got out of the car. Now, Ember couldn't even fit inside the car to ride with her. He was as big as the car.

"Ready to get started?" Davyn inquired.

"Yeah. Are we going to stay here?"

Sometimes, they went farther afield, training in different environments or trying different tasks. Lately, they had been staying at Davyn's most of the time, which Reg suspected was because of Ember. Davyn didn't want to take him out where he might be seen.

"Yes, just into the woods." Davyn left his coffee cup behind and picked up a backpack that Reg knew contained emergency supplies, including water bottles so she wouldn't get dehydrated, burn dressings in case of an accident, and whatever else Davyn thought might be needed.

If one of them got accidentally burned, which was extremely rare, they could heal from it quickly, as long as it was not a catastrophic burn. But the same was not true of tourists or hunters who ventured onto Davyn's property despite the fences and numerous *Danger* and *Private Property* signs. Reg had some basic healing powers, but healing took time and, if she were exhausted, she would need to recharge before she could do anything more.

They started with the usual exercises, getting warmed up and giving Davyn a chance to evaluate Reg's mood and condition, pieces of information vital for the training session. It was all pretty routine, and Reg normally flew through the warm-ups without any problem.

But today, things were not going as they were supposed to. Reg didn't know if it was because she was short on sleep or distracted by thoughts of what had happened in her visions of ancient Egypt, but she kept slipping up on skills that she had previously mastered.

CHAPTER SIXTEEN

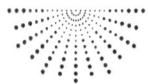

*A*gain," Davyn prompted, watching Reg carefully, having her repeat the last exercise. He mirrored her movements as she formed a fireball the size of a basketball between her hands and took it through various stages, heating and cooling it, allowing it to grow, and then shrinking it down to the size of a marble before absorbing it again. Ember sat on the gravel nearby, watching. He made a disappointed noise. Reg glanced at him.

"Reg, focus," Davyn warned.

"I am."

"I don't think you are. You can't be distracted by what Ember is doing. You can't let your thoughts wander."

Reg sighed in exasperation and started over.

"Have you been doing your meditation?"

"Yes, I always do my practice assignments."

Almost always. Usually. She *had* missed a few sessions the last few days, but that was not enough to affect her performance.

"You should be meditating on your own as you need to as well. Not just because it is an assignment. If you have something on your mind, need to work things out, or are having difficulty with something, you need to take time out of your schedule for meditation."

"I do. I just don't need to do it very often."

They continued with the practice but, a moment later, Davyn stopped her again, dampening her fire, which had grown much bigger than Reg had intended.

"Slow down," he advised. He wiped sweat from his face with the back of his hand. "What's going on today, Reg? You have something on your mind."

"No," she insisted. "I just made a mistake. I'm a little tired."

"Why are you tired?"

"Because I haven't been sleeping very well."

He opened his mouth to respond and Reg jumped in before he could.

"It *isn't* because I'm worrying about something. I just haven't been sleeping well. And when I do, I have a lot of dreams, and you know how that can make you feel more tired than if you hadn't slept at all."

"Yes, that can be frustrating. How long have you been having trouble sleeping?"

"I don't know." Reg didn't really want to give a truthful answer. At least Davyn didn't have the lie-detection gift that Damon did. "It's been a little while. I'm sure I'll sleep better tonight."

"Have you seen someone about it? Sarah probably has some sleep-inducing teas."

Reg wrinkled her nose. Sarah's potions might work. Reg wasn't sure whether they did or not, but she did know that Sarah's teas tasted awful. Reg had been shocked the first time she'd had a healing tea made by one of the fairies, and it had actually tasted good as well as doing what it was supposed to. All of the herbal preparations that Sarah made were bitter and foul-tasting, a challenge to even choke down.

"I saw Marian yesterday, and she gave me valerian tea and

lavender. But it didn't help much. I'm sure... tonight will be better."

"Why? Did you get a prescription? I don't see how it will be any better if nothing has changed. Do you know why you're having trouble sleeping?"

"It will be fine," Reg insisted, trying to close the subject. "Can we get back to playing with fire?"

Usually, the phrase brought a smile to his face but, today, he just shook his head. "Not while you are so scattered. This is dangerous. I know you want to play, and I do, too, but sometimes you have to recognize your limitations and realize this is not the right time. Just like sometimes you want to go out to an event but you can't because you are sick. You still want to go, and you would if you could, but you stay home in bed and look after yourself because that's what you have to do."

"I'm not sick," Reg grumped.

"No. But you know that an accident with your fire could have disastrous consequences. We cannot risk it. Why don't we finish up by working on meditation? Maybe that will settle you down enough that you will be able to sleep tonight and get back on the right track and, next week, you will be able to play like normal. But I won't risk it while you're so distracted."

Reg opened her mouth to argue but, this time, it was Davyn who held up his hand and overrode what she was going to say. "You're not going to talk me out of it. It is too dangerous. So we can work on meditation, go inside, have another cup of coffee, and chat for a while."

Ember snorted, not liking this any more than Reg did. He loved it when she came over to play. He was just as excited to see her using her fire and playing a game or two with him as she was to be able to use it.

He came over and nudged Reg as if trying to get her to conjure fire even though Davyn had said not to. Reg wanted to comply but knew she couldn't go against what Davyn said. He was the only one she knew who could work with her on her firecasting skills and, if she didn't listen to what he told her, he would no longer work with her. As frustrating as it was, she had to obey her mentor or lose out on being able to cast fire at all. Reg scratched Ember's ears and jaw.

"I'm sorry, bud. I'm just not feeling very well today, so I can't. We'll meditate for a while with a little fire, okay?"

He put his head on her shoulder, grumbling.

"Let's sit down," Davyn suggested. He sat on a tree stump, and Reg on the tree that had been cut down. She looked it over, wondering whether it had been harmed in a storm or had been diseased. She knew Davyn wouldn't just cut down a tree for no reason. But it looked like it had been there for a long time; it was old and gray and weathered.

Davyn kindled a small flame in his palm, and sat staring at it. Reg tried to focus, looking into the depths of the flame. Reg tried to clear her mind of everything else and just focus on the flame. The very heart of it.

It calmed her anxiety somewhat. She hated to admit that maybe Davyn was right. She should have been more diligent in her meditation exercises while going through this disruption in her life, rather than skipping it because it was too difficult and she was too easily distracted.

That was when she needed it the most.

CHAPTER SEVENTEEN

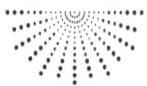

*S*he relaxed her muscles, loosening them up the best she could, feeling for any tension in her body as she gazed at the flame. She was aware of Davyn working around her consciousness of the moment, trying to understand what was going on with her, like a doctor prodding an injury.

If she could just sleep... She was sure that sleep would make her feel better. It wasn't the first time her sleep schedule had been a problem. It happened with regularity. As a child, her sleep schedule had been unmanageable. It was better as an adult when she could set her own schedule to a certain extent. She knew what times were usually good—or not good—for her.

If she went home and tried to sleep for an hour or two, that wouldn't be so bad, would it? She knew that sleeping out of her circadian rhythm could really screw things up, but it couldn't get much worse. Sleeping during the day to catch up was not the worst thing she could do for herself.

But what would she dream if she fell asleep now? She knew that when she fell asleep during the day, she tended to have wild nightmares. She was already having disturbing enough dreams without adding another ingredient to the mix.

She knew the end of her dream about life in ancient Egypt,

so she wouldn't dream that again, would she? She was pretty sure that she wouldn't. Once something in a dream was resolved, she would stop dreaming it. She already knew her brave warrior died and the priestess and her court died. There wasn't anything left to dream after that.

She thought of El-Sayed's clear green eyes. Very much like October's. It made sense, she supposed, that she would dream of someone like him. They had been together when she had seen the first part of the vision, so she had given the warrior some of his attributes. His strength and bravery. His muscular figure. His beautiful clear green eyes.

Suddenly, she was looking at another pair of clear green eyes. This time, it was not the warrior but the Greek athlete. He, too, had those crystal-clear green eyes—or she had assigned them to him in her dream.

"Most esteemed poetess," Petros whispered, pulling her to him for a brief embrace. It was disconcerting to see him in a cloak when she had seen him fully naked while he had been training. He graced her cheek with the whisper of a kiss, and looked around, hoping no one was in a position to observe them. While neither of them was married, it was unthinkable that they would meet each other alone, without an entourage, even though they intended to do nothing other than talk in private.

The only person who might be nearby was Reg's lady-in-waiting, who had received the message from the street urchin the wrestler had sent and had escorted her to the meeting place. Reg had sent her away, but she might still be close, still within earshot, monitoring the situation.

"I'm so glad we could meet," she said softly. "Thank you."

A smile played across his face. "Of course, my lady. It is an honor to spend time with you. I would give up my opportunity to compete in the games to be with you."

She knew that he wouldn't really. Competing in the games

was the most important thing in his life. His reason for being. The reason he was here in Olympia. Without the games, he would be half a world away. It was just flattery.

"Let's sit down," she motioned to a bench in the grove. "Where we can talk."

It took a moment for them to both get comfortable. She looked at him, again amused at her own reaction to seeing him clothed. She wanted him to remove his robe so that he looked like he always did. It was silly and made her smile.

"Tell me all about your training," she encouraged him. "You have come such a long way, done so much. Have you always wanted to be an athlete?"

"Did you always want to be a poet?" he countered.

"Yes, always. I have always loved words, loved putting them together, seeing what beautiful things I could create with them. I love the way words flow, how I can drink them, and breathe them out for others."

"And you do," he agreed. "I have never heard such beauty."

"And you…" She stroked his muscular arm with a teasing forefinger. "You carry beauty with you wherever you go."

His smile softened the more rugged planes of his face. "The human body is a beautiful thing and I have done my best to perfect mine. Everything we do—training, education, diet —is all aimed at perfecting the body, making it operate as the gods intended."

"You look like one of them."

"One of whom?"

"One of the gods. You look like Zeus. Or Heracles."

He made the sign of the fig to ward away evil. "You must be careful what you say. A warrior, no matter how hard he works, never aspires to godhood. We cannot hope to achieve anywhere near their beauty and perfection."

They both looked around as if waiting for one of the divine ones to approach and either praise him for his modesty and humility or strike him with a lightning bolt because Reg

*had dared to comment on how he neared the gods in his
perfection of form.*

*The grove was quiet. No one approached. Reg's lady had
apparently gone home, and no gods chastised them for
worshiping the human body.*

"Reg."

He shook Reg's arm—only it wasn't Petros; it was Davyn.
He had extinguished his fire and was looking at her with
concern.

"Yes? What?"

"You were... are you okay?"

"Yes. Of course. I'm just fine. Why?"

"You were in a trance, just staring..."

"Did you see it, too?"

"See what?"

She was going to say "the vision," but then she would have
to explain what she had seen. And she didn't want to have to
bring someone else into it. If Davyn hadn't shared the vision
with her, as October had, then he wasn't meant to know
about it.

"Nothing. I was just meditating. That was what I was
supposed to be doing, wasn't it?"

"What were you thinking about?"

"That's... personal, isn't it? I don't need to tell you what it
was."

"No, of course not," he agreed quickly. "I don't expect you
to tell me what you are thinking about privately. I was just curious, but it is none of my business. You were just so focused
that... I was worried."

"Nothing to be concerned about," Reg said lightly, with a
shrug. "Just doing what you told me to do."

"Then I'd better not complain about it," Davyn said good-
humoredly. "I'm sorry I interrupted you. You have definitely
improved in your meditative focus." A slight blush colored his

cheeks. "I'm sorry for criticizing you and asking whether you were doing your meditation. You have clearly been working on it."

Reg shrugged. She couldn't very well tell him the truth.

"Should we go into the house, or did you want to continue with your meditation?"

"Let's go inside."

They walked back to the house. Ember took flight and wheeled in circles overhead until they reached the house. Ember landed and gamboled up to Reg like a puppy, playful and excited.

Reg scratched the soft, smooth scales around his ears. Then she reached into her pockets and gathered a few coins she had set aside during the week. She would have used only electronic payment for all her goods, but she knew she had a dragon who needed cold, hard cash and jewels. She presented the coins to Ember, and he took them from her delicately with his clawed hands. Then he flew off over the woods and out of sight. Reg watched him go.

"Where is his hoard, do you know?"

"Not exactly, and I would never go looking for it! When he started getting too big to fit down in the basement, he moved it away, bit by bit, to whatever cave or other hiding place he has chosen. It is well-hidden."

"Full of pennies," Reg laughed. "He doesn't seem to mind that they are not gold coins."

"No, and he finds glittery costume jewelry just as entrancing as the real thing. I am not going to try to dissuade him. I can't afford to give him my hard-earned gold."

Reg laughed. "Me neither. I've given him a few real gems but, mostly, he'll just have to settle for the glass stuff."

They entered Davyn's house. There was not yet a fire burning in the fireplace, which was big enough for a man to stand up in. But when Ember returned from stashing his new treasure, he would insist on one being kindled. Reg didn't sense

Julian's presence, so they could have a fire without worrying about his roasting in the heat.

Reg sat on the couch while Davyn brewed coffee in his big, fancy machine.

She thought of the clear green eyes of the athlete. Had she given him green eyes because she was obsessed with October and his alluring green eyes? She didn't think that the single feature had affected her so much. October was gorgeous, like Petros in the vision. But had Petros had anything else In common with October? He worshiped the human form rather than being concerned with others, as October was. The games were all that was important to him.

CHAPTER EIGHTEEN

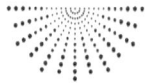

*H*ere you go."

Reg returned her attention to the room as Davyn handed her a cup of coffee. She inhaled the steam, reveling in the rich, aromatic brew.

"Your coffee always tastes so much better than mine. I even got a fancy machine that grinds the beans and does all of the work, and it still isn't the same as yours."

"What beans are you buying?"

"I don't know. Whatever's on sale at the grocery store."

He snorted. "You get what you pay for. If you want good beans, I can give you the details of a few places to order them. But you won't find them on the shelves of the Big Mart."

Reg had money now. She could afford to pay for a better bean. But her penny-pinching ways were ingrained from many years of barely scraping by. Or not scraping by. She grimaced. "I guess I'll have to bite the bullet if I really want to make a good brew."

He nodded and took a sip from his cup, settling on the sofa beside her.

"So, long thoughts today? You looked very far away."

Not to mention her distractions when trying to do her firecasting exercises. And losing herself in ancient Greece when she was supposed to be meditating.

"Do you believe in reincarnation?"

He shrugged. "Whether I believe or not does not change the immutability of the soul. You are fully aware of the existence of a life force that is not confined to a physical body. I don't know the nature of that soul or whether or not every one passes through more than one joining with a physical body. I don't know the ins and outs of how that works. But I'm open to it. I have certainly seen evidence of it more than once."

"So you believe a person can actually be reborn as others in multiple lifetimes."

"Why does what I believe matter to you? Why don't you tell me what you have seen or have evidence of."

"Well, I don't have any evidence."

"No? You have *something* on your mind."

"Do you think... that we can remember people from other lives? That we might meet them again in another life?"

"It seems that some relationships do persist across lifetimes. That the same two souls may be intertwined, even if they are in different relationships in each life."

"Different relationships?"

"Maybe lovers in one life, mother and child in another, brother and sister, best friends..."

"Really?"

"There are many different names for these karmic bonds or life-crossers. But they are a part of many different religions and philosophies. When you have a very strong bond with someone in this life, many people would consider that a sign that you had somehow been involved with the other person in a previous incarnation. I don't think that is always the case. I think we can 'click' for other reasons, but I wouldn't dispute the power of previous life connections."

"So you and I could have met in a previous life."

"Certainly."

"In more than one?"

"How many previous incarnations have you had?"

Reg was taken aback. "I don't know. I didn't think that I'd had any until recently. Now... I don't know. How could I know that?"

"And I don't know how many I have had either. Given the fact that both of us could have had countless existences before... I certainly think there is the possibility that we have met and been friends or otherwise familiar with each other in other lives. Multiple lives."

"Do people just keep getting reborn again and again? You just die and then... are immediately born again somewhere else?"

"I told you I don't know how it works or how many different incarnations I might have had. I am just as ignorant of the process of transmigration as you are."

"I don't think so," Reg shook her head, disgusted at how little she knew about this. "Considering I've never even heard the term before."

"Well..." Davyn chuckled and took another sip of his coffee. "Maybe I have studied it a little more than you, but it is not possible to know the unknowable."

"Then why study it?"

"Like you... I have had questions and have sought the answers. I may not have been successful in unwinding the mysteries of the universe, but I have satisfied my curiosity as much as possible. Come to a belief that this... recycling of souls or progression through different states of being is the basis of belief for many religions."

Reg's mind boggled at the thought. She had a hard enough time unwinding her own heritage and origins in this life.

"But if I'm one thing in this life... a medium or a fire-caster... or a part siren... then that wouldn't be the same across all lives? A fairy couldn't be reincarnated as a skinwalker or a goblin, right?"

Davyn laughed. "Some religions believe you could return as a dog. Or a flea. If you do not fill the measure of your creation, you could be... demoted in the next life. On the other hand, if you do well, if you are all that you can be and complete your life mission, you could be *elevated* in the next, become a higher life form." He smiled. "Maybe a dragon."

Reg heard the whoosh of wings and flapping as Ember landed outside the house, then squeezed in the porch door to join them. Inside the house, it was even more apparent how much he had grown. It wouldn't be long before he couldn't enter through the door any longer. And then what? Would they meet outside? Make a new, bigger door? Would Ember establish a home somewhere else? In the mountains far away?

Ember approached Reg and rubbed his head against her shoulder, making little purring noises. In answer to Reg's thoughts, he sent Reg a picture of himself curled up on a pile of gold coins and jewelry, with Reg tucked under his arm like a favorite doll. She laughed and scratched the fine, smooth scales around his ears.

CHAPTER NINETEEN

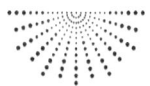

*C*an we meet at Psychic Beginnings?" Reg asked October over the phone. "Marian's place?"

He didn't respond immediately. "Why?" he eventually asked. "I don't think that my friendship with Marian has any impact on... what you and I are going through."

Reg tried to unwind that. His friendship with Marian? So he wasn't seeing her in a professional capacity. He didn't even sound like he had considered her profession before answering the question.

"I don't know anything about your friendship. But I have been consulting her about these dreams and wanted to talk to her more about... you and I. Sharing this dream, I mean. Not our relationship." The conversation was growing awkward. Reg didn't want to claim a relationship with him that they didn't have. They were friends, not anything else. Even if they had experienced crossings in previous lives, that didn't give her a special position with October. And she didn't want it to make things awkward between him and Marian. Or to make it look to Marian like she was butting in.

"You've had more of these dreams?"

"Well... not that one specifically. But I have been having

trouble sleeping lately, and having these dreams. I can't always remember them when I wake up, but I have been able to remember a couple of them, and Marian thinks they might be memories of past lives. I thought... we should talk to her about... developments. About you and I sharing a vision and a dream. I guess... I want to know whether this is just something produced by my imagination or... if it is really something we shared."

"And you think Marian could help with that?"

"She is a psychic. And not a bad one. I'm hoping that she can sense something. Give us some direction."

"Direction. To do what?"

"If I knew that... I wouldn't need direction."

"I say we just chalk it up as a bad dream." October was much more cavalier about it now than he had been when they had both just awakened from the dream. "Move on with our lives."

"Can you really just forget it?"

"Forget it? No, probably not. But I can put it behind me. Move on with my own life."

"You don't believe that *was* your own life?"

"Maybe it was. But if it was, it happened millennia ago. It's time to move on."

"So you won't meet with Marian?"

"We can, if you insist. But don't get your hopes up that it is... something significant. I don't think this is anything earth-shattering. I don't think she'll have any grand answers for us."

* * *

Reg called ahead this time, setting up an appointment with Marian so they wouldn't find her there with another client or have to wait for an opening. October sounded like he had lost interest in the whole thing and, if she made him wait, he might just leave after a while and not be interested in trying again.

Marian sounded pleased that Reg was coming back. Reg got the feeling that she was often alone and didn't have many good friends. Marian was surprised that October was going to be coming with Reg so, obviously, he hadn't talked with her about the vision at the restaurant or the dream, even if they were good friends.

Reg didn't know why she had such difficulty picturing the very handsome werewolf and the middle-aged psychic as friends. Age and looks had very little to do with friendship and the ability of two people to connect, so why did she have so much trouble with it?

Maybe it was because her relationships with each of them were so different. A friendly, professional relationship with Marian. And with October? A sometimes flirtatious friendship? Two practitioners who had worked a job together, who had worked together to save the wolf pack.

She tried to arrive at Psychic Beginnings before their appointment, thinking maybe she would have a chat with Marian while they were waiting for October to show up. But despite her best efforts to arrive fifteen or twenty minutes early, she was late getting in the door and found October and Marian with their heads together, turning the tables. Instead of having a chance to talk about the situation with Marian ahead of time, they had been talking about her.

Reg's cheeks and ears burned. Despite the calming emotions Marian attempted to send in her direction, she was flustered and embarrassed. Things were not turning out at all as she had planned.

"Hi," she tried to cover how rattled she was. "I'm sorry I'm late. Things just kept happening to slow me down. I don't know why."

"That is the way things go sometimes," Marian assured her. "Maybe it was meant to be. It is funny how often a series of misfortunes turns out to be positive in the end, causing us to avoid a larger disaster, make a connection, or be where we are needed at the time. October and I have had a nice chat while we have been waiting, so you don't need to worry about that."

Reg did worry about it, just ever so slightly. She glanced at October for his response, wondering whether he was happy she had been delayed. He gave no sign of what he was thinking.

"Well, why don't we all make ourselves comfortable," Marian suggested, motioning to the table and chairs in the middle of the store.

They weren't exactly comfortable chairs, but they weren't hard metal or plastic chairs, either. They were at least upholstered, but they weren't the kind of chairs she could settle and get cozy in. The three of them sat down. Reg could smell tea, but Marian didn't bring any over to the table immediately, so Reg had to assume Marian had something different in mind.

"October told me a little bit about your situation," Marian began.

Reg shot a glance at him. She had assumed that they would not begin until they were all together. She would explain the situation herself, since she was the one who had started having the dreams and visions, and October could contribute his thoughts afterward. He didn't seem too eager to have the consultation with Marian, so she could only assume that everything he had told her about their shared vision and dream had been cast in a negative light. She would now have to overcome all kinds of obstacles before they could move forward and get anywhere.

October raised his brows, fixing Reg with his bright green eyes, and did not apologize or give any sign that he understood her disappointment in how things were unfolding.

"Maybe we should start at the beginning," Reg said, hoping to get better control of the situation.

"I think I have a pretty good grasp," Marian offered. "You came to me earlier, and I understand you are having somewhat disruptive dreams about past lives. These incidents are keeping you from being able to get a good rest. Did the valerian and lavender help?"

Reg shook her head. "No. Not really."

"I'm sorry to hear that. We might need a stronger preparation to help you to get the sleep you need."

Reg didn't say anything to this. She was no longer there about her inability to sleep. Things had gone far beyond that.

"Now October has... become involved," Reg said, unsure how else to explain how he now figured into the equation. "He shared my vision at the restaurant. He touched my hand and it... triggered something. Then last night... I dreamt more about that life with him. And I guess..." She looked at October.

"I also had a dream," October acknowledged. "It was very disturbing, very emotional. But I thought it was just because I was disturbed by the previous vision. My brain was trying to fill in details and resolve the unfinished story. Except that right after I awoke, Reg called me, and it was clear that she had just had the same dream."

Reg nodded. Marian asked for more information about the dream, and the two of them told the story, stilted at first, and then filling in details for each other and finishing each other's sentences so that the story flowed without a break.

Marian listened attentively. "I think it is pretty clearly a past-life memory rather than something Reg has invented or hallucinated," she advised. "The consistency of details between your two experiences. Historical accuracy. I assume neither of you is an Egyptologist."

Reg laughed. October shook his head seriously. "It's not a history I've ever been that interested in," he said. "It always seemed like they had more interest in cats than dogs."

Reg and Marian both raised their brows at this. It seemed like a very shallow reason for not being interested in a particular country or culture.

"What about Anubis and Wepwawet?" Marian challenged.

October shrugged. "The culture worshiped cats. What can I say?"

Marian shook her head. "So neither of you has had any particular interest in ancient Egypt, and yet the story you tell is full of historically accurate detail. Where did that come from if it is not a former life memory?"

Reg sighed. She didn't know why she was still fighting it, still trying to tell herself that she had not lived any previous lives. Why was it such a sticking point for her? Because she was proud of herself for all she had overcome in this life and did not want it to be overshadowed by another life? Because she had grown up with scant community or friends, and rejected the idea of former associations and meetings?

She should be happy that she'd lived other lives where she'd had more power and success or friends and lovers. She should be happy that her life spread eternally in both directions and what she knew would not be her only existence.

Instead, she felt overwhelmed by the possibility, the pressure of all those lives weighing heavily on her shoulders. If she had been so successful in former lives, why had she fallen so low in this life, barely scraping by an existence on the street at times? Sarah and the other practitioners told her how powerful she was, and she had thought that power had come from Norma Jean, her mother, and Weston, the immortal who claimed to be her father. But if it was something she had brought with her from other lives, then what did she really know about herself and her heritage?

She rubbed her forehead, the third eye position pulsing with pain.

"So I've lived other lives. How many? And October?"

Marian nodded. "Probably many lives. There have been many generations since ancient Egypt and, as far as anyone can tell, there is not usually much of a gap between death and rebirth."

"Many lives." Reg tried to calculate how many lives they were talking about. Life expectancy had been much shorter in ancient times—other than people like Methuselah, apparently. If she calculated that the average human lifespan was fifty years, and she had been cycling through lives continuously since ancient Egyptian times...

She couldn't even calculate out how many lives that was. Hundreds? Why did one life stand out more than the others? And had she lived before that, or was that her first? Davyn had talked about souls progressing from lower animals to human lives and, if that were the case, how many times had she had to cycle through before reaching her first human life?

"This is all academic," October said impatiently. "Why does it matter how many lives we may have lived before now and whether there were gaps in between? I already live two different lives in this world. I don't need more overflowing into the present. Why can't they just stay in the past?"

His eyes slid over to Reg and he spoke directly to her. "The question is, what has triggered these memories now, thousands of years later?"

Though he didn't exactly say it, Reg thought that he meant what had *she* done to cause him this trouble. What digging around in the past or dark magic had she done to bring these memories to the forefront now, where he had to deal with them?

"I didn't ask for these memories any more than you did," she told him testily. "I just started having these dreams out of nowhere. It wasn't because of something I did to conjure them up."

"No," Marian agreed, her voice low and soothing. "This isn't anyone's fault. I think... there may be unresolved issues or unfinished business from those past lives that are affecting you now."

"Unresolved issues?" October repeated, at the same time as Reg said, "Unfinished business?" They both looked at each other. Reg wanted to laugh at their simultaneous reaction, but she couldn't. It was too serious.

"It may have been triggered just by the two of you being together. Until now, you have not met in this life. You've both lived in other places and have not had any contact with each other. Now you are both in Black Sands, have worked closely on a project and become..." She hesitated. "Friends? Acquaintances? But being around each other has brought up these old memories. This ancient crossing in Egypt."

"What could be unresolved from thousands of years ago?" October pressed. "And how can we resolve it?"

"Is it because they both died?" Reg suggested. "Maybe something was going on between us, a relationship, and we died without ever acknowledging it?"

"Okay," October said stolidly. "Mery, whatever your name was back then, El-Sayed loved and cared for you and never acknowledged it."

They both sat there, staring at each other. October looked around and shrugged as if he had been expecting lightning or another dramatic reaction to his pronouncement. Reg frowned and shook her head.

"I don't think that is even true," she said. "I don't think it was a secret. Maybe it was a secret from the rest of the world, her staff and his men, but I don't think it was... unrequited."

"Then what do we need to resolve?" October smiled and shook his head, but the smile, as well as his voice, seemed very forced. "I hate to tell you this, but I am not getting into a romantic relationship because we may have had one in a past life thousands of years ago."

"I'm not either," Reg agreed. Although she had been attracted to October from the first time she had met him. It wasn't her fault that he was so handsome. Those green eyes made him hard to ignore. The way that Mery and El-Sayed had interacted with each other as he was preparing to go to battle had such emotional depth, as did their subsequent deaths, that she couldn't see him as just another man or just a friend. There was something much stronger between the two of them.

They both turned their eyes back to Marian.

"So what can we do?"

CHAPTER TWENTY

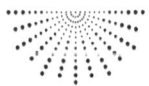

*M*arian's answer was less than satisfying. Figuring out what had triggered their memories and how to resolve any past issues would take a lot of work. She suggested past-life regression, hallucinogenics, talk therapy, and a book on dream symbolism.

Reg wasn't too open to any of these solutions. She wanted the instant fix. Perhaps an incantation, a potion to swallow, and the memories of past lives would recede into the distance, not to bother them again.

She gathered from October's expression and his brief, flat goodbyes that he had a similar viewpoint. He did not suggest they go to dinner again to talk it out. Reg feared that if they did, they would be plunged even deeper into the memories. If October's presence had triggered the reappearance of the memories, then perhaps they should stay apart and not have anything to do with each other for a while.

They said cordial goodbyes and went their different directions. Reg was exhausted from her firecasting, the past-life memories, and the new tension between her and October. She drove herself home, made a mug of the valerian tea, and sat down on the couch with her phone and the TV to scroll or channel surf until her brain grew numb and she fell asleep.

Starlight jumped up on the wicker couch and rubbed against her, yowling and demanding attention. He didn't need more food or water, he just wanted to know what was wrong and for her to give him pets and cuddles.

After a good amount of stroking, he finally curled himself into a ball beside her, warm against her leg.

"It is all going to be fine," Reg told him. "We'll just avoid each other for a little while, and the dreams will fade away into oblivion."

Starlight made a small trill and covered his nose with his tail. Reg yawned, more to convince her body that she was getting tired and she would like to have a nap than because she really was.

She would nap for an hour or two, then get up and prepare for her evening appointments, feeling renewed and refreshed.

They had become more comfortable on the bench, naturally getting closer to each other and exchanging fleeting touches as they spoke, lost in conversation. She loved having someone to talk to. She knew the power of language, and Petros hung on her every word. At the same time, she was entranced by the beauty of his body and the strictness of his training regimen, interested in every detail of how he and the other athletes ate, slept, moved, and exercised to improve their bodies and functions, disciplining them until they were images of the gods they worshiped.

Perhaps others would see it as a strangely unbalanced relationship, with their interests being so opposite. But instead, it was as if they completed each other, she with her words and intellectual pursuits, and he with his physical perfection and goal to compete in—and perhaps even win laurels in—the Olympic games.

She didn't know how much time had passed so pleasantly

when they heard approaching footsteps. They froze, listening. Whoever was nearby would surely simply pass them by, uninterested in the couple in conversation in the grove. Her hand landed on his arm, his on her leg, as they reached out to still and quiet each other until the passerby was gone.

At first, she couldn't see who it was. The owner of the footsteps carried a lantern, and the brightness prevented her from seeing the face beyond the light. But she recognized the voice when he spoke.

"Esteemed lady," the lantern-bearer's tone was disapproving, shocked at her public display. "We have been concerned by your absence. Have you been detained by this... young dog?"

Reg pulled her hand away from his arm and he also withdrew his from her leg. They were still too close to each other, their bodies nearly touching. Not how she had been taught to behave in public by her mother and other esteemed ladies.

But they had not been in public. They had thought themselves alone.

Which, of course, was even worse. A virtuous woman and man must never find themselves alone together in circumstances such as these. They both knew better. They had thought to escape the ridiculous strictures against men and women conversing together by meeting away from the rule-enforcers.

"I am fine, Phylakas," she said, "We are merely talking. It is so hard to get the chance when Petros spends so much of the day training. You know how he is the favorite for the Olympic wrestling competition."

"All the more reason he should be sleeping at this hour of the day," her chaperone told her severely. "This shocking behavior is just what one would hope a young man of such promise would guard against. His minders have not been very diligent."

She swallowed.

"Sir, all blame cannot be laid at his feet. I am, in truth, the guilty party. He was merely indulging the whims of an esteemed guest."

"I have never known you to take such liberties. You are shameless. I promised your parents I would guard your virtue and care for you as if you were my own daughter. And now I find you here, in this compromising position. You will return home immediately."

"Yes, Phylakas. I am… very sorry. I am mortified. But I meant no harm."

"Come now."

She rose from the bench, her legs stiff and cramped after sitting on the hard bench for so long. It must have been much longer than it had seemed. She felt like they had only been there for a few minutes; the time had flown past.

She did not look at the young wrestler, but kept her eyes demurely on the ground, just ahead of her feet. With the lantern raised high to guide her, her guardian ushered her through the grove to the city streets and back to their lodging. There seemed to be many more people on the streets of the polis than there should have been. Perhaps it was just that, in her shame, it seemed that all eyes were pointed at her. Their whispers rose to her ears. Words that she had never thought would be aimed at her. Names that made her cheeks flame.

But the entire time she was walking back to their house of lodging, she was thinking of her young wrestler. Men were not shamed as much as women for small indiscretions. Hopefully, his fellow athletes and trainer would laugh and nudge each other and, while Petros would be embarrassed at being found out, his reputation would not be damaged.

* * *

Her hopes were not to be realized.

The next morning, before her ladies even entered her room

to help her with her ablutions and preparation to see the officials she was to recite before, she heard them talking about Petros, the city's favorite for the wrestling competition, and how he had been shamed and was to be brought before the competition officials today to try to defend his behavior.

But there was no excuse, besides the one she had provided to her guardian. She had prevailed upon him and he had simply been accommodating a lady greatly esteemed by the metropolis, including the Hellanodikai in charge of the games. Perhaps Petros could be excused if he said he had been doing it for the sake of the Olympic games. But she feared that would not excuse his indiscretion.

After she was properly dressed and prepared for visitors, the man appointed her guardian during her travels appeared before her. His eyes were not lowered as they usually were when he appeared in her presence. Instead, he met her gaze boldly, and she found it necessary to drop her own, her cheeks growing warm under his brazen stare.

"Your recitations have been canceled," he told her in a tone of satisfaction. "The Hellanodikai are all in agreement that they do not wish a woman of such wanton reputation to be part of the ceremonies."

She swallowed. "All of my appearances during the games?"

"All of your appearances in Olympia. We are making arrangements for your immediate return home."

The lump in her throat was not going away. It was a struggle to keep the tears from springing up in her eyes. She had worked so hard to get there. It had not been an easy journey. Rising to the top of her profession, putting out the word that she wanted an invitation to the games, getting sponsors for her trip, and, not least of all, convincing her parents that it was safe for her to go on the journey and what a privilege it was for her to appear in the various venues that had been arranged for her.

She nodded her head in submission.

"And Petros?" she asked.

"The young man is also being sent home."

She caught her breath. "No!"

"He will be banned from the games." He folded his arms. "His career as a wrestler is over. He will need to find an apprenticeship elsewhere. After this disgrace, few places would take him. Perhaps he can become a fishmonger."

She had done this to Petros. If it had not been for her invitation, for the way she had encouraged his affections, he would have been able to compete in the Olympic games and, perhaps, even be crowned with laurels. And now his career, his entire life, was ruined by her indiscretion.

She put her hands over her face before the tears could come, but she could not stop the flood once it had started.

CHAPTER TWENTY-ONE

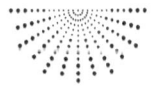

*W*aking after this dream of Greece was not as devastating as waking from her dream of the death of the Egyptian priestess and her warrior. But it was still crushing. The poetess had been among the best in her craft, had worked hard to get the recognition she deserved. To be called upon to recite her work at the games in Olympia was a great honor. Her god-given talent had been appreciated. Everyone knew her name.

Her admiration of the young wrestler had grown almost to an obsession, and she had been excited when Petros returned his affection and agreed to meet her.

Knowing that she had ruined both of their hard-earned careers with her actions shattered her. How could she have made such a terrible mistake? She had told no one who she was meeting and had thought she would be home long before anyone had reason to be concerned. He had made similar arrangements with his fellow athletes, telling them only that he was going for a long walk to condition his legs. How had they been discovered? How had her guardian known where to find her?

Reg rubbed her brows and forehead tenderly. She had hoped

that the nap would make her feel better. She would be able to work through the situation with October and her dreams, and handle her evening appointments with a clear head. But instead, she was now even more emotionally drained. How could she handle all of the deaths and disappointments of her past lives as well as the one she was living? She couldn't let herself get caught up in them. The past needed to stay in the past. There was no benefit to reliving these terrible disappointments.

"I need coffee," she told Starlight, who stretched all four limbs, quivering with the effort. "Lots and lots of coffee."

He gave an understanding meow. Acknowledging the fact that Reg was going into the kitchen where there was food for cats, rather than any interest in her coffee drinking habits.

Reg chuckled at this. She swung her feet over the edge of the bed, and Starlight was off like a shot to beat her to his food bowl and make sure it was the first thing she focused on when her lazy human legs eventually brought her to the kitchen.

Reg was brought up short when she saw Harrison waiting for her in the kitchen. He had picked Starlight up and was cuddling him to his face. Harrison loved cats, and Starlight in particular. From what Reg could understand, they had been friends in one or more of Starlight's former incarnations.

Harrison might be a good person to ask about her dreams of October and her previous lives.

Was October having the same dreams as Reg was about the young athlete in Olympia? He hadn't mentioned them to her in front of Marian, but that didn't mean that he wasn't, just that he wasn't ready to talk about an additional dream in front of an outsider.

Maybe October wasn't sure whether it was a shared dream either. Perhaps the dream of Greece was an additional complication neither of them was ready to discuss.

Reg's eyes went to the kitchen island, where about sixty filled coffee cups were crowded together. The rich aroma of freshly brewed coffee filled the kitchen.

"What's all this?" she demanded.

"Lots of coffee," Harrison intoned. "Lots and lots of coffee."

Reg gave a little laugh of disbelief and drilled a knuckle into the tight knot of muscles in her forehead. Maybe the caffeine would help her headache.

"I can't drink that much."

Harrison nuzzled the top of Starlight's head. "Lots and lots of coffee."

"Yes, you got me lots and lots of coffee. And that *is* what I said. What are you doing? How long have you been here?"

"You did tell me not to watch you sleep."

"Yes, I appreciate that. I'd much rather find you in the kitchen than wake up with you watching me in the bedroom. That was very thoughtful of you."

"I have come with a warning."

Reg took one of the cups of coffee off the island and looked at him, dread knotting her guts. She took a long drag of the hot, bitter coffee and tried to tell herself that it would just be something silly. Harrison had acted as her guardian in the past, but she wasn't a child anymore. The dangers she had faced back then were past. Maybe his warning was that she was now out of coffee beans, since he had used it all up making her afternoon coffee for her.

"What is your warning?" she asked in a calm, even voice.

"He is a danger to you. A threat to this existence."

"He? Who is a danger to me?"

"He goes by many names," Harrison said meditatively. "But he is here again, as he has been in the past."

"*Here* where?"

"Here in this time and place," Harrison tried to clarify. "Reg needs to take care."

"Do you know his name here?"

"Names are not important. He can change names. He cannot change who he is. Not... not in the now."

"Can you show him to me? Take me to him?"

Harrison looked pained. He shook his head. "I do not know his current shape. Only that he is here again. I can feel him."

It was hard to understand the limitations of her guardian. Reg thought of the immortals as being all-powerful and all-knowing, but it had been pointed out to her more than once that immortal was not the same as omniscient or omnipotent, and just because that was how she had been taught to see deity. The Christian god that had been worshiped by some of the foster families she had lived with knew all and could do anything He wanted to.

The gods in other cultures, however—the gods of Greece, Rome, and other pantheons—were more human-like. They had human limitations and foibles. They had preferences and personalities. Like Harrison.

She didn't even know if he were truly immortal, as long as he was not killed by violence. He might just be long-lived. His apparent ability to conjure food and drink out of nowhere had been lifesaving to her as the starving child of a negligent junkie.

It was hard to understand how he could be aware of a dark entity that threatened her existence and not be able to tell which direction the danger came from.

"How do you know he is here? Has he… done something to attract your attention? How close is he?"

"He has been in your life before, in different forms. I see this… he has… ended other existences."

"What do you mean, ended other existences?"

But Reg knew exactly what he meant. She wanted more clarity, but Harrison's explanations tended to get even more obscure and difficult to understand the more she questioned him. What was real and concrete to her as a human was never straightforward to Harrison. Her existence and movement through time and space were linear, but his were not.

"You should sit down," Harrison told her gravely.

CHAPTER TWENTY-TWO

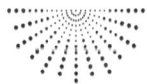

*T*he response was startling. Harrison rarely used "you" when talking to Reg, referring instead to "Reg" as if she were out of the room.

And advising her to sit down when he was about to break something to her was also out of character, as he didn't necessarily understand human emotions and how what he told her might affect her.

She suspected Harrison was echoing something he had heard on TV. Maybe a cop or hospital show.

She took her coffee to the living room and sat down on the couch. Harrison sank into one of the wicker chairs, still holding Starlight, sprawled with his long legs akimbo, looking comfortable and awkward at the same time.

"Okay. I'm sitting down. What else can you tell me?" Reg asked.

"You know there is a danger. You have been warned of this."

Reg reflected. She hadn't received any portentous warnings she was aware of. No spirits or elves had appeared with cryptic messages. She had not received any messages or signs.

Or had she?

What about the X's in the fortune cookies? What about the dreams and visions that had been plaguing her? She had been upset by her lack of sleep, but had never considered that there might be a reason she was having the dreams. Not just a reaction to something in her environment, but an intentional and directed warning. But from whom? From Harrison? Another life force? The universe itself?

"Is that why I have been having dreams? What does the X mean?"

"X can mean many things," Harrison said thoughtfully.

X could be an unknown, a variable to be identified, a secret identity.

"I know, but did you put it in my fortune cookie? Or did someone else?"

He shrugged. "Someone else?" he echoed the questioning note, so Reg wasn't sure whether it was an answer or not.

"So... I have lived other lives," Reg said conversationally, deciding to approach the problem from another direction.

He leaned forward, his eyes probing hers. "Yes?"

"Did you and I know each other in other lives?"

His head cocked to the side slightly. "Perhaps."

"You can't remember?"

"I remember *many* times and places... but not all of them yours."

Reg had never subscribed to the idea of a multiverse; but then, Harrison taking her to her own past and changing things there had not had the same Star Trek-ish results she had expected. There had, apparently, been no time-and-space-ripping paradox. She had still been able to remember the details of the past life she had lived which had been overwritten. And it had not changed her present, or had changed it very little.

But maybe Harrison could see crossings that he and Reg had experienced in other lives, not just previous incarnations but a multiverse of diverging timelines that had not actually occurred for Reg.

"But some of them… in this world. In my timeline."

He still seemed uncertain of his answer. It must be just as perplexing for him to understand her linear timeline as it was for her to envision how Harrison experienced life, time, and place.

"This Reg," Harrison said, making a motion with two parallel hands as if to pin her in time and space, where she sat on the couch drinking her coffee, "has past experiences."

"Previous lives? Incarnations?"

He nodded, brows drawn down. He adjusted Starlight on his lap and petted him with long, gentle strokes.

"And you have known me in some of those past experiences?" Reg prompted.

He gave a quick nod, as if worried the answer might change if he waited too long.

"And in some of those incarnations, this *person* has… caused my death?"

Harrison nodded again.

Reg blew out her breath. There was, apparently, some sinister force that had hunted her throughout more than one lifetime and had succeeded more than once in killing her.

"Why?"

"X," Harrison corrected. "He is unknown."

"No, not the letter Y—I mean, *why* did he kill me? Or kill my previous incarnations?"

"Ah." Harrison scratched Starlight's ears. "Human motives are… difficult."

"They're actually pretty simple. People kill for money, sex, revenge. Or maybe just because they enjoy killing."

"Yesss…"

"But you don't know which one is the reason?"

"Yes."

Yes, she was right about his not knowing, or *yes*, he knew the reason?

"What about October?" Reg asked.

Harrison held up a finger to stop her as he thought about it, composing the answer in his head. Eventually, he announced, "October is the tenth month of the year. It is thirty-one days long. It is... a time when humans wear costumes and burn things."

"Yes. Uh... I meant my friend named October. Have you seen him?" She tried to envision October clearly in her mind so that Harrison would be able to see it.

"Oh..." October's brow furrowed in confusion. "He is a human and not a human?"

"Yes. He can shift between man and wolf. He is a werewolf."

"In all lives or in one life?"

"In this life." Reg was glad she had asked Davyn about the possibility of being another species in other lives, so she was prepared to answer the question. "I don't know what he has been in other lives."

All at once, October was standing in the middle of the living room. Reg's mouth dropped open. October stood frozen for a moment, eyes darting around, and then fixed on Reg.

"What is going on? How did you summon me here? Is something wrong?" He eyed the flamboyantly dressed Harrison, sprawled in the chair with Starlight, and didn't know what to say.

"Uh... sorry, I didn't bring you. I just asked Harrison if he knew you, and *he* brought you here, not me. I'm sorry..."

October didn't move. His eyes caught on the counter full of filled coffee cups, and he couldn't help grinning.

"Reg, I knew you had a problem with drinking too much coffee, but this seems excessive even for you."

Reg laughed, glad for the release of tension. "Please, have a cup. I'm not going to be able to drink all of it. I know you don't usually go for coffee, but..."

October considered, then went over to the counter and picked one up. "Are you expecting a lot of company?" he asked.

"No. It was just a... slight miscommunication."

He took a small sip, found it acceptable, and returned to the living room to sit on the couch with Reg.

"So, as unexpected as it was to find myself here... I would like to talk with you privately, at the first opportunity."

"I think this might affect you, too. That's why I was asking Harrison if he knew you when he had you brought over."

"What affects me?"

"He was warning me of... a danger. A person or entity that is a danger to me, who has ended my life in previous incarnations."

October's eyes widened at that. He considered this possibility. He glanced at Harrison and then back at Reg. "Can I ask who... or what Harrison is?" He looked at Harrison to address him directly. "*What* you are, sir?"

"He is... an immortal," Reg explained. Harrison gave a nod. "He has known me in other lives. He has been... a protector in this life."

"Little Reg," Harrison contributed, "was very cute."

"Yeah, she was," Reg said, shaking her head at the bizarre twist in the conversation. When she had seen herself as a five-year-old child, she too had been very taken with little Reg. She *had* been cute.

"What do you know of this danger?" October questioned, looking from Reg to Harrison to include them both in his question. "And why would it have anything to do with me?"

"I think... you and I have known each other in more than one life," Reg suggested.

He sipped his coffee, thoughtfully considering his answer. "Why?"

"X," Harrison corrected again.

Reg waved this off. "Have you... had any other dreams? Any other visions or insights into a previous life?"

"I've had other dreams," October said slowly, "but I don't

know that they have been anything special. Or had anything to do with past lives."

"I had one earlier about ancient Greece."

October looked interested, but didn't immediately jump in to say that he'd also had a dream about Greece. Maybe he hadn't. Maybe Reg had been wrong about the green-eyed wrestler. Maybe the green eyes in her dream did not signify that it was October, as she had thought it did. Of course, October would not have had green eyes in every one of his previous incarnations, but she might still dream that he did, as a way for her to identify when he appeared in other lives.

"I dreamt about a lady poet and a wrestler," she told October. "I thought... I thought maybe the wrestler was one of your previous incarnations. He wasn't?"

"Each of us could have many incarnations; I doubt either of us can remember each one of them."

"He was going to compete in the ancient Olympic games. But then... something happened and he couldn't."

Reg thought she saw a reaction to this suggestion, but October was being careful not to give anything away in his expression or to allow her access to his mind and emotions. That caution itself made her wonder how much he knew or remembered. Before this, he had always seemed pretty open with her.

"If you're having similar visions, perhaps we can piece things together," Reg urged, "and figure out who is a danger to me. And maybe to you."

"Why would he be a danger to me, if he is targeting you or your previous lives?"

"If you and I have had more crossings... I don't know. If what happened in Egypt was the result of something he did, then your life was ended too."

"What do you mean? How does what happened in Egypt have anything to do with him? Is that what Harrison said?" October looked at Harrison.

"You were betrayed in Egypt. Someone gave away your position and your plan, so they knew what to expect before you even started. That betrayal had to come... from inside our own forces. Someone under your command. Maybe someone who eavesdropped on us. Those plans were not widely known."

"How do we know it wasn't one of *his* kind?" October nodded to Harrison.

CHAPTER TWENTY-THREE

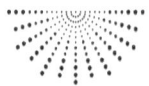

*R*eg looked at Harrison, her stomach again tying into knots. One of the immortals?

It certainly wasn't outside the realm of possibility. She had been targeted in the past by an immortal. She had been in danger from more than one of them, and who knew how many more still existed? They would be impossible to track.

Her heart pounded hard in her chest, making it hurt to breathe.

"Uncle Harrison, who is the danger from? You said he has a lot of names and you don't know what form he is currently in. So... is it one of the immortals? I know you are not able to do anything that would harm one of your kind."

"He is mortal," Harrison advised, giving her a straight answer for once.

And that in itself was odd. Was it the truth? Or was he trying to cover up the truth?

"It isn't the Witch Doctor?" she demanded. "Destine, I mean. He isn't coming after me again?"

"Destine is bound," Harrison pointed out. "He cannot do anything to harm you in that form."

"And the other immortals? What about Weston? Where is he?"

"Weston?" Harrison looked around, and Reg saw Weston standing in the kitchen, considering the cups of coffee in the kitchen. The little cottage was starting to feel crowded.

The charms and wards that she and Sarah had set in the cottage were supposed to keep uninvited guests out and to keep her safe. But they had no effect on Harrison and his powers. The immortals had different rules.

Reg looked at the immortal who claimed to be her parent. She didn't look very much like him, that much was certain. Weston was tall and husky, handsome and rugged. He rubbed his chin, looking around. She didn't think her personality was anything like his. Had she inherited anything from him? Any of his powers? She could attribute a number of her traits and gifts to her siren mother, Norma Jean. But Norma Jean was not a fire-caster. She could not transport herself or other objects or people. She did not have the significant psychic powers that Reg had, though she could communicate with their siren sisters telepathically. The ability seemed to be much more developed in Reg.

"Weston," she said.

Reg didn't explain her relationship with Weston to October. She would rather he didn't know that she might have immortal blood in her veins. That would not make her more trustworthy in his eyes.

Weston picked up a cup of coffee and sipped it before looking in her direction. "The child is here," he said to no one in particular.

Harrison watched his friend. The two of them could behave like two naughty little boys when they got together, and there was no one who could send them to their rooms for time-out until they could behave themselves. Reg was wary of them. Doubly so when they were together.

"Yes, I'm here," Reg agreed. "We need to talk. Do *you* know who it is that is a threat to me? Someone who has been the cause of my death in previous lives?"

Weston looked at Harrison. "Is it him?"

Harrison nodded. "It is him."

"Who?" Reg demanded.

They could clearly share more exact information with each other than they could with mortals, who demanded inconsequential things like names, which changed with each incarnation and sometimes even during one lifetime. Reg herself had a number of aliases.

"The one who threatens you," Weston said, as if this were elementary. He sat down in the other chair and looked at October, who sat beside Reg on the couch. "It is a wolfman," he said with interest. "Be a wolf."

October shook his head. "I do not transform for entertainment," he said through gritted teeth.

"Be a wolf," Weston repeated firmly.

Before her eyes, October began to shift. It was slower than Reg had seen him transform before. Maybe October was trying to fight the change being forced upon him. But in the end, October dropped to hands and feet as he started to change. In a few seconds, he became a beautiful big wolf.

Starlight spat and hissed and climbed up to Harrison's shoulder, where he perched to look down at October and hissed some more.

"Starlight," Reg remonstrated. "It's just October. He's not going to chase you around the cottage or something."

"A wolf," Weston said, looking at October in his canid form. "They are better than humans."

"He is still human," Reg told him. "He's just in another form. Now let him shift back."

"You too can transform," Weston looked at Reg. "Most humans cannot."

"If you force me to take another form, you will be sorry," Reg told him flatly.

Weston looked at Harrison, who shook his head. "Drink your coffee."

Weston settled back in his chair and had a few swallows of the coffee. That was apparently pleasant enough to satisfy him for the moment. Harrison might be communicating more to Weston that the rest of them could not hear.

I'm sorry, she told October in her mind. She was used to communicating with the wolves telepathically. She didn't know whether the immortals could hear their telepathic communications. *I didn't intend any of this.*

If they are not going to be any help, send them away.

It isn't that easy.

"Let October resume his human form," she told Weston. "And tell me... who is it that is a danger to me? Is he also a danger to October?"

"You are not safe," Weston told Reg, deigning to actually talk to her about what she wanted to talk about. "You must... cleanse your life."

"What does that mean? A ritual or spell? What should I do to protect myself?"

Weston leaned back in his chair, sipping the coffee thoughtfully. "Root out this evil... and eliminate it."

Reg swallowed. She didn't like the sound of that. She hadn't even figured out yet if the danger were in the form of a person or something more insidious. If it were a person, the thought of "eliminating" the threat was not particularly palatable. She considered herself a nonviolent person, even if she had been forced to protect herself in the past.

"How can I do that? How can I identify the danger if you can't tell me who or what it is?"

"Vigilance. Constant attention." This advice came from Harrison. He had no idea what kind of energy it took to remain constantly vigilant.

The cryptic answers were not helping Reg find a concrete solution to the threat.

October was able to transform back to his biped form, though he looked a little worse for wear. He smoothed his hair and his clothing and tried to look as though he was not affected by the involuntary transformation.

Reg nodded at him, again repeating the apology in her head. She had not called him there and was not the one who had forced him to transform, but her questions had prompted everything. His eyes flicked between Reg and the immortals.

"So you're saying I need to stay on high alert?" Reg asked, trying to get a more direct answer. "Forever?"

Weston shrugged as if this should be obvious. "Strengthen your bonds with those who can protect you. Fortify your home." His eyes flicked around at the wards Reg and Sarah had established. "These are not adequate."

"Starlight," Harrison added, petting the cat who had settled back down after October's transformation back to his human form. "Is more than he seems."

Starlight stared at Reg inscrutably. She knew his powers were much greater than anyone would have guessed by looking at him, but he used them rarely.

"What about this enemy?" October asked after a period of silence. "If he's ended Reg's lives before, how do we stop him from doing it again?"

Weston shrugged as if this were little matter. "Be ready when he reveals himself."

"Great," Reg muttered. "That's incredibly helpful."

He smiled at her and nodded.

"Remember," Weston added cryptically, "it is your choice."

Reg looked at October to share a frustrated glance with him. She looked back at Weston, but both he and Harrison had vanished.

CHAPTER TWENTY-FOUR

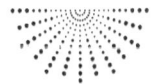

Since Harrison had stranded him at her cottage without a vehicle, Reg drove October back to the hotel room he was using when he wasn't in the woods with the pack. They spoke little on the way. Reg was trying to figure out how she was supposed to stay vigilant for this dangerous person or entity until he made himself known.

She didn't remember anyone showing his hand in either the dream of Egypt or of Greece. If an unknown person could turn fate against them in both of those cases without detection, what were the chances Reg would be able to recognize the entity at work in this life?

October didn't have much to say either, probably angry and embarrassed by what had happened to him. It wouldn't be easy to keep him on her side if Harrison and Weston thought they could just play with him like a pawn. He wouldn't want anything to do with Reg.

"Thanks for the ride," he told Reg gruffly before getting out of the car. "I appreciate it."

"I'm... I'm sorry again. I don't know what is going on, and I'm sure you don't want your life being torn up anymore because of this guy... or this entity or whatever it is."

"Reg…" He frowned, hesitating and trying to find the words to express himself. "I know that none of this is by choice. If it is true that our souls crossed in Egypt and Greece, and maybe in other lives… maybe that explains the affinity I felt with you from the moment I first saw you. And… as much as I would like to be left out of this and just to live my own life and protect the pack… I'm not going to abandon you. We already have a relationship… maybe we did even before we met in this life. I'm not going to shut you out or pretend that I'm not a part of this."

He paused with his hand on the door handle.

"I need time to think about it and get my head around the whole past lives and previous crossings thing. I'm not sure how to handle that. Not that there is anything I can do about it. But I'm not going to abandon you."

He rested his hand on her arm before he got out of the car. It was warm and reassuring and, while it lacked the electric charge she got when she and Corvin touched, she was grateful to him for his words and attempt at comfort.

They had been close in previous lives. Did that mean they were destined to be close in this one, too? He had not picked a mate from the pack. Maybe that was because he had sensed there was someone else out there for him.

After dropping him off, Reg wasn't sure where to go. While Marian had given them some clarity about having had past lives and Weston had told them to remain vigilant, Reg lacked any strategy she could put into action.

Who were her enemies? Was it possible he had already revealed himself, and she had simply not realized it? The immortals did not think in terms of a linear timeline like humans. That might mean the enemy had already revealed himself, and it was time for action.

Corvin was the first enemy she had made upon coming to Black Sands. The fact that they had a psychic connection and were on speaking terms with each other made it a difficult and confusing relationship, but she still had to consider him an enemy more than a friend. He had stolen her powers before and would again, given the opportunity. And if he did it again, he would not return them as he had the first time. To do so once had been unprecedented. To do so again would be unthinkable.

Since then, Corvin had gained immense power in their battle with the Witch Doctor. The powers that immortal had wielded were so great that it had taken Corvin a couple of years to begin to access and exercise them. Reg didn't know whether he now had enough control to wield them all. He had already been a powerful warlock. Now, he had the Witch Doctor's powers and anything else he had consumed since he and Reg had first met. However much he could control was too much.

As the new leader of the warlock coven that Davyn had previously led, Corvin also had influence over the warlocks in the coven. He might not be able to seduce men into doing his will as easily as women, but he could still use his significant charms to influence their actions.

Not only that, but Corvin's son, John, was now also a member of his coven. He had the same ability to consume the powers of others as Corvin, and he had been raised by a witch who had not believed in the need for him to obey the rules set out by other practitioners for power eaters. While his mother, Verity, had been killed, Reg was sure that Verity's ghost had attached to him and was still whispering her poisonous directions in his ear. It was possible he was even more dangerous than Corvin, and he had reason to hate Reg.

Was it possible that John was X, the entity Weston and Harrison had warned her about? He had only recently come into the picture. Maybe it was his presence in town that had triggered Reg's memories and dreams. Maybe he was the enemy.

She couldn't decide which of them might be more dangerous. And there was another possibility that worried her, too.

Ever since they had bound what remained of the Witch Doctor, Francesca's spell had been unwinding. She had initially assured Reg that the Witch Doctor would remain bound for at least a thousand years. Something she wouldn't have to worry about. Reg would be gone long before that time came.

But that was not how things had turned out.

Reg didn't bother to call Francesca. She knew where Francesca lived and was afraid that if she tried to set up a time to see the Haitian witch, Francesca would put her off, claiming to be too busy with other duties. They were friendly, but Francesca didn't always put that relationship first. And Reg needed to talk to her this time. It couldn't be put off.

Francesca answered the door and looked Reg over with a sour expression. The gorgeous blond did not look anything like what Reg had once imagined a witch would look like—or a Haitian, for that matter. She had imagined that all native Haitians were black-skinned, like the Witch Doctor himself. But Francesca was white with glamorous blond curls and looked diametrically opposite to what Reg would have imagined a Haitian witch to look like.

But she did have that beautiful accent and lilt in her voice, even when she was annoyed. "Reg, this ees a surprise."

"We need to talk." Reg hoped that her flat, curt response would be enough to convince Francesca that she was serious and could not be talked out of this or put off even for a day.

"Of course. Come in." She opened the door the rest of the way for Reg to enter. Francesca led the way to the sunny kitchen. "Tea?"

"Sure." Reg wouldn't have minded something a bit stronger than tea.

Or a lot stronger than tea.

She sat down at the table while Francesca put the kettle on and prepared the tea service.

"Tell me there haven't been any changes in the status of the Witch Doctor," Reg said.

Francesca turned and looked at Reg, one delicate eyebrow arched.

"There have been no changes," she insisted. "The sah that was attached to Horace is trapped in the void, where you bound it. The other eight pieces are still bound to the eight remaining kattakyns."

"For sure? None of them have been released? When did you check last? Have you talked with all of the cat owners?"

The kettle started to whistle. Francesca moved slowly, pouring it into a teapot and then bringing the service over to the table.

"You do not think that I stay in contact with all of the owners?"

"Do you? Don't they wonder why you are still so involved if they don't know about the piece of the Witch Doctor's sah in each one of them? Isn't it kind of strange that the old owner would keep calling to find out how they were doing and if anything negative has happened?"

"I have relationships with them. I send them pictures of Nicole," —NEE-cole in Francesca's charming accent— "and of course, they update me on how her kittens are doing. It is natural."

"And you've been able to reach all of them and gotten stories back? You're sure that none of them have deceived you? They could pretend everything is fine while trying to steal the sah to access its power, like Kareem did."

"I am not a diviner," Francesca admitted. "But I do not believe any of them are lying to me. I have no reason to believe that any of them are."

Reg breathed in and out slowly, trying to calm the knot in her stomach.

CHAPTER TWENTY-FIVE

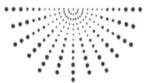

*W*hat is it?" Francesca demanded. "Why are you asking this? What has happened?"

"I don't know if anything has happened," Reg said slowly, and tried to think of how to explain everything in a few simple sentences so that Francesca would comprehend the seriousness of the situation. "I have been having dreams and visions of past lives."

Reg selected a tea bag and poured hot water over it in her cup. No loose-leaf tea this time. No portentous symbols. The soothing aroma of chamomile filled the air.

"You remember past lives? Your own?" Francesca asked.

"Yes. My own. And sometimes a crossing with October, a… man who has recently come to Black Sands."

Francesca nodded her encouragement, not challenging the idea as Reg had thought she might.

"In some of those dreams… there was an entity working against me. Someone who prevented me from achieving something or did something to end my life. Harrison and Weston said that it was… a danger for me here. That I need to be on the lookout for him. To be vigilant to protect myself."

Francesca shook her head. "It will take more than vigilance.

If he has killed you in other lives... he must be very powerful. And you don't know what form he might take."

Reg hadn't thought of him being in any form other than that of a human. What if he came to her in some other form? She shook off this stray thought and forged ahead with her explanation. "Anyway, I thought... perhaps it was an enemy I have already identified. And maybe it was the Witch Doctor. He targeted me from the time I was a child, so maybe... he has some kind of grudge against me. Something that carried over from another life."

She remembered the chill she had felt when the Witch Doctor had remembered her and gloated over the fact that he was going to kill her. How powerless she was in front of him. Was that the entity that had followed her from life to life to ensure she did not progress?

"If you have just started having these visions, they were not caused by the Witch Doctor," Francesca assured her. "He is still bound."

"I had to be sure."

Francesca nodded. "Of course. But the pieces of the sah have been spread all across the world, kept apart from each other, and remain that way. The Witch Doctor cannot re-form until those pieces are all brought together."

"All of them? Including the one I trapped in the void?"

Francesca wrapped her hands around the teacup as if to warm them. "As you found, even just one piece can... be troublesome if unbound. Especially if reunited with the powers that the spirit drinker holds. But the Witch Doctor cannot re-form and become what he once was without all of the pieces. He will not be whole without them."

"He could still be a danger."

"Of course. But he remains bound. You are safe from him."

Reg turned this over in her mind. It was not the reassurance she had hoped it would be. She still felt uneasy. Even if the Witch Doctor had not re-formed, she still knew that there was some kind of danger out there, some entity that had caused her death in multiple lives.

If it had been the Witch Doctor, then at least she would have known what she was facing and had some idea of how he would react. But if it wasn't the Witch Doctor, then the face and shape of X was still a blank. It could be anyone.

"I don't know how I'm going to do this."

Francesca nodded. "What about the other immortals? One of them could target you across multiple lifetimes without dying himself."

"The only others I know are Harrison and Weston, and it isn't either of them."

"You know this?"

"They were the ones who warned me that this... someone is after me."

"That does not mean it is not one of them. The immortals... they are tricky. They do not follow the same rules as humans. They do not have the same feelings."

"Or see time and space the same way."

"No."

"But Harrison has been my guardian since I was a child. And Weston... I don't know. Would he kill his own blood? I thought they protected their own."

"Perhaps. Perhaps not. Maybe the rules have changed or his feelings have changed. Or maybe it is another immortal you don't know. There are others, but they are elusive. We don't know where they are or what they may decide to do. Weston broke the rules by allowing your birth."

"But he already served his sentence for that. He is back now, and they will not harm each other."

"Immortals are unpredictable," Francesca said with a shrug.

Reg sighed. "Do you think that is the most likely? That it was an immortal because they can follow me across lives?"

"That is the easiest. If he lived and died, he might not always cross paths with you."

"How does it work? If I have had multiple crossings with October, how did that happen? Why did we cross with each other so many times?"

"Something bound you together. Perhaps unfinished business, love, a debt. We don't understand the way it works. We do know that some spirits... do seem to continually cross with others." She gazed at Reg. "I envy you that. To have a relationship that transcends lives. It is very romantic."

At the moment, Reg didn't think it seemed very romantic at all. She really hadn't needed another danger to add to her list. Corvin, strangers, magical species she wasn't familiar with, magical laws she didn't understand, curses, her heritage...

But, when she thought back to how she had felt with her consort in Egypt and Greece, she did feel warm and a little surge of... affection? She wasn't willing to call it love. But what the priestess had felt for the warrior she sent off to battle and what the poetess had felt for Petros had been more than attraction or admiration. She couldn't recall more than a few minutes or hours of each life, but she knew the connections had been profound, not just passing flirtations.

It pained her that El-Sayed had been betrayed by someone passing information about his campaign on to the enemy. Who would have done such a thing? He hadn't even told his men what they would be doing before the campaign. No more than the bare bones. The priestess had been the only one to know the full details.

Reg couldn't blame herself. She wasn't the same person she had been then. But she was sure she would not have betrayed his plans. She wouldn't have told anyone what El-Sayed was doing. She had known that if the usurper found out, he would destroy everything she knew and loved. No amount of money or glory would have been worth that.

She *had* been careless in Greece. Clearly, her guardian there had been watching her more closely than she had realized, or someone had tipped him off to what was going on. Since he had been the one who had discovered her and the athlete together, the destruction of both of their careers had to be laid at her feet. Unless one of them had been unaware of a spy in their own household. Reg couldn't be blamed for that.

"How do I recognize someone else who may have crossed with me in past lives?" she asked Francesca. "When they are reborn as someone else, with different physical features, different gender, maybe even a different *species*, how am I supposed to recognize them?"

"I don't know. How did you recognize October?"

"I just… had a feeling. We were having shared visions, so he knew what I was seeing and could tell me about it from his perspective. And his eyes…"

"So I guess… you would recognize an enemy the same way. The feeling you had around him… maybe some physical feature he carried across more than one life. With October, did you feel an attraction toward him when you met?"

"Yes! And it was like… I knew what things he was going to laugh at, what he was going to say. Like we'd known each other forever, even when it had only been a few seconds."

Francesca sipped her tea. "Maybe the opposite if it was an enemy. Maybe you would instantly dislike him, without knowing why."

Reg thought back to John, Corvin's son. He was one that she hadn't really liked from the start. But he wasn't really an enemy. Was he?

CHAPTER TWENTY-SIX

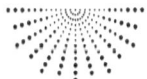

*a*t the end of the day, Reg wasn't any further ahead than she had been when she had woken up that morning. She understood her situation a little better but still didn't know who X was, why he had targeted her, or what to do with all that coffee.

In the end, she'd dumped it all down the drain, which was a shame because Harrison had used up most of her coffee beans in the venture. Maybe she would ask Davyn where to get the good stuff. Splurge a little for once and get something special for herself instead of going for the cheapest possible purchase.

Reg talked to Starlight as she got him his dinner, hoping the immortals were right and he might know something that would help her.

"Can you show me who X is?" she asked him. "You're very good at telling the good guys from the bad."

Starlight had always hated Corvin, had attacked him when given the opportunity, and let it be known how upset he was every time she was around him.

So maybe he had already been telling her; she just hadn't been listening.

Of course, Starlight also didn't like her hanging around with

Ember, and Reg was quite sure that the young dragon was *not* an enemy. Ember loved her and would never knowingly do anything to hurt her.

Ember had been just fine with October when they had met. He hadn't attacked October in either human or wolf form. Likewise, October had not felt anything negative about the juvenile firedrake. He had been excited to meet a real dragon.

So she didn't have to worry that the young dragon was an enemy. Or October. But Corvin...

For once, Reg remembered to strengthen the wards protecting the cottage before going to bed. Maybe tomorrow, Sarah would help her to fortify the house further with even more wards or protections. She should do everything she could to protect herself. That was what Harrison and Weston had said. She needed to be vigilant all the time, talk to Starlight, and fortify her wards.

It didn't feel like very much.

Wolves were crepuscular creatures. A few months before, Reg would have had no idea what that meant. But now that she had contact with wolves, she knew that it meant that they were most active at dusk and dawn. Like cats. It was not quite the same as being nocturnal. Reg considered herself more nocturnal than most humans. Or homo sapiens, anyway; she couldn't speak for other magical species. Pixies were underground dwellers, so she wouldn't be surprised if they mostly came above ground at night.

But October was a wolf, which meant that dawn was one of his more active times. Reg awoke to her phone ringing and could barely pry her eyelids apart enough to look at the screen. Her phone was on sleep mode, so it should not be ringing unless it was someone she had set as an exception or someone was calling her repeatedly, so the phone considered it an emergency and allowed the ring to break through her *do not disturb* settings.

Reg squinted at the too-bright screen.

October.

Reg groaned.

If it had been anyone else, she would have just rejected the call and gone back to sleep. But not only did she like October, but he might have thought of something about the dark entity targeting them, and Reg needed to know about it.

"Yeah?"

"Reg, I—" October stopped abruptly. "Were you asleep?"

"Nobody gets up at dawn."

"Well... some people do," he said lamely. "I'm sorry, but since you're awake now..."

"I'm not. I'm not going to be awake until I've had about five more hours of sleep and the same number of cups of coffee."

"Oh."

Reg sighed. "What is it? I'm not going to be able to fall back asleep wondering what was so important that you had to call me at dawn."

"I've been thinking about our problem. The identity of X."

"Yeah. I haven't been thinking about much else."

"Have you come to any conclusions?"

Reg lay back on the bed with her eyes closed. "Well, even though they said it wasn't one of the immortals, I had to look into that and make sure." She realized at the last moment that October didn't know the story about the Witch Doctor, and she probably should not give him all the details. "I had... an encounter with one when I first moved here, and I had to be sure it wasn't him. Somehow escaped from being bound."

"And is it?"

"No. There have not been any changes. He is still bound. No danger. It could still be another immortal, I guess, but..."

"But the whole point is that if it is someone who intends to do you harm, or me, then it would be someone that we knew. Not an immortal that you've never met."

Reg thought it was a good deal more complex than that, but she accepted October's conclusion. She thought he was probably right. Whoever it was that wanted to kill her in life after life; it was more than likely someone she had met. And met since her arrival in Black Sands.

Besides, she couldn't know about anyone she hadn't ever met. She could only identify people she knew.

"I've heard about the trouble you had with Corvin when you first arrived in Black Sands," October said. "And even with being disgraced and shunned, he has remained close to you. He didn't leave town. He didn't decide that he needed to avoid you. He is around all the time. Watching you. Trying to convince you to be with him."

"Yeah."

"I don't know if you've thought about him, but he is very possessive of you, and maybe when I came to town, he decided that I was a threat to his relationship with you."

Reg didn't think that Corvin needed any special encouragement to be possessive of her, but he might have grown more jealous knowing that she had met someone else. At any rate, he hadn't actually tried to kill her or October since October had come to town.

Maybe Harrison and Weston were wrong. Maybe there was no immediate threat. Perhaps the dreams had just been triggered by October's presence, and neither of them was in any danger.

CHAPTER TWENTY-SEVEN

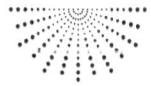

*R*eg?" October prompted. "Did you fall asleep?"
"No. I'm just thinking."
"About Corvin?"

"I wondered about him too. He's been *interested* in me since I got here. Maybe he was in other lives, too… but in other lives, he was different; he wasn't a power drinker. So it wasn't my powers he was interested in; it was romantic. Or maybe if I was in a position of power, it was my political power he wanted rather than my gifts."

"Sure," October agreed. "It might have been different motives in different lives. But something kept drawing the two of you together, and then you would do something that upset him or made him think that he'd lost you or wouldn't be able to hang on to you. Something that made him think that he had to act. But then…"

"What, instead of chasing me, Corvin decided it made more sense to kill me? And you?"

"Maybe he blew up. He strikes me as the type who has a temper."

"Yes… but he doesn't usually blow up. He gets mad, but it's

usually quiet mad. I don't know. Like a grumpy toddler. Irritated at everything until he gets his own way."

"So, do you think it is possible? That he is the one that the immortals were warning you about?"

Reg sighed. "Yes, except for one thing."

"What's that?"

"They know him. If they knew this X, this dark entity, was seeking me out and was a danger to me, then wouldn't they know that it was Corvin? Harrison has warned me about him before. And he never said Corvin might kill me or had killed me in a past life; it was always about him being able to steal my powers."

"Hmm." October grunted and thought about this. "But they did say that they wouldn't know what to look for. That they wouldn't necessarily know him. Maybe they just don't realize he is the one."

"Maybe. But Francesca thought I would be able to feel something from the entity if it was someone that I met. That I would know it was someone dangerous."

"And the immortals said you would know when he revealed himself."

"If I should recognize him by how I feel around him or recognize him when he reveals himself, then if it was Corvin, couldn't they tell me who he is?"

"Maybe they already know. Maybe they just figure you should have to figure it out on your own."

That would be just like Harrison. She didn't know about Weston. She really didn't know him well enough to know if he would be the type who believed his offspring needed to be confronted with danger in order to learn and grow to overcome it. Like mama birds that pushed their babies out of the nest to force them to fly.

"I guess it could be Corvin," Reg said slowly. "But if it is... he's not going to kill me. At least not until he takes my powers."

"Maybe he would come after me instead," October said. "If

he has ended your other lives, perhaps he has ended others of mine, too, not just in Egypt."

Was it jealousy? Was it something to do with Reg's relationship with October? Corvin did not want them to be together? Whatever unresolved issue was between them, whatever drew their souls together in life after life, also drew their foe?

"Then what do we do?" Reg asked. "Are we just supposed to wait around and see if he tries to kill one of us?"

October was silent.

"It isn't like we could do anything about it, anyway," Reg pointed out. "Corvin is too powerful for either of us to fight and win. And growing in power. Able to access more of the powers he had already absorbed and to absorb new ones."

"I may have an idea about that."

"And there's also John," Reg pointed out.

"John? The young warlock? He seems a little…" October hummed, clearly trying to find the appropriate, politically correct word. "Bat-crap crazy?"

Reg snorted. "Maybe," she admitted. "Or maybe his dead witch of a mother is still whispering in his ear, which comes out to the same thing."

"Do you think he is a danger to you?" October asked. "I don't know anything of his gifts, but he does not seem to be particularly powerful."

"But he is. He's also a power drinker."

"Him too?" October sounded stunned. "Two of them in the same coven? That is very unusual. They are a dying breed. I would not expect to find two in the same place—the same hunting grounds."

"John is Corvin's son."

October whistled. "You're kidding me. I didn't even know he had a son around here."

"He hasn't always been here. Just for a few months. And Corvin didn't know that he existed until he showed up here. His mother had kept him a secret. Split up with Corvin while she was pregnant. Too early to know it."

"One of them has to be the cause of this," October said strongly. "One of them is the dark entity... I'm sure of it. Hunters are power hungry. They will always get power wherever they can take it. You've prevented Corvin from getting what he wants. Your gifts are powerful in this life; they were probably highly sought in other lives as well. I don't know how long-lived he is. He may have terminated several of your lives just in this lifetime. That would create a powerful bond between the two of you. Fate trying to bring you back together to right the balance."

"I don't know. Corvin claims to be centuries old. But wouldn't I remember him? Wouldn't he have started triggering memories when I first saw him? Weston and Harrison said I would know him when he revealed himself."

"Not even the immortals understand how it all works. We only know what has been recorded, what people have reported about discovering past lives while under hypnosis or through other means of recovering memories. Trusting that what they have reported is the truth and not manipulated."

"I don't think it's Corvin. I thought at first that it might be, but... if he wanted to kill me, he would have done so. But he... we have a strong psychic connection, and I think that would hurt him if he did."

"What is a little bit of psychic pain for the reward he would get? He has already held your powers once. He would put up with the discomfort if it meant getting those powers back again."

Reg shook her head. October really didn't understand about the connection between her and Corvin. But how could he? Reg had tried to explain it to others many times and had never been satisfied that she had managed to communicate it. Maybe even she and Corvin didn't understand it.

"What about John, then? Could it be him?" October asked, when Reg's silence had drawn out.

"I suppose so. How would I figure it out?"

There was no immediate answer from October. Reg started to drift again, falling back asleep even though she was holding the phone to her ear.

"What about meditation or hypnosis?" October suggested, making her jump and nearly drop the phone. "That might help you to remember your past lives and the people who were a part of them. And then you would recognize him. Maybe."

"I only knew that you were the other man in my visions because you were having the same visions and dreams as I was," Reg said, which was a bit of a fib. There was also October's eyes, but she couldn't count on her enemy having the same physical characteristics in multiple lives.

"I don't think we can force him to have the same dreams as you."

"No. I don't either."

CHAPTER TWENTY-EIGHT

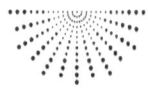

*S*he finished her set and walked up to the bar of the speakeasy, readjusting the long string of beads and her cloche hat. It was crowded and she was sweating. Hopefully, her makeup wouldn't run.

The bartender, Gus, smiled at her and handed her a shot without her asking. She boosted herself up onto a barstool and tugged down the hem of her dress, which reached the middle of her thigh while she was sitting, showing off her long, slender, brown legs to their best advantage. She crossed her ankles and downed the shot, looking around to see who had arrived while she had been singing, the glare of the lights preventing her from being able to see the room.

She was expecting Marco tonight. He could, of course, show up any night, expected or not, but he had told her he would see her after Valentine's Day and, so far, she had not seen him. After what had happened, he was probably lying low, but the establishment paid the cops well to keep them away from the speakeasy, so it was as safe as anywhere for him to visit. Maybe safer than most.

But she still didn't see him. Instead, she was approached by a man she didn't know, though she had seen him around before.

He was nattily dressed, with a slim, well-tailored pinstripe suit with a red tie and pocket square. His wingtips were shined to a mirror finish, and his fedora was cocked to a rakish angle.

He looked at her, openly ogling her short skirt and long, exposed legs. He lingered at her shoulder for a moment before taking the stool next to her, and she thought he was trying to catch a glimpse down the front of her dress. She focused on not flinching or readjusting her clothes and pulled a cigarette case out of her tiny purse.

He produced a gold lighter as she put the cigarette in her mouth, and she drew on the cigarette as he applied the flame to the end. Their faces were close together as if he were bending in for a kiss.

Then he settled back on his stool and pulled out a cigarette of his own. He signaled the bartender for drinks, and they were each supplied with a shot.

"The name is Frank," he introduced himself. "And you need no introduction, Miss Lucy May."

They each downed their shots. Lucy noticed that the liquor had not come from the same bottle as her previous drink. It was much smoother, much higher quality than the moonshine the speakeasy normally served. Frank nodded in satisfaction.

"That's the good stuff," he informed her. "From my private reserve."

"It's very nice," Lucy told him.

His eyes were sharp, predatory. While it was fine to be drinking with him in such a public place, where there were plenty of people around to witness what happened, she would not have wanted to meet him on the quiet street at night.

"I enjoyed your set. You've got a great set of pipes."

Lucy was already warm, but her cheeks heated further at his compliment and the leer that went with it. Like she had been doing something dirty up on the stage rather than just singing about love, loss, and freedom.

"Thank you so much. I'm glad you enjoyed it."

"A lot of people are not happy with women being granted the vote and being so much more… liberated in public. But I, for one, am all for it. I love to see women gaining ground in society, being given the opportunity to do more and be more. I like an independent-minded woman."

Lucy had her own mind; that much was certain. Her mother was horrified by the liberties Lucy took, the decisions she made about her life. It was, after all, her own life. She did not belong to her parents. She didn't need her father's protection or direction. She didn't need a husband to guide and shelter her. God had given women minds; why not use them?

"You are enchanting," Frank told her. "What happens up on stage when you start to sing is… magical."

He smiled his most charming smile but, somehow, it looked like the grin of a shark. The scent of roses washed over Lucy. His cologne or aftershave. His eyes glittered as he watched her.

Beyond him, Lucy saw Marco making his way through the crowded floor and knew he was coming to see her. She wondered if she should try to separate herself from Frank some-how, to make it clear that she was not there with him. But it was too late for that. Marco's eyes were already on her, and changing seats or turning away from Frank would only emphasize the fact that she had been talking to him before Marco's arrival.

He looked angry. That wasn't a good sign. Lucy liked it when he showed up in a mellow, expansive mood, when nothing was likely to set him off. When he would just smoke and drink and brag, and she could enjoy herself with him without fear of his temper.

He was dressed in the same style as Frank, though his shoes were not as shiny and his pocket square a little crumpled, as if it had fallen out of his pocket and been stepped on, and then replaced. He had a cut on his face. A long, deep slash that had only just started to heal, still red and a bit puffy.

Marco did not take a stool. He signaled to Gus and stared at Frank.

"Well, look who is here," he growled. "You have a lot of nerve showing up here."

"Why wouldn't I?" Frank countered. "I have as much right to be here as anyone. You and the other boys are very generous with your donations. Isn't it within my best interests to make sure that the place is safe and everything is operating smoothly?"

"You are paid to stay away. What part of that didn't you understand?"

Frank smiled. "I wasn't told to stay away. Just to be sure it didn't get raided."

"You gotta lotta nerve," Marco repeated.

Frank looked at Gus, who didn't need to be told to supply him with another drink. Frank motioned to Marco, and Gus poured him a drink from his private reserve. Marco drank it down and looked down at his empty glass.

"That's not the usual rotgut."

"No, it's not," Frank agreed.

They stared at each other. Marco's green eyes were challenging. They were like two dogs circling each other, deciding whether to attack. Two wolves, teeth bared and slavering.

The musical number ended, and Lucy looked up at the stage to see who was next. There were still a few sets to go before she would need to appear again. Lucy took a long drag on her cigarette, looking at the men. Neither of them even seemed to know she was there. That was one of the problems with the political and social climate these days. Too much distraction. Why couldn't they just enjoy themselves and the company?

CHAPTER TWENTY-NINE

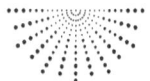

*R*eg awoke from the dream, her heart pounding, anxious and excited at the same time. She knew that face, that charming smile, that heady scent of roses. It hadn't been a previous incarnation of Corvin, but the same one as she knew, his ageless face as familiar to Reg as her own. She wasn't sure if he were truly centuries old as he claimed, but she knew for certain he had been alive and well in the 1920s.

Her mouth was dry as she considered the implications. He and October had been rivals. They had both known Lucy. She didn't know how Lucy had died, whether it had been an accident or by violence, whether she had died young or lived to a ripe old age, dying just before Reg was born. Reg reached for the water bottle beside the bed, but it was empty. She grumbled to herself. She should have filled it before bed. Now she would have to go back to sleep without a drink or to get up and go to the kitchen.

If she went out to the kitchen, she might have a shot of Jack Daniels instead of water. The satisfying smoothness of the drink in her dream had dissolved with the dream. While she had tasted it, she could no longer appreciate the warm buzz she'd gotten from a couple of shots drunk in quick succession.

Reg closed her eyes and tried to go back to sleep. Her phone didn't ring. She had thought that it might, that October might have shared in her dream again and might call her to discuss it and the possible implications.

But October didn't call and sleep didn't come. Reg was still thirsty and craving a drink. She didn't normally drink alone, but just one nip wouldn't hurt anything. Eventually, she was too restless to do anything else and dragged herself out of bed. Starlight was snoozing on the windowsill and gave a sleepy trill as Reg ran her fingers through his soft fur, but didn't follow her out to the kitchen. He apparently recognized that she wasn't on her way to make breakfast or a post-midnight snack.

As Reg walked to the counter to get herself a drink, she saw lights on in the big house. And the back door light was on, winking at her to come over.

Sarah, her landlord and friend, was apparently not only up and around in the small morning hours, but also open to company. Reg wondered sometimes if Sarah ever slept. Maybe the emerald that slowed the progress of time so that Sarah did not visibly age also gave her the ability to function without sleep. She was often up as late as Reg, yet still humming and cheerful early in the morning, hours before Reg would be able to function.

It would be better to visit with Sarah and see if she had any insight into Reg's situation than to drink alone. Reg slipped on a pair of sandals and walked across the yard to the back door of the big house. The air was cool and refreshing. The screen door was closed to keep bugs out, but the inside door stood open in invitation.

Reg knocked on the screen door, then opened it to let herself in.

"Come in, Reg," Sarah called from another room. "Put on the kettle, and I'll be right in."

Reg obeyed, putting the kettle on to boil and then checking the tea service to make sure everything was in order. A basket held a variety of commercial teas and Sarah's homemade blends. Reg would not be drinking one of Sarah's bitter concoctions.

The warm scent of freshly baked cookies lingered in the kitchen.

Sarah appeared before the kettle started to whistle. Her gray hair was in pink sponge curlers and her slightly plump figure swathed in a green silk robe. "I thought you might come over tonight," she said with a smile.

Reg wasn't sure how she knew that. Sarah did not claim to be psychic or prescient, but she often knew way more than Reg told her about what was going on in her life or percolating in her brain.

"Have a seat, dear. There are some cookies."

Reg took her place at the table. A plastic container held several short stacks of chocolate chip cookies. Reg helped herself to a cookie. Sarah's teas and potions might leave something to be desired, but her baking was top-notch. The cookies were still just slightly warmer than room temperature, the chocolate gooey.

"These are wonderful."

Sarah patted her hips. "Don't I know it! I'm glad someone came over to help me eat them."

In a few minutes, Sarah was seated across from Reg and they were both waiting for their tea to steep.

"How have you been?" Sarah asked. "It seems like ages since we had a good heart-to-heart."

"Well, things have been a little strange. I've been having dreams…"

"We all have dreams."

"I know. But these ones… have been confusing." Reg considered how much to tell Sarah, then launched into an explanation, telling her of the dreams she could remember and the suggestion that X, some dark entity, had stalked her across several lives, ending them prematurely. Then she told her about the latest dream, seeing Corvin in the speakeasy.

Sarah looked thoughtful. "Prohibition," she said thoughtfully. "A very turbulent time. I remember it well."

"Did you know Corvin back then? What was he, a cop?"

Sarah shrugged. "We have all been many things during our lifetimes. I have known Corvin off and on at various times during this life, but I have not always been in contact with him and aware of what he was doing."

"I just have... a hard time imagining he was ever anything like that. I mean, if this dream was a memory, then obviously he was, but I have only known him as... a professor, warlock, leader of the coven. Just sort of... retired in Black Sands. I never thought about him being anything else."

"Well, of course he has been. But I don't know all of the things he has been or places he has lived. It doesn't surprise me that he would be right in the middle of things during prohibition times. The chaotic times would have allowed him to cover up any of his activities, giving him access to many of the type of people who would not be missed."

"There weren't a lot of practitioners involved in the activities around prohibition, were there?" Reg asked, trying to wrap her mind around it. When she thought about that time in the country's history, she thought of gangsters, flappers, and cops, not about witches or other magical practitioners.

"Of course there were," Sarah said with a laugh. "Home brews, flying below the radar, vanishing from sight... it was a perfect fit." She hesitated and shook her head. "It was a time of terrible evil, though. It ran rampant and was part of everyday life. The violence, even massacres... it was splashed across the headlines every day. Terrible pictures published in the paper. Many innocents were killed, not just the gangsters and law enforcement."

Reg nodded. It seemed like she could remember some of that. Some of Lucy's memories still banging around in her brain. An exciting and terrible time to live.

"Do you think... do you think it is Corvin whose life has

been intertwined with mine throughout these other lives?" Reg asked tentatively. "Do you think he is the one who has terminated past lives and may be trying to… may be a danger to me now?"

"It would make some sense. It would explain why the two of you have been so close despite what he has done to you. If you have impacted each other's lives that much in the past, you might have been drawn to each other."

"Marian talked about unfinished business."

"Yes, if there was an issue to be resolved that never was, or a wrong done between you, anything like that, we *think* it can cause lives to cross again in future incarnations."

Reg shook her head. "But I don't remember anything like that."

"From what you have said, you haven't actually remembered a lot. A few interactions with October, one with Corvin. It isn't a lot to draw from when you have possibly had countless interactions over dozens of lives. You might have been lovers in a past life. Siblings. Parent and child. Brothers in arms. Sworn enemies. You need to remember more to come to a conclusion."

More.

Reg would have preferred to remember less. The dreams and visions were troubling. She woke up feeling all played out, like she had been fighting all night long. She wished she could return to the way things had been before the dreams had started. Only worrying about what happened in her current life, not having to deal with questions raised by other existences and interactions.

"Do you think that would help?" she asked Sarah doubtfully. "I mean, really? Would it make a difference? Would I know whether it was Corvin who has been my enemy all of these years, through all of these lives? Do you think he is a threat to me now? To my life?"

"I have told you from the beginning how dangerous he is. Could he end your life? Of course. You know he could suck the life force right out of you. He may say he is only interested in your powers, but would he stop at that?"

Reg remembered the episodes in the past where Corvin had apparently been unable to stop himself. There was good reason to think that if he were to seduce her thoroughly enough to steal her powers again, he would not stop there.

And she wasn't sure she would want him to. She had lived only a few minutes without her powers, without the clamor of voices in her head, and it had been paralyzing. She had never felt so alone and desolate. She didn't want to go through life feeling that isolated. She didn't know how normal people could handle it.

"So if I have to remember more... then how do I do that?" October had suggested hypnosis or meditation. Reg was only too aware of how hypnosis could change her memories or implant new ones. And she had never been very good at meditation, to which Davyn could attest. She did better meditating with a flame, but she wasn't sure how long she could manage that, or if she could meditate deeply enough for it to be of any value.

She wished she had a memory like Ember's. He had not only his own memories but also generational memories from his forebears. And he was able to access all of it. It wasn't something he had to meditate about or concentrate on.

"There are memory spells and charms," Sarah said slowly. "I don't know how efficacious they will be at accessing memories of other lives, but you won't know if you don't try."

"Well, I suppose I should try, then."

"There are certain risks involved," Sarah cautioned.

"What kind of risks?"

"Memories can be traumatic. I think you know that from your current life."

There was a lot that Sarah didn't know about Reg's life, but she knew enough to know that she already had a number of traumatic memories.

"Yes."

"If you are inundated with traumatic memories from a number of lives, all at once… it could be overwhelming. It could do damage."

As if Reg didn't already have enough damage from her current life, including when she had been possessed by a force that had basically taken all of her accumulated memories, shaken them around, and dumped them on the floor. There were still more gaps than she would like to admit.

Sarah nodded at Reg's expression. "You need to think about it and carefully consider your path forward. I am glad you did not immediately jump at the possibility of recovering all those memories. It is not a simple solution to your troubles."

"No," Reg agreed.

"Don't decide right now. Think about it. Sleep on it, if you can. It isn't something to decide without a great deal of consideration."

"Okay," Reg agreed. She sighed. Back to bed. She didn't know if she would have any luck getting back to sleep, but she hoped she could get a few hours in. She couldn't operate for long on such a large sleep deficit, let alone make important, far-reaching decisions.

"Would you like a sleeping potion?" Sarah suggested.

"No, no, it's all right."

"Are you sure? They can be very helpful. I have tea, a syrup, sachets of lavender, a cream to rub on your temples…"

"Uh… maybe I'll try the cream," Reg conceded. At least she didn't have to drink that. If she did, it probably couldn't taste any worse than the tea.

Sarah disappeared into her pantry to rummage through her stores before returning with a small jar of cream.

"Just a dab on each temple and rub it in," Sarah advised. "It is a very effective sleep aid."

CHAPTER THIRTY

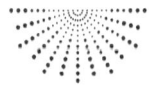

*R*eg did sleep after returning to the cottage and rubbing the cream on her temples. It had a pleasant floral smell, which was a surprise. She had expected it to smell as bad as Sarah's other potions tasted. She watched videos on her phone until her eyelids started to droop, then plugged it in and closed her eyes, drifting off to sleep.

She slept soundly until Starlight decided it was time for her to get up. Reg awoke to his rough tongue rasping over her face repeatedly. Disoriented, she wasn't sure what was going on or where she was. It took a few minutes to decide she didn't want cat slobber on her face and to push him away.

"Ugh! Why would you do that? Gross." Reg scrubbed at her face. Starlight had never done such a thing before. Jumped on her, pawed her, meowed and yowled piteously about how he was starving, but he had never licked her face to wake her up.

"Ugh," Reg repeated, and headed to the bathroom first to scrub her face clean. "Never do that!"

Starlight didn't dignify that with an answer. He marched into the kitchen and sat like a statue next to his food dish, imperious.

"Coffee first," Reg told him.

First, she had to check to see if she had any coffee grounds or beans left and, eventually, found a half-bag of grounds. She had no idea where they had come from or how long they had been there, but it was coffee. She put the grounds into the coffee machine and started it brewing.

While Reg waited for the coffee, she rummaged through the fridge to find something for Starlight. It would be a lot easier if he would just eat the cat food that came in a bag but, while he would pick at the kibbles left in his dish during the day when she was not there, he demanded people food when she was there to dish it up for him.

Real food. Would Reg have been happy with dry kibble?

Reg saw Starlight's glare. No, of course she would not be happy with dry kibble either.

"I'm sorry," she apologized. "I know it's not that picky to ask for real food. It's just that most cats eat whatever their humans feed them."

Starlight was *not* most cats.

Certainly not.

The coffee machine spat out enough coffee for Reg to start her day. She swapped the half-full cup for an empty one and let it keep filling. She didn't have the patience to wait for a full cup.

The sleeping potion cream had not left her with a foggy hangover like prescription sleep aids, and she was feeling more like herself.

Time to fill October in on her latest dream and Sarah's thoughts on the subject. Maybe they were actually moving in the right direction. With enough sleep under her belt, she was actually optimistic that they might be able to do something.

And if not... well, she had another life coming, and maybe it would work out better. She couldn't have all negative experiences.

October answered the phone after a few rings. His voice was slow, maybe a little drowsy. "Ah, Reg. Hey, I'm sorry about this morning. I didn't even think before calling you. I should have known that you would be asleep. I hope you managed to get back to sleep again…?"

"Well, I got up and had tea with Sarah for a while, and she gave me a sleep-inducing cream, and that really seemed to do the trick. I'm feeling a lot better now."

"Good," he declared. "Glad to hear it."

"You sound like maybe I woke you up, though," Reg suggested.

"Oh, just a nap." He chuckled. "Since we have several active cycles during a twenty-four-hour period, we also have several less-active times when we might rest for a few minutes or a few hours, depending on what is going on both personally and with the pack."

"I never really thought about it before. I just thought that you would have the same sleep schedule as everyone else."

"Like you?"

"Well, I know I'm not normal…"

"What's normal?" October sounded cheerful. "So, I have been thinking more about Corvin and the dark entity, and I'm even more convinced they are one and the same. I have been talking about the situation with a couple of close packmates—"

"I didn't know you were talking to anyone about it." Reg didn't like the idea of his going to others to talk to them about her situation. It should have been up to her to control the flow of information.

"Well, yes," October's voice was cautious. "You and I have both been talking to trusted advisors about the situation."

They had talked to Marian together. Reg had talked to Francesca and Sarah. Did she have any right to say October should not have been talking to any of his fellow wolves about it? They might have knowledge that was not well-known in Reg's circle of acquaintances. Knowledge that was closely guarded by the wolves. Learning everything she could about past lives and the threat she faced was important.

"Uh… I guess so," Reg conceded. "Though… you might have asked me first. I don't know these packmates."

"I wouldn't discuss it with anyone who I didn't trust. They're not going to spread it around to anyone else."

"Okay. I guess."

"It is not just *your* situation," October pointed out. "It is mine too. We are in this together. I think I have the right to consult with my own people about it."

"Sorry. I wasn't thinking about it that way. So… did you find anything out?"

He held back. She should have known that her attitude would make him reconsider what he told her. Maybe he didn't want to share specialized wolf knowledge with an outsider, now that he'd had a chance to think about it.

"We are still looking into it," he told her. "I'll tell you when I know something. In the meantime…"

"Yes?"

"Did you have another dream last night?"

Reg didn't know whether to assume he had shared the dream with her again or not. Was he testing her? Was it just an idle query? Curiosity?

"Well, yes," she admitted. "Just a short one. About the twenties. Prohibition time."

"Really. Tell me about it."

Reg again had the feeling that he was testing her. Checking to see whether she would tell him about a dream they had shared.

She tried to remember all the details to prove to October that she was being open and honest. Her face got hot as she told him about Corvin, how he had looked at her, and how he had made her feel. And then the approach of October's alter ego, Marco.

October started to chuckle. "So I was the gangster, and Corvin the cop? That's a switch. I guess he wasn't the soul sucker he is now in that life."

"But he had to be. If Corvin is as old as he and Sarah claimed, then that wasn't a previous life for him. It was just a few decades ago in the same life. It was a different life for me..." That much should have been obvious from both her age and race.

"The same life. So Corvin was a cop—not just a cop, but a cop on the take—during prohibition. Not going by the same name, obviously. I imagine he changes at least every hundred years."

"Probably by circumstances. Different jobs in different states. Different communities or cultures."

"Right," October agreed. He breathed heavily into the phone. "So that proves it, doesn't it? You have remembered him from one of the past lives. He was jealous of you and me. Didn't like you being interested in someone else, so he took action..."

Reg shuddered. "You think Corvin ended Lucy's life?"

"Don't you?"

"I don't know. I didn't see that much. Just one meeting in a bar, and that didn't tell me that much. You knew each other. Didn't get along. But that wasn't necessarily reason enough for him to want to kill me. Or you. I don't know what happened to either of us. We might have both lived a long life. Unless *you* remember something I don't," Reg challenged.

"No... I don't remember what might have happened to either of us. But it was a violent time. I don't imagine Corvin would have hesitated if he wanted to take you from me. Or, from what you said, maybe you had some gift that was undiscovered, and that triggered Corvin Hunter to do what it is he does."

"I didn't have any magical gifts," Reg said with certainty. "I would have known that. It was just... I was a singer. A good jazz singer. That was what he was complimenting me on. That was why he was interested in me. It was just... entertainment. A diversion. He's not interested in women who don't have powers."

"You seem pretty certain of that, for such a short dream."

Reg was uneasy. She didn't know that Corvin had done anything in that past life and didn't want to give October a reason to retaliate against him.

"I know Corvin," she told October. "Maybe he is the one we are looking for, but maybe not. There isn't any proof."

"What proof do you think you're going to find?"

"Well… maybe a memory of who it was that ended my life. How I died. Right now, I don't know anything about how Lucy May died. It could be anything. A car accident. Influenza. Childbirth."

"Do you remember who caused your death in any of the other lives? We both know that we were betrayed in Egypt, but by whom? This enemy sticks to the shadows. He is good at not being seen, at working covertly so no one knows. If he continues to follow that pattern, how will you get proof? To remember who it was?"

"I don't know. I think we should keep working on it. Sarah said I need to remember more."

"I think that we need to act now, before Corvin acts. You don't know what his plan is or when he may strike. Harrison thought you would know him when he reveals himself, but look to the past. He hasn't revealed himself. He's been very careful not to."

"If it was Corvin, he would have acted by now. What is he waiting for? He's been a part of my life for a couple of years. If it was him, wouldn't he have acted by now?"

"You don't know how long he took in those other lives. We don't know if something specific has triggered him or whether his actions were planned or impulsive."

"We can't just *assume* it is him."

"For the moment, we can. Why not? Let's look at him seriously. Figure out what his motive is and what he is planning. Figure out how to mount a counterattack."

Reg hesitated. "I just don't know."

"Meet with me. Let's go over it. You convince me that Corvin has no ill intentions toward either of us, and I'll believe you. We'll move on to the next suspect. But so far, who else do we have for suspects? John? Who else? You haven't seen anyone else you know in your dreams."

"But I don't know if I would. I have to be able to recognize someone who has taken a different form than the one I know."

"You have seen me. You have seen Corvin. You'll know if there is someone else."

Reg was silent. She couldn't help wondering about October. What if he were a traitor? What if he had betrayed her? He was happy to jump all over the idea that maybe it was Corvin. Was that because he needed her to look elsewhere? What if it had not been an outside intruder, but October himself?

"Meet with me," October prompted. "We'll discuss it."

CHAPTER THIRTY-ONE

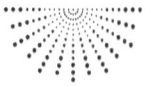

*O*f course Reg agreed to meet with October. There wasn't any harm in doing that, and it was vital that they put their heads together to try to sort it all out. They were both potentially in danger from the dark entity. They desperately needed a plan of action. A way to identify the force behind their former deaths.

If it were Corvin... then they would act on that knowledge. Reg had considered him an enemy almost the entire time she had lived in Black Sands, but he had also been an ally at times. He had given her strength or healing when she needed it. They had solved mysteries together. She had saved his life from someone who had been determined to kill him. She knew they were enemies and that their fates were somehow intertwined. She had come to understand that there was nothing she could do to break that bond between them. It was something she just had to accept.

October agreed to meet at The Witches' Brew. Reg liked it because she knew she could get good coffee there. They did all of the fancy stuff, all of the shots and flavored coffees and special blends that she couldn't do at home. With the pack moving into the wilds adjacent to Black Sands, the shop had also begun to carry a few items to entice them. Artisanal waters. Pate. Beef jerky. Quiches and hard-boiled eggs. They were advertised as part of the shop's new "low carb" menu, so they appealed to some of the trendy crowd as well as the wolves.

October reached the coffee shop before Reg. She always felt like she was arriving late to the party. But it had taken her some time to find her keys and get everything she needed to get out the door. In her head, she heard all of the criticisms from foster moms of the past about how she needed to pay attention to where she put things down, that she needed to put things away every time and not be lazy about it, and all of the other good and practical advice she had been given on keeping herself organized.

None of which had ever worked.

Reg inhaled the rich smell of fresh coffee and pastries deeply, looking forward to a treat. She was halfway across the cafe to greet October before she realized that there was someone else with him. She stopped and stared at the young woman for a moment. Then she continued toward the table, raising an eyebrow in query. Was October trying to pick up girls at the coffee shop now? Did he have interests other than just finding out who was trying to kill them over and over again?

"Reg, this is Channelle," October introduced. "You might have met before. She is part of the pack."

Reg took a closer look at the woman. She had rescued a lot of wolves that night and had not been able to stop to get to know any of them. And there had been a few wolves who had been in hiding when Jake was running his experiments who had rejoined the pack later.

She didn't recognize the woman with the brown, flowing hair and glittering dark eyes. Reg held out her hand to greet her. Channelle reached out an arm with a full sleeve of intricate tattoos. She squeezed Reg's hand briefly and let go.

"Nice to meet you, Channelle."

She looked at October again, trying to understand what

Channelle was doing there. Maybe she had just accompanied him or met him there to get herself a treat, and she would now be going on her way.

"Channelle is something of an expert on past lives," October said. "I thought it would be wise to bring her along. She can help us in our considerations."

"Oh." Reg reassessed the woman. How did someone become an expert on past lives? Especially someone so young?

"It is a passion of mine," Channelle told her, a faint French accent detectable in her voice. "I think it is very important to know your heritage. And that includes where you came from before this life. We are all a combination of all of the lives we have lived, are we not?"

Reg gave a brief nod as she sat down with them. She wasn't sure it was true, but she would go along with the idea for the sake of the conversation. She was there to learn, not to argue or theorize.

On the table was a plate with thin slices of various meats on skewers, and two bowls of bone broth. A waitress came over to the table and took Reg's coffee order and request for a muffin.

"This is nice for you," Reg commented, motioning to the wolves' food.

"They are always very accommodating," October agreed. "There are not a lot of establishments that would adjust their menus to our tastes."

"It means more business for them."

They made excruciatingly boring small talk until Reg's coffee arrived. Then, once the waitress had left them alone again, they turned to the serious topic of conversation.

CHAPTER THIRTY-TWO

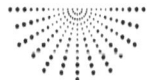

I have told Channelle the basics of what we have discovered," October informed Reg. "The basic outlines of the previous lives we are aware of and what happened when our lives crossed."

Reg pressed her lips together, a little irritated that he would tell such private matters to someone without asking her for her permission first. But she supposed he was entitled to tell her his story and, to him, Reg was only tangential to it. He had been killed in Egypt too. His life had been ruined in Greece by the exposure of their unchaperoned assignation. She still didn't know what had happened in the prohibition era. But despite what she had said to October about the possibility they had died of accidental or natural causes, the violence had been so rampant in that time and place that she doubted that the ends of their lives had been peaceful.

"It is fascinating," Channelle said. She didn't gush, exactly, but it was obvious that she was excited to have learned of their past life revelations. "It is so rare that we can identify crossings such as yours. Especially across multiple lifetimes. These experiences can expand our understanding of past lives and how they affect our present."

"It's interesting," Reg agreed. "But I'm not sure what we can learn from it. There is so much more that we don't know."

"I think it is meant to be kept from us," Channelle said. "Obscure, with only a few of the experiences leaking into current lives. Having too much knowledge of past lives could make it difficult for us to continue with the here and now. We can't spend our whole lives looking back instead of forward."

Reg nodded. "That is... really what it feels like. That I'm stuck looking back on the past, and it is keeping me from moving forward. There isn't anything we can do about what already happened in past lives... I'm not sure how knowing helps us now."

"But in your case, it is different. Because now you know that the two of you are connected and that there is someone who has... who may intend you harm in this life. I do not know of anyone who has been in that situation before. It is unique and can tell us so much about how reincarnation works."

"Does it?" Reg shook her head. "I've found it all pretty confusing. It's disturbing, and I feel like I am stuck in this repeating loop." She looked at October, trying to mask her grief. "Are we just doomed to keep repeating the same thing, life after life?"

"I don't think this is something that has happened through every life. The lives you have remembered are all similar—you as a woman and me as a man, in prestigious positions. You haven't remembered any where our positions are reversed or we have had other relationships. There must be many other lives where we weren't in those same roles."

"But here we are again." She met his eyes. "So, are we doomed to repeat the same pattern?"

"I don't know. I think that we have been given the opportunity to discover who this entity is that is working against us. Why would we be shown that unless we could do something about it? Identify the person working against us and do something about it. Maybe save ourselves from repeating the same cycle in this life and future lives."

"You think it's fated for us to stop it? Or repeat it?"

October had a sip of his soup, frown lines wrinkling his forehead.

"There are... opposing forces. We see it all the time in nature. Forces that push or pull in opposite directions. And maybe it is true in our past lives as well. Things that pull us together and things that push us apart. Being allowed to discover this person and root them out of our lives, or to repeat the cycle, and then maybe next time... we figure it out."

"Does that mean we had the opportunity before and didn't take it?"

"Perhaps... maybe we weren't able to figure it out. Or maybe this is the first time enough has been revealed for us to take action on it."

"Maybe it is just a fluke," Channelle said with a shrug. "Because of your psychic gifts. Without those, you might never have been able to remember your past lives in such detail. You might have simply had a dream and not realized it was a past life. Or not even had a dream. It wasn't until you and October were reunited in this life that you started having these visions, right?"

Reg nodded. "I guess so. I have been looking for another trigger, another person who might have come into my life in the last couple of weeks that I've been having problems sleeping and having vivid dreams. I thought maybe there was something else, because I've known October for a few months but only been having these issues for a few weeks."

"Maybe your contact with Corvin?" October suggested.

"No... I was in contact with him before you ever came to town. That didn't just start the last few weeks."

"Have they increased? Has his behavior changed at all?"

"No... I don't think so."

"What about John?"

"Who is John?" Channelle prompted.

"John is Corvin's son. He has only been here for a few weeks," he looked at Reg for confirmation.

"Months," Reg corrected. "Before you."

"Have you had any more contact with him recently?" October asked. "Any reason to think he might have been more interested in you? Showing up more often?"

"No, I haven't had any contact with John. I avoid him whenever I can, to be honest. I'm not comfortable around him and I... hear his mother's ghost when I'm with him. She was a very scary creature."

"Scary in what way?" Channelle asked, leaning forward, her expression rapt.

"I don't really want to get into it. She was... John was feeding his powers to her, so she became really powerful. She was intent on taking her revenge on Corvin for the way he treated her in the past."

"And what happened to her?"

"Uh... she was killed."

October and Channelle both looked at Reg, expecting more.

"It was... she was incinerated. By a dragon." There was a bigger and bigger pause between each phrase. "By my dragon."

"Oh, my," Channelle murmured.

"So John has a pretty good reason to target you," October pointed out.

"Yes. Of course. Which is one of the reasons that I try to stay away from him."

"Has he tried to take his revenge on you?"

"No. Nothing I know of. Corvin is kind of trying to mentor him, but I don't think he has very good control over him. And I think John is sort of..." Reg remembered October's own suggestion. *Bat-crap crazy.*

She didn't like labeling anyone as crazy. How many times had people used that word to describe her? And all along, she hadn't been crazy at all. She'd been psychic, with a sprinkling of other gifts. That, and traumatized by her past. Trauma had definitely contributed to her behaviors as well.

"Between Corvin and John, it's *bound* to be someone in the coven," October said.

"I don't know..." Reg didn't think there was enough evidence to jump to that conclusion.

"Corvin was the person in your latest dream. You know he was there. You haven't seen anyone else that you know, have you?"

"I don't know."

"Corvin is the only person other than me that you are sure crossed with you in another life."

"Yes... so far. But there could be others. I don't know how common or uncommon it is."

"Out of the billions of people on the earth, how many of them do you ever cross paths with? The vast population of the earth now or over the progress of time will never cross paths with you, especially not in a significant way. So there has to be a reason for it. If it was not a close bond, then it is the opposite. Someone who did you wrong. An ancient wrong that needs to be righted."

Reg sipped her sweet mochaccino with caramel topping. She could just imagine the look on Corvin's face if he saw her drinking it; he always commented about her drinking her desserts.

"I could still have more than one enemy who did a wrong that needs to be righted. Even just here in town—Corvin isn't the only one. There's Julian, for one. There have been others... sirens, pixies, the Witch Doctor, Hakeem, the Cabal of the Withered Paw..."

"Jake," Channelle provided.

Reg sighed and nodded. "Jake," she admitted. She hated putting him in the camp of her enemies. They had been so close. She had thought once that she would be with him for the rest of her life. She knew now that part of it had been a binding spell he had placed on her, but that didn't make her feel any better. She had thought that she loved him, and she'd participated in taking him down. She was no longer bound to him and he could no longer continue his experiments on the wolves. Or anyone else.

"Jake hasn't shown up in any of your dreams?" October asked.

"No. Not that I have noticed."

"I am sure you would have felt something if you had crossed paths with him."

"Yeah..." Reg thought about the way she had felt whenever she was around Jake. She felt a longing just thinking about him. "I think I would."

"So that brings us back to Corvin or John. Do you really think it is one of the others that you named? Or didn't name. It didn't escape my notice that you couldn't mention the individual members of the other groups you mentioned."

"What about Julian?" Reg shot back.

"Julian?"

"Davyn's... friend. And he's an inspector of magical whatever. Law enforcement. He used to be a foster brother, used to bully me all the time, and then came back to investigate... something that happened in the Everglades. So he's crossed with me twice in this life."

"An interesting possibility," October admitted. "Where is he?"

"I don't know. Davyn said he was off on business. Investigating somewhere else, I guess."

"Not here in Black Sands."

"Not right now. But he is sometimes."

October ignored the comment. He looked at Channelle. "I think we need to focus on the coven. Don't you?"

"Yes," she agreed immediately.

Reg was frustrated. She didn't know how to convince October that the coven wasn't responsible for what had happened to them in the past. Maybe Corvin had crossed paths with her in another life, maybe more, but that wasn't proof that he was the mysterious X.

She couldn't just let October lead the charge against Corvin and John, but she didn't know what else to do.

"You don't need to do anything," October told her. "This is my life, too, and I am not going to sit around waiting for someone to attack me again. Channelle knows about past lives, and she is going to help me figure out how to put a stop to it. You only need to stay out of the way. I will take care of everything."

If Channelle knew a magical way to neutralize the threat, why would Reg want to stop them? She didn't want to wait around for an attack any more than October did. If they needed her to provide a lock of hair or a chant or some other contribution to their efforts, they would let her know.

CHAPTER THIRTY-THREE

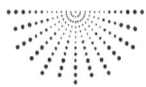

*S*he shifted in her sleep and sniffed the air, making sure there were no intruders. It was second nature. Awake, sniff, process, and go back to sleep. Nothing had disturbed her sleep for a long time.

Her lair was well-hidden deep within the mountains, where faint echoes of dripping water mixed with sulfurous air filled her cavernous home. As long as she did nothing to attract the attention of any of the pitiful humans in camps or small gatherings around the mountains, no one could find her hoard. The weakling two-legs didn't need all of the riches. What were they going to do with them? They scattered gold around like the worthless wheat and rice they grew in their fields. They had no respect for it, shuffling it from one place to another and keeping it in their tiny boxes. They didn't understand how to treat the riches they had, so why should they have access to any more?

But something made her pause this time. Something tickled her nostrils—just the barest hint of human sweat, oil, and leather—something that immediately made her eyes fly open, and she looked all around without moving, which might draw attention to her.

It was probably just an explorer. Lone humans occasionally broke away from their tribe to go wandering, looking for interesting new places. Places where there were no other humans to join with. She didn't understand why. They were not like adolescent dragons, in need of new lairs to accommodate their increased size and riches. They were not looking for mates, not when they were searching places where there were no other humans. Perhaps they were sick. Shunned by their tribe or looking for a quiet place to die.

Whatever the reason, she knew she did not worry about explorers. They were not a danger to her.

She kept her ears pricked alertly, listening for a footstep, the brush of clothing, the squeak of leather. Anything to indicate where the lone human was and what he was doing.

Her eyes were like lamps in the darkness. To her, there was no such thing as dark. She could always see around her cave even though no sun reached this place. On the contrary, she preferred to avoid the blinding light of the sun. It gave her a headache.

A clink. The scraping of a body against the tight tunnel walls. Much too big for the tunnels herself, she regarded them as ventilation ducts, not entrances or exits. She sniffed the air.

Stronger this time. More sweat. Closer to her. The rank smell of fear, and yet the tiny human persisted, drawing closer and closer, navigating the fissures and lava tubes that ran through the mountain. She remained motionless, waiting. The human was unlikely to be drawn to her lair without any light or movement. Her breathing was far too slow for humans to notice.

But he kept coming. Slow and awkward, like all of them. The clumsy humans never seemed to grow out of that awkward baby stage, but continued to bumble around as if they were too blind to see all of their surroundings and too deaf to hear their own stumbling gait.

Her worst fears were realized when the human reached the

end of a tunnel that led to the cavern. She waited, motionless, hoping it would see nothing and return the way it had come.

There was a gasp and a few muttered words. Not as blind as she had hoped. What was it there for? For her, or her gold?

She watched the curious human emerge from the tunnel slowly and carefully. He had a string to climb down, a shiny exoskeleton, and a needle to jab her with. He carried a small light in a cage to help him navigate in the darkness.

His heart beat like a sparrow's, so light and fast. She knew it would not take much to kill him, even with the exoskeleton armoring his body. It might withstand a little battering, but not crushing. Not fire. Not a long, piercing claw.

It's true!

She heard his words in her head. It was difficult to interpret them. Her ancestors had learned some human words over the centuries, passing them down in generational memory from parent to hatchling.

Gold! Untold wealth!

She stirred. Until then, her body had been in the shadows of the cavern. Scales encrusted with gold helped her to blend in with the piles of gold. Her gold, safe and protected from avaricious human hands. But when she moved, the human froze, light held in the air.

Dragon!

She slithered along the surface of the treasure hoard, keeping the angle between herself and the human steep to avoid any projectiles. She got closer to the intruder, drawing breath and letting it burn in her chest, waiting for the exact point at which she would release it, eliminating the threat.

How long have you been here?

She was startled at the question. Humans did not talk to dragons, only to each other. Why would this one speak to her?

It must be a very long time.

She breathed out slowly and, after due consideration, shared with the human a vision of the years that had passed *since she had moved into the lair and settled herself on the piles of gold.*

What is your name?

She drew closer to the human, studying him, trying to make out all of the nuances of this dragon-speaker.

A male of the species. Larger and stronger. The females stayed at home, bearing live young, until their bodies wore out and they died. The males were hardier, but many still died young, killing each other, falling, creating machines to kill themselves, and making many other foolish choices.

With the mask of the glittering armor lowered, she could see the human's face. Young. Rugged. Curious green eyes caught the light he held in his hand.

What is your name? *He repeated.*

She was unsure how to answer. This one seemed able to understand dragon memories, but dragon names were difficult to communicate without a shared language. She worked through several memories, trying to assemble something that would make sense, laying them out and examining them like the pebbles on one of the paths the humans created.

Wind... thunder... storm...?

She focused, trying to narrow it down.

Storm Bringer?

It was as close as she thought the human tongue could get.

Storm Bringer.

That's a beautiful name. A strong name.

He would not think it so beautiful if she were to create a firestorm to consume him. Humans and dragons did not associate, and she immediately regretted giving the human intruder any clue as to her name.

She conjured up memories of dragons chasing down and killing the tiny, defenseless humans, pushing them back away from their mountain lairs, away from the treasure they accumulated and watched over.

The man took a step back. At first, he raised his needle in defense as if the pinprick would be enough to protect him against Storm Bringer.

I came for gold. I need money to protect my family. To put food in the little ones' mouths. To help them grow up to be strong warriors instead of starving to death or freezing in the cold with no walls to shelter them from the weather.

So he thought he could come here? To steal it from her hoard? Such a thing could never be done.

The audacity of this creature, to think he could simply walk into her domain and take what was rightfully hers.

You risk your life for gold?

The human nodded slowly, his eyes never leaving hers. For my family. For their survival.

Dragons did not raise their own young. Hatchlings came into the world alone, forced to rely on their generational memory, instinct, and experience to survive. They were hardy, but not all survived. There were predators out there big enough to kill a new hatchling.

She would never know how many of the eggs she had laid and left behind hatched and grew up to become strong, full-grown dragons. She had occasionally seen dragonlets or hatchlings from a distance, gamboling and experimenting, testing their limits. But she would never know their parentage or what happened to them after she left. She would never stay in the vicinity of a young dragon. She would do nothing to attract the attention of humans or other base predators who would kill a young dragon simply because it was not human. They would not even eat it.

I do not wish to steal from you, but I do not know where else to go. I came to the mountains to find precious ores or gems.

His eyes roamed over the precious ores and gems of her hoard. Such a trove would feed many humans for many years if they traded the gold for their meager food.

Take what you want *Storm Bringer told him impulsively. Feed your hatchlings.*

He looked at her in disbelief. She waited and, eventually, he started to move. Storm Bringer watched intently as he cautiously approached one small pile containing mixed coins and precious gems. He reached toward it with his free hand, watching her.

Storm Bringer leaned closer, watching to see how much he would take. Perhaps he thought she was going to kill him for what he had already picked up. He dropped it and stepped back, raising his weapon, which he had never let out of his hand.

It is yours, *Storm Bringer told him,* Take it and go.

A few seconds passed, not even one heartbeat for Storm Bringer, but many for the intruder. He was sweating profusely.

With a weak yell like a songbird, he lunged at her, thrusting the needle forward so that it made contact.

It was not strong enough or sharp enough to penetrate her armor, hardened by years of growth and crusted with gems. He raised it and tried to pierce her several times, trying to reach her throat and eyes which, even lowered to look at him were far beyond his reach.

Eventually, she put an end to his struggles and put the gems and coins he had pilfered back onto her pile.

CHAPTER THIRTY-FOUR

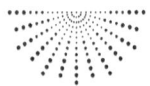

*R*eg awoke from the dream with a sense of foreboding. She turned over, pulling the blanket over her head to block out the sun, and tried to go back to sleep again. But her brain was already alive with worry about what the dream meant and she didn't know how to deal with it.

Her relationship with October had developed over the past months, so she considered him a friend and ally. She had felt close to him from the time they met, and realized that was the result of what they had experienced together in their past lives. All of her memories of past lives with October had been positive, their relationship as man and woman, lovers and allies. She understood that they could have had other relationships in other lives, but she had believed that they would all be positive. Their souls knew each other. That was why they had been drawn together, wasn't it?

She had not anticipated the memory of a life in which they had not been friends, but enemies. Or a situation in which October had betrayed her.

She had reached out to him, had done something against her nature, a kindness, and he had responded with betrayal. Had tried to kill her. He had not been there as a simple woodcutter who needed to supplement his poor family's income. He had approached the dragon's lair in full armor, which would have weighed him down and made the journey into the mountain cave that much more difficult. He had known that there might be a dragon there and had intended to kill her and steal her hoard.

He had tried to deceive her, to somehow evoke her sympathy and, when she had allowed him to take a tiny portion of her hoard, he had not reacted with gratitude but with violence.

Could a man like that be trusted in another life? Did his nature change from one life to the next, or did he remain the same person at his core?

And if he had betrayed her trust in one life, what about others? She didn't believe he had been at fault in Egypt or Greece, but could she really know that? And what about other lives she did not remember?

Maybe nobody could be good in every life and every circumstance. Reg herself had done plenty of things she knew were considered wrong or sinful. She blamed it on her circumstances, her upbringing, the necessity of protecting herself and surviving all that she had been through.

In the end, she had chosen to do things that she knew broke the law or society's ethical standards, and didn't feel guilty about it. If someone let himself be conned by her, that was his fault for being so gullible. And she never stole from the needy, only those who could afford to lose what she took from them.

Besides, most of those accused thefts were not outright thefts at all. Reg had never intended to take what she had, but because she didn't know of her powers, she had unwittingly called them to her. She said the owners had given them to her because she had found them among her possessions. What other explanation was there? It had not been intentional theft.

Was she a bad person? Had she betrayed October in other

lives? Had she ever hurt him in the past for reasons other than to protect herself from a predator?

It was his own fault that he had been killed in the dragon cave. He had attacked her, and she had merely protected herself the only way she could. And she hadn't wasted his body and left it there to molder, as he would have hers. With her slow lizard metabolism in hibernation mode in the cave, the tiny morsel provided her enough sustenance for a long time.

Her mind kept returning to the question. Could October be trusted? Was he a different person in this life from what he had been as a medieval knight? Or was her incarnation the difference? In that life, she had been a natural enemy, and he couldn't be expected to see her as anything else, no matter how long they had gazed into each other's eyes. In this life, she was a woman, in human form as he was, so did that automatically make them friends or allies?

Or was he still the same predator he had been in the dragon lair? Trying to sneak up on her unaware, then trying to kill when she had offered him untold riches, because he wanted more.

CHAPTER THIRTY-FIVE

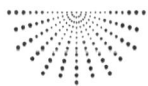

*I*n the distance, an owl hooted softly. A cool breeze blew in off the ocean, filling the air with its salty tang.

"Now is the time to act," Channelle encouraged. "We may not get an opportunity like this again. We know the coven will be performing the ceremony at the equinox when it will be the most powerful."

October nodded. He didn't want to rush into anything. But at the same time, he did. He wasn't about to wait around for anyone else's approval. He had found the proverb "it is easier to get forgiveness than permission" to be true in the past. Sometimes, there was a penalty to pay, sometimes just disapproval or a lecture. But it was easier than trying to get a consensus from others with a diversity of opinions. He tended to be a lone wolf, preferring to make a decision on his own. He participated in councils when required, but he found them annoying and frustrating and frequently did not have the patience to wait them out and get an official decision. He jumped in and acted when he saw the need was greatest. Sometimes, it worked out; sadly, other times, it didn't.

Channelle was right about the timing. They were not likely

to get an opportunity like that again for a long time. Who knew what could happen during that time? If they had to wait weeks, months, even years for another similar opportunity, what could happen during that time? Corvin could make his move and steal Reg's powers, then dispose of her body like the husk of a fruit crushed for its juice.

Or he could recognize the danger posed by October and try to take him on. Corvin's powers were very strong. Overwhelming. If he were to breach the laws and treaties between their kind and attack October or the pack, he could annihilate them.

October couldn't wait around for that to happen. He knew that Corvin would not hesitate long to break the rules. He had before. October had to act before Corvin decided to come after him.

October must not hesitate to act when the opportunity was presented. He would seek forgiveness from the authorities for his actions later, when he was safe. When Reg was safe. When they were able to be together without fear of the dark force ending one or both of their lives.

"I suppose it is my only choice," he told Channelle finally.

She nodded, her eyes bright and eager.

She was young and new to the pack. October found her quick to act whenever an opportunity arose. Impulsive. More than once, he had seen her make a serious misjudgment on the hunt, losing the pack their prey. They were forced to choose an alternate target or to go out again another day.

Not such a big deal when they were close to town and could go to the supermarket in biped form and feed their families meat that had been raised and slaughtered by others. If they were forced to live on what they had caught, the young pups might have gone hungry more than once due to Channelle's impulsivity.

October had to act as a steadying force for her. To be the voice of caution and reason and not allow himself to be swept up in the excitement of her suggestions.

"This needs to be carefully planned. And we have to use caution with who we recruit to help us. Some will not think it is a good idea. Better that we take a few of the pack who we know will be strong supporters and give us the backup we need than to reveal our plan to naysayers and nervous Nellies who will counsel caution."

Channelle nodded her agreement. "I know. I'll listen to your advice on who to talk to. I don't want to wreck this. Not when we don't know when we will get another chance. And if we got banished from the pack..." She trailed off, and October heard a faint whine as she considered the consequences for them. She looked at him sidelong, wondering, he supposed, whether he would stay by her side. Whether he would become her protector, maybe even her mate, if they were banished.

He hadn't really thought about banishment. It was a harsh punishment only meted out for the worst of offenses. Surely not in the case of someone who was merely protecting himself and his loved ones. *Himself and his pack,* October amended mentally.

Another wolf would not expect him to ignore the danger to his own life or the lives of his pack. If he always acted for the benefit of the pack, he would not be banished. He might have to deal with other consequences, but not banishment.

"We will act," October told Channelle grimly. "We cannot stand by and just watch this soul eater wreak havoc in this town."

CHAPTER THIRTY-SIX

*O*ctober's ears were pricked for the sounds of the coven. Midnight was approaching, and they would be sure to be performing the ceremony at the equinox when it was most powerful.

The darkness magnified the sounds around the ancient temple grove. The moon was bright but occasionally covered by drifting clouds.

Corvin was an incredibly powerful warlock due to his ability to consume the powers of others and, from the stories October had heard, he'd had the opportunity to acquire great powers over the past couple of years. Powers that made him almost invincible.

But this was his first equinox as the leader of the coven, and he would be sure to put his extraordinary powers to use to show his coven they had made the right choice in electing him. He would give them all extra power, and they would be bound to him even more strongly, building a fortification around him that was even more unassailable.

But to perform the ceremony to transfer considerable powers to the coven members without any noticeable diminution on his part, he would need to align the ceremony with the equinox. October had no doubt of this fact.

Corvin would be at his most vulnerable during the ceremony.

Standing at the edge of the ruins in his biped form, October listened intently as the wind rustled through the leaves. He called to the other members of the pack he had invited to join him in his mind. This was no time for howls or other audible signals. They needed to work in complete silence for the ambush to be successful and to take Corvin unaware.

The ceremony began. The gong struck, unifying the voices of the coven. The chanting began and rose up to October's ears. It started an itching in him, an uncomfortable restlessness that needed to be acted upon. But he had to bide his time. Wait for just the right moment.

The wolves moved into their agreed-upon positions. October checked in with Channelle, making sure she understood where she was supposed to be. She would not act until they were all ready, and October gave the signal.

I know, Channelle agreed. *I wait.*

The chanting swelled up, growing in strength and intensity. Their voices blended as one. Then October heard Corvin's voice diverge from the rest as he gathered strength and prepared his part. It was a low rumble that October felt deep in his gut. It resonated like the gong that had begun the ceremony, and October's body responded.

The others were awaiting his signal. October waited until he could barely stand it. The magic pulled him in and, at the same time, repelled him. It was not *his* kind of magic.

Finally, he could stand it no longer. *Now,* he gave the command.

They moved in concert, following the preplanned attack pattern, each member of the team following a precise path that would take him to the coven without alerting them before the attack.

They all burst into the clearing at the same time. The members of the coven stood in a circle with Corvin at the head. An altar with an offering of herbs was at the center of the gathering. Symbols or runes were carved into the stone. The chanting stopped abruptly, but no one moved, shocked by the unexpectedness of the werewolf attack.

October had remained in biped form while most of the pack had taken canid form for an easier attack. October needed hands to carry the vials he had brought with him. Mandrake, rosemary, and other herbs blended with oil.

He threw the first vial on the altar, smashing it and releasing its contents. After the tinkling of the breaking glass, everything was silent, but a shock wave rippled through the temple grove, expanding outward and swallowing up all sound. The pungent scent of the herbs burst forth.

Still, everyone in the coven remained frozen, too shocked to fight back. Corvin stood before October, looking powerful and mysterious in his black robe, yet too stunned by the attack to react quickly. He was vulnerable in the midst of a ritual that opened him up to those in his coven, a ritual that could only be performed in a safe place. But they had misjudged, not knowing that October and his packmates were planning an attack.

October knew that even with surprise on his side, he had only seconds to act. The shock and vulnerability would last only so long and, if Corvin had the chance to gather his thoughts, he would be a foe too powerful for October to deal with. Too powerful for all of them to defend themselves against. October put the other vial between his teeth and transformed.

Precious seconds passed as he shifted from biped to canid form. He could hear the howls of his packmates around him, calling to each other, growling and threatening the warlocks, keeping everyone pinned in place so that the circle remained intact, the coven's spell unbroken.

Focusing to remain balanced on his two hind legs, October dragged his claws across Corvin's arm, ripping open the skin and exposing the vulnerable veins. He clamped his long teeth down on the glass vial, breaking it, and dribbled the mandrake tincture into the open wound.

Corvin let out a shout of pain, the first sound he had made since the attack began. The sizzle and steam from Corvin's arm told October that it was working; it was not just Corvin's surprise at being attacked that made him yell.

October knew from Reg that Corvin had some telepathic powers. Though whether he could communicate with anyone or only to Reg or a limited number of people, October didn't know. It didn't matter. He wanted his words to be heard, but the spell would work whether he spoke them aloud or not. So he pushed the words into Corvin's mind.

> In the name of ancient bonds betrayed,
> With mandrake's force, your powers are stayed.
> Guardians of magic now hold sway,
> Cross us again, and you shall pay.

Corvin stared back at October, stunned. He stepped backward, finally breaking the circle.

Wolves howled around them. Some of the members of the coven fell to the ground with the breaking of the circle, others staggered with the force of it but remained on their feet. Corvin raised his hand to point at October, presumably to curse him or perform some other magic but, as he did so, his injured hand spasmed, and he clutched it close to his chest, letting out another cry of pain. The spell, October saw with satisfaction, had taken.

Corvin would not be able to use his magic, especially against October or Reg, without causing himself excruciating pain. The mandrake thrown in the middle of the circle while it was still active would seal the curse on all of them, preventing the rest of the warlocks from being able to cast a spell against Reg or October as well.

Remember this night! Channelle howled. *Remember the night the werewolves bested the most ancient coven in the country!*

The other wolves took up the howl.

Remember this night!

October dropped to all four paws. He gave a bark to call the others and loped away from the broken coven. They would need the veil of darkness if they were to avoid the immediate consequences of their actions.

CHAPTER THIRTY-SEVEN

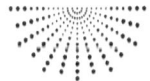

*R*eg's head pounded like she had a hangover, but she was too tired and queasy to do anything about it. The pounding continued for some time, and then it was gone and she drifted, as if floating in a deep pool of water.

"Reg! Reg, you need to wake up!"

Reg fought back against the command. She didn't want to wake up. She wasn't ready to deal with the day. She was incredibly tired, sore, and nauseated. She needed sleep. It was not time to get up. Anyone who needed her could wait a day or two until she felt better.

"Reg."

Reg shook her head. She kept her eyes tightly shut. She didn't want anything to disturb her sleep tonight. She was going to get all of the sleep she needed this one time.

A hand shook her arm, and Reg tried to push it away. Eventually, the persistence of her tormentor paid off, and Reg pried her eyes open to stare up into the face of Detective Marta Jessup. Her dark, almond-shaped eyes reflected anxiety.

Reg didn't think she had a girls' night or spa day set up with Marta. So what was she doing there? She knew that Reg slept in late and needed that sleep to function.

The only reason she could think of for Marta to be there without a prearranged appointment of some kind was...

Reg forced herself to sit up. "What is it? Is Sarah okay?"

"Sarah? Sarah is fine." Marta frowned, confused. "Why would something be wrong with Sarah?"

"I just..." Reg shook her head. "What are you doing here, then? Why are you waking me up? I thought something must have happened to Sarah."

Marta shook her head. But she didn't smile or joke around about Reg thinking something was wrong when she just wanted a little girl-to-girl talk. Instead, she had her *cop face* on. Reg didn't like the cop face.

"What is it?" she demanded.

"You should come out to talk..." Marta suggested, gesturing toward the open bedroom door. "There will be less repetition that way."

Repetition? Why did they need to have a serious talk? Reg had no idea what had happened to require Marta's frown and the need for a serious talk with Reg.

"Okay. Okay, just give me a minute. I'm feeling kind of..." Reg grabbed the water bottle from the side table and had a long pull on it. "Kind of awful," Reg muttered. She tried to remember whether she had been drinking the night before and, if so, why. She didn't normally drink enough to affect her the next morning. Not anymore. Not since she was a teenager.

"I'm sorry," Marta said. She gave a little grimace, "I know it must be the middle of the night for you. But we need to talk right away. Things are... going to get out of hand pretty quickly."

"What are you talking about?" Reg rubbed her eyes, which felt sandy and sore. She would need eye drops. More to drink. Maybe a cold compress over her eyes.

And another five hours of sleep.

She finally got unsteadily to her feet and made her way

toward the coffee machine. If she was going to have to have a real talk with anyone, she was going to need some fortification.

Sarah was in the kitchen and handed Reg a cup of tea. Reg looked down at it. English Breakfast tea, not one of Sarah's vile concoctions. She sipped the scalding hot tea. It wasn't coffee, but it was a start. When she finished it, maybe she would also have a couple of cups of coffee. If she weren't allowed to go back to bed.

"What is this? What's going on?"

"I'm sorry about letting Marta in, dear," Sarah apologized. "You know I don't normally let anyone but myself in; that's our understanding."

They didn't actually have an understanding. Reg had come to accept that Sarah would let herself in from time to time to schedule clients on Reg's calendar, put food in the fridge, clean, decorate, or do any number of things she saw necessary to keep the cottage in tip-top condition. There was no point in arguing about it when Sarah was helping Reg both by charging her very low rent and providing all kinds of other perks no other land-lord would have.

Reg shrugged and looked at Marta, hoping she would now explain what was wrong.

"Let's sit down," Marta suggested.

Reg didn't argue. She shuffled over to the couch and tried to make herself as comfortable as possible under their scrutiny. Was she in trouble? If so, for what? She couldn't think of anything she might have done lately to attract police attention. Or that would put that solemn, worried look on Sarah's wrinkled face.

"There has been an attack," Marta explained. "A werewolf attack."

Reg gasped. Her mind went back to the slashings by the tortured, crazed werewolves that October had released from their cages in Jake's lab and the subsequent tragedy. Her heart felt like it was being squeezed.

"Oh, no. Is everyone all right?"

Sarah and Marta shook their heads in unison. Reg clutched the cup of tea too tightly in her hands, afraid it would break, but unable to feel it.

"Who…?" Reg didn't know whether it would be an injured wolf or an injured human. Or both. Or multiples. She had grown close to some of the members of the pack. Especially Zora and cubs. She prayed that nothing had happened to the puppies. But what would have happened to them? They would not have been involved in any kind of attack. They were too young. Wolves didn't usually get aggressive until adolescence, and the pups were not that old yet. Though, of course, Fenris had turned Jake when he had been only hours old. And Zora was always saying how precocious they were. Who knew what changes Jake's experiments might have caused to their physiological development?

"Corvin and the coven were attacked during their equinox observance last night."

"By werewolves?" Reg gasped. She couldn't even imagine such a thing. Why would werewolves attack the coven?

Equinox was a time of peace and harmony. That was what the witches had taught her. A time of goodwill, sharing, and growth.

Not a time of violence.

A werewolf attack? It made no sense.

"Have you talked to October?" Marta asked.

"October? No, not for a few days. Was he involved? That doesn't make any sense."

But once the words were out of her mouth, she regretted saying anything.

A werewolf attack. October.

An attack on the coven. Corvin and John, while they were in the midst of an equinox ritual. Reg set her cup on the coffee table and put her hands over her face.

"Oh, no. Are they okay? Is everyone okay?"

If there had been deaths, she didn't know how she would forgive herself. Or forgive October. She had told him that she wasn't sure about Corvin. That she didn't think he'd had anything to do with their deaths in the past. There were many times since Reg had moved to Black Sands that Corvin could have taken her life if he'd been inclined to do so. Didn't the fact that she had never seen him betray her in her recovered past life memories mean anything?

"No one was seriously hurt or killed," Marta assured her. "Some superficial injuries. The worst was Corvin's, and I'm not sure…" She looked at Sarah. "Maybe you'd better explain."

"I'm afraid I don't really know what to say," Sarah said, frowning. "It would appear… to be a magical injury. A curse. He was slashed, but the appearance of the wound and the way that Corvin is behaving… it is more than that."

Reg shook her head. "That's horrible. But I'm not sure…" she drew down her brows. "I'm not sure why you are telling me that. What does it have to do with me?"

Other than that October was trying to protect her life from a perceived threat.

"Well, for one thing, to find out if you have talked to October lately," Marta said.

"Like I said, not for a few days. Whatever he got into his head to do… it didn't have anything to do with me."

"Corvin said that is not true."

"What did Corvin say? I didn't know October was going to do anything."

She hadn't been sure he would do anything. She hadn't anticipated that it would be so quick or that he would undertake a physical attack on Corvin. Especially while he was with the coven. That seemed like an incredibly risky thing to do.

"October is okay?" she asked. "Was he hurt?"

"None of the werewolves were injured. Only warlocks."

"Werewolves," Reg repeated.

"Yes," Marta was impatient. "I told you it was a werewolf attack."

"But I thought you meant... just October. But you said *werewolves*, plural."

"Yes," Marta agreed. "At least half a dozen of them."

"Half a dozen!" Reg tried to identify in her mind which six wolves would be involved in something like that. Who would October have been able to talk into it? Who would have been so brazen? Attacking the coven? It made so sense. There were laws. Treaties. Societal expectations.

"Good grief," she said, for lack of anything else to contribute. What else could she say? It was something so totally unexpected, she was too stunned to think of anything to say.

"I know," Sarah said with a sympathetic nod. "It's hard to comprehend, isn't it?"

"What does it all mean?" Reg asked. "Does it mean you charge October?" she asked Marta. "Or does he get judged by his own people?" She knew that each species was supposed to be self-governing, but they had all agreed to certain rules to be followed in their dealings with each other.

"First, we need to find him," Marta said, frustration evident in her tone. "They've gone underground. There isn't a trace of any of the wolves who were involved in the attack. I was hoping you might have some idea of where October would go. He might have told you his plans..."

"No, why would he? It isn't anything to do with me."

"Corvin said that you and October seemed to believe that he had done something to harm you, and this was your revenge."

"Me? No. I didn't know what he was going to do or where he went afterward. I had no idea, honestly."

"This wasn't revenge for something that Corvin had done to you?"

"No. I don't know. October might have thought that it was.

But I told him…" Reg tried to find a way that she had told October that it was not Corvin who had been stalking her through her previous lives without sounding crazy. And how to avoid giving Marta the impression that she had known something about what October was going to do, because she hadn't. She had not thought that he was going to attack Corvin. She had thought that he would investigate. Maybe give Reg a chance to do some past life regressions to find out what had happened to them in their previous lives. She didn't think that he was going to go immediately to a violent attack.

"You and October thought someone was targeting you," Sarah suggested.

Reg gave her a sharp look. She had hoped that Sarah would just keep quiet and not give Marta any information about their theory. Though it was evident that Sarah had already said too much. And Corvin, too, had known too much. Reg hadn't even had a chance to talk to him yet about their past crossings. Or Corvin's crossing with Reg's previous incarnation.

"Yes, we thought someone might be targeting me in previous lives. Or me and October. But… we hadn't really established anything yet. I only had one memory that even included Corvin for sure."

"Did you tell October about that?" Marta asked.

"Well, yes. But I told him… I told him I didn't think that Corvin was the one."

"It would appear that October disagreed."

Reg shrugged. "I can't help what October thought."

"Did he have any memories of his own?"

"I don't know. Not that he told me."

"Do you think he would have told you?"

Reg thought back to their last conversation. Probably not. October knew that Reg disagreed with him. Maybe he didn't want to reveal anything else that he knew.

She couldn't help thinking of her memory of the knight who had broken into her cave. He had been offered riches beyond his wildest dreams, but he had chosen to attack instead. Choosing violence over wealth. Or choosing to take all instead of just a small portion.

And he had been the one to release the wolves from Jake's lab against the council's decision.

Did October ever act for anyone other than himself?

CHAPTER THIRTY-EIGHT

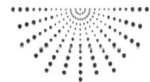

*D*o you know where October is?" Marta asked sternly.

Reg didn't like her cop voice. At least Marta wasn't calling her "Miss Rawlins" yet. Reg wasn't a suspect, but she knew October, which was apparently enough to put her into the spotlight.

Reg had only known October for a few months; she didn't know how she was supposed to know where he would go after something like this. If he wasn't with the rest of the pack, Reg didn't know where he might be.

"I have no idea."

"You and he are friends. You must know something about where he goes."

"He goes with the pack. I don't know where. I'm a city girl. I don't know my way around the wilderness. When I visit October or Zora, I don't track them or run with the pack. I just meet them in a park or something."

"I don't think October is likely to be in a park," Marta said.

"I don't either. That's why I said I have no idea where he is or where he would go. That's his own business."

"Do you have any way to contact him?"

"No."

199

"He must have a cell phone."

"Well…" Reg couldn't deny that part. Everyone had a cell phone, including October. Maybe the wolves who spent most of their time in canid form did not, but those who spent their time on two legs in the human world did, just like the rest of the population. "Yes, he has a cell phone. I can text him and see if he responds, but I won't try to fool him."

"Did I ask you to do anything like that?"

Reg gave Marta a look. She knew the way it was. She knew that the police or whatever council was over werewolf law enforcement would want to get in contact with him, and it wouldn't be long before they were asking Reg to help bring him in.

They both knew it.

Sarah made a little noise as if trying to break them up and make peace between them. She knew it, too.

"If you could text him," Marta said reasonably. "Maybe… just ask him how he is."

Reg considered this. She wasn't going to try to trap October or to make him talk, but she *did* want to know if he was okay.

She pulled out her phone, paused to rub the sleep out of her eyes to see the screen more clearly, and considered what she wanted to say.

Police here R U OK?

She didn't expect an immediate answer. If October was on the run or amid some kind of turmoil, then he had more immediate concerns than communicating with Reg, especially when he knew the police were eavesdropping on the conversation.

Reg ran her fingers through her box braids. She gathered the tiny braids together in both hands and pushed them all behind her shoulders. She had another sip of tea and wished that it were coffee instead. She needed a bigger kick. Maybe an espresso. Or maybe a hit from the bottle of Jack in the cupboard. Something to wake her up or to steady her nerves. She didn't know which she needed more.

The screen of her phone had gone dark. But as she looked at Sarah to ask her a question, she saw it light up from the corner of her eye. She picked it up before Marta could lean over and see what it said, even though she knew that October would not type anything he didn't want the police to see. He would be careful of what he said.

But she still wanted to see it before Marta.

CHAPTER THIRTY-NINE

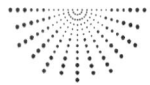

I am fine

Not much of an answer, but maybe all he could manage for the moment, or all that he cared to write for law enforcement's eyes.

They want to know where u r

The answer came back more quickly this time. He was still holding the phone in his hands, taking the time to have a conversation with her rather than putting it back away while he did whatever he had to do.

I'm sure they do

Reg couldn't help snickering. She had known that October wouldn't tell her, of course, but she might as well ask the question so that she could show Marta that she had done her bit for law enforcement.

Everything fine now, October's words appeared on the screen. *You don't have to worry.*

What did that mean?

Marta, leaning over to look at Reg's screen as she wrote, obviously wanted to know the same thing.

"What's that about?"

"I don't know."

"You don't."

"You can see what he wrote. Did he explain anything to me? He didn't. So I don't know how you expect me to know more than what he said."

"You had conversations with him about your fears that Corvin had done something to you in your previous lives."

"No, not exactly. We talked about how he had been in one of my dreams. One of my memories. But I told him that I didn't know if he'd had anything to do with other lives. And that I had no idea how that life had even ended, let alone whether Corvin had been involved in any way with it. I didn't tell him to attack Corvin." Reg could hear the frustration in her own voice.

In fact, she had told October that Corvin was probably not involved, and he hadn't listened to her. Instead, he had gone off and done his own lone-wolf thing.

Well, except that he had taken half a dozen members of the pack with him.

And they had attacked Corvin in the middle of a ritual. And not just him, but the entire coven.

"Who else was hurt?" she asked. "I can't believe that they would do that... that they would go after the whole coven. That's crazy."

"I can see why they would," Sarah contributed. "Corvin is a very powerful warlock. I don't know if there is anyone else that could rival him. Other than you and the immortals, but other mortals... I don't know. But during his equinox rites... he was probably channeling power to others in the coven. Opening himself up, making himself vulnerable. He was elected with the understanding that he would share his power and gifts with members of the coven and that he would use them to help them. So he had to show that he was willing to do that."

"So October...?"

"He realized that it was the time that Corvin would be at his most vulnerable. That it might be the best chance he had in the next year or more to ambush him. And to do… whatever it was that he did."

Reg swallowed. She understood why October had decided he couldn't wait until they had more evidence that Corvin was the one targeting her. He knew that Corvin had appeared in one of her memories and that Corvin had attacked her for other reasons in this life, so he had decided to take matters into his own hands—or paws—and to get retribution while he had the chance.

"What exactly did he do? Just attack Corvin? You said that he and the others were slashed?"

"And cursed," Sarah reminded her. "Corvin was the only one who was cursed. The others were probably only hurt because they tried to fight back."

"Cursed how?"

"We don't know the extent of his injuries or the curse," Marta said. "He wasn't very forthcoming about what had happened. The other members of the coven are keeping mum as well. But Sarah…" Marta's eyes went to the older woman.

"His arm is injured, but it was bandaged so that I couldn't see the injury," Sarah contributed. "But his aura and especially the aura around the injury… it was very dark. I thought I perhaps got a whiff of mandrake with the other herbs used in the spell. That is a potent substance. And mandrake near opened veins…" Her face was pinched and pale. She shook her head. "That would be very powerful magic. An attempt to purify the blood… to prevent evil intentions from being put into action…" She nodded. "I can see the shape of that magic. Mandrake is known to be used for protection or breaking curses. It is very powerful medicine."

"So you think that *could* prevent Corvin from following through on any evil intent?" Reg asked curiously.

If that were possible, why hadn't anyone done it earlier? Why hadn't the tribunal performed that kind of magic when they had judged and sentenced Corvin for the wrongs he had done in the past? If they knew that he was the type of warlock to break the rules and to do harm to others, knowing that he was a power drinker, that he had a gnawing hunger that would make him target magical practitioners over and over again and not follow the rules agreed upon for his kind, why hadn't they tried to perform a spell that would stop him?

"I don't know the details of the curse or spell put on Corvin with the mandrake," Sarah said cautiously. "I don't know whether it is possible to stop him. And I don't know what kind of power October has, whether he is a skilled spell caster or not. He might be an amateur trying something out of desperation. Or he might be a master who knows exactly what he is doing and how it will work."

Reg looked down at her phone screen. October had not sent her any additional messages. He hadn't asked how Corvin and the other injured members of the coven were. He hadn't even asked Reg how she was. He had only told her that she didn't have to worry anymore. He had taken care of the problem.

But only if Corvin was the problem.

What if it was someone else? She typed and, after a moment of hesitation, tapped the button to send the message.

She couldn't answer the unasked question. Just how skilled was October? Had he known what he was doing? Did he know what effect he wanted and was he able to design a spell that would work?

He had known enough to attack Corvin when he was most vulnerable. October had known that and had put his plan into action immediately.

It was Corvin, October responded.

How u know?

Did he have some information that he had not given her? Some insight that he had not passed on? Maybe a memory he had chosen not to share. She'd had dreams that she had not shared with October.

He is the only one it could have been.

Reg shook her head. She shrugged and put her phone away. "He is not telling me where he is or what he plans to do next."

Marta looked like she was going to argue with Reg, insisting that she take her phone back out and try to get October to give up more information. But then she didn't. She knew how stubborn Reg was. And there was no point in trying to talk her into giving up more information, since he knew that the police were there and had access to the messages he sent.

"What's his phone number?"

Reg didn't think she should give it to Marta. They would use it to trace old calls and messages, track his GPS, and do all kinds of other things that they wouldn't be able to do unless Reg gave them private information. She'd seen it on TV.

Let someone else give the number to Marta. Reg was sure she was not the only person who knew it.

"I can't give it to you. He told me it was private and not to give it to anyone else," she lied. October *would* have told her that if he had thought there were any possibility of the police using the information to track him.

"Why?"

"I didn't ask. Maybe he has a jealous ex. Or maybe he just doesn't like spam calls. If he doesn't want me to share it with anyone, I can't share it with anyone."

"Even the police?"

"Especially the police. Besides, the police aren't going to want to hear that it was a werewolf and a curse and all about past life crossings. They'll think that's crazy. They're going to want to hear that it was gang activity and one gang banger slashed another with his knife. Right?"

Marta sighed and shrugged. She wanted to know what had really happened and had brought Sarah in on it to provide advice as to the magical aspects of what had happened. But when the time came to report to her superiors or put something into writing, she would have to give them a boring, everyday explanation.

"October's pack will need to decide how to handle this," Marta said, focusing on how the Black Sands practitioners would handle the curse and October's motives rather than how the police would handle the physical assault. "He broke the rules of the werewolf-human treaty. They won't be happy about that. But that isn't the bad part."

Reg frowned at Marta's tone of voice. She sipped her tea. "What do you mean?"

"An organized group of werewolves attacking a coven during a ritual…" Marta shook her head. She looked at Sarah, who mirrored her grave expression.

"The problem isn't really how the werewolves will handle October's breach of the treaty," Sarah said. She gave Reg a long, sad look. "The problem is… this being seen as a declaration of war."

CHAPTER FORTY

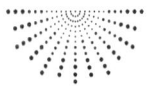

*R*eg didn't like going to Corvin's house alone, but she couldn't think of anyone she wanted to take with her to witness the conversation she wanted to have with him. She wanted it just to be her and Corvin. No one else.

It was dangerous to be alone with him; she knew that. Especially in his own lair, where he was at his strongest.

From what Marta and Sarah had said about the attack on Corvin, it sounded like he would not be performing magic for some time.

She didn't understand how it all worked. She didn't know what October had done or how it had affected Corvin, which was one of the reasons that she wanted to see him. She needed to understand what was going on and the impact it would have.

Would the warlocks really hunt the werewolves to the uttermost regions of the earth until they had bound or killed all of them? Was that the only solution to the situation they found themselves in?

She didn't tell Corvin that she was coming to his house. It didn't seem like a good idea to give him time to prepare for her arrival. There were ways to harm a person even without magic, and Reg didn't want to give him time to prepare any surprises.

Let the surprise be on her side.

Even so, she did not need to ring Corvin's doorbell. He sensed her proximity even before she parked in front of the house, and he opened the door as she was walking up the sidewalk.

He didn't look too bad. A little paler than usual. Worn and tired looking. Older around the eyes and maybe grayer in the temples. But that was probably just a trick of the light. He wouldn't actually have aged since she had last seen him.

"Regina. This is a surprise."

"You didn't expect me to bring a casserole?"

"Oh, please. Not another casserole. The old biddies from Sarah's coven have been burying me in casseroles since word got out about the attack."

Reg presented him with a fabric shopping bag, which he peered into and laughed.

"Much better," he approved. He pulled out the bottle of Jack Daniels. "You have outdone all of the old crones." He jerked his head back toward the interior of the house. "Are you coming in?"

Reg nodded and stepped forward. He looked mildly surprised, but stepped back and allowed her into the house before closing the door.

He had been half-hidden by the door when she had handed him the bag. Now that the door was shut and there was nothing obscuring her view, Reg could see a large white bandage wound around his arm. His fingers were purplish in color. *Dusky* was the word Reg thought would be used to describe them.

"How is it?" Reg asked. "I don't know exactly what was done, but it must have been painful."

Corvin nodded. He moved slowly, leading her to the kitchen where she had been once before. It looked much better than it had on that occasion, when it had been blown up in an attempt to kill Corvin.

Everything had been redone in gray tile, oak, and white

marble. It was a beauty to behold. Other than the dirty dishes, a pizza box, and other fast-food wrappers. The ladies might have been bringing Corvin casseroles, but he appeared to have been comforting himself with junk food.

He swept a pile of wrappers into one hand and shoved them into a trash can.

"I don't normally eat like this," he told her.

She knew this was true. She had seen the kind of food Corvin ordered when he went to restaurants and the types of restaurants he chose when going out. His tastes were much more highbrow.

Or maybe he just enjoyed showing off when he was with someone else, and the fast food was truer to his preferences. Someone who preferred a cheap box of wine could still order the most expensive thing on the wine list, smell the cork, and proclaim it satisfactory—or not.

"Do you want me to open that for you?" Reg indicated the bottle. "Is that arm out of commission, or can you still use it?"

"I have another open. I'll leave this one until later." He met her eyes. "But thank you for bringing it. I am going to need it."

He was able to prepare drinks for them one-handedly, and he invited her into the living room, or parlor, or whatever he preferred to call the luxuriously decorated sitting room they settled into. Reg sank so deep into her chair she wasn't sure she would be able to get back out again.

"So... I know this is nosy, but what exactly happened?" Reg asked. "And... how badly are you hurt? It isn't any of my business, I know, but... Sarah was talking about a war. That affects all of us, so it kind of is my business."

"It was an unprovoked attack," Corvin said. "So yes, it will cause conflict between October's kind and mine. They dropped the bomb, but they are the smaller force, so I don't know how they think they are going to survive. I have no idea what October thought he was doing."

He sipped his drink and shook his head. "I know he didn't particularly like me. That feeling is shared by many practitioners, human and wolf alike. But most people are satisfied with simply avoiding me. Most do not attack me or try to kill me."

Reg rubbed her forehead and tried to decide what to tell him. Did he actually know what had prompted October to attack him during the equinox ritual? Or had it been as much a shock to him as to Reg?

"October thought… that you might be the person who has been… uh… responsible for our deaths in past lives."

"Past lives."

"Yes." Reg searched Corvin's face for some guilt or understanding. "He thought that you were dangerous to us."

"To *us*. Who do you mean by 'us'?"

"Me. And October. We had… there were a number of crossings in our past lives. Lives where we had known each other, had been together one way or another over the centuries."

He gave a slow nod. "Okay. Maybe that is the case. I don't see what that has to do with me."

"These other lives… There was a dark entity trying to cause trouble. To end our lives or our happiness together. And Harrison said—"

"Harrison? You're trusting that crazy immortal to tell you anything? I've told you before that they are not omniscient. They don't know everything. Not everything in the past, and not necessarily anything in the future."

"But they *do*. They can travel through the past and the future and know all kinds of things about it. They knew that someone had betrayed me or caused the end of my life in other times, and they said that I was in danger of it happening again."

"And that I was the one responsible? I was the one who was going to hurt you?"

"I didn't think it was you. October did."

"And the immortals?"

"They didn't know. They said I would know the person when he revealed himself to me. But by the time I know who it is, it will be too late to do anything about it."

CHAPTER FORTY-ONE

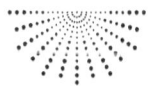

a war. Reg had not even considered the possibility of an armed conflict between the two groups.

From what she understood of the history of witches and magical species in the country, a tenuous peace had been in place for a number of years. A few centuries, maybe. Some time after the Salem witch trial, of course, a tentative peace had been established. A number of treaties were in place to set out the rules of interactions between species whose territories overlapped and whose practices had frequently caused friction between them.

There were international treaties governing sirens and where and how they could hunt. Sirens and mermaids were not allowed to hunt on land and were subject to penalties if they did.

Soul eaters like Corvin had to gain the consent of their victims before draining them of their powers. They used several different approaches to fool their innocent victims into surrendering themselves to the will of the hunter.

Certain territories were set aside for endangered species like swamp goblins. The goblins could act with impunity. After all, it would be wrong to let the species die out.

Reg wasn't sure why that would be wrong but, apparently, it was.

She wasn't sure whether there were any laws governing the immortals. They seemed to be able to get away with doing whatever they wanted. How could humans enforce any consequences on an immortal? Reg knew from experience that it was difficult to get them to enforce even their own values on each other.

A war.

"What is going to happen?" she asked Sarah, not sure she was going to like the response.

Actually, pretty sure she was going to hate it.

"The pack will not be safe," Sarah told her. "Even if October split away from them to do this, the pack will be targeted. People will not believe this was done without their consent."

"But... Zora and the cubs. And all of the other wolves who were completely innocent in this!"

Sarah nodded. "I know. They will all be seen as having participated in this. They will all be targets of retribution."

"No."

Marta nodded her agreement as well. "We need to find October and get him into custody. Show people that the offender has been dealt with and that no other action is needed. Cut off any talk of war immediately."

"What about the other wolves who were with him?"

"We'll need to arrest all of them. Have the pack judge them."

"And... what if you don't?"

"Witches and warlocks are going to take it into their own hands."

Reg looked at Sarah. "But you know that it was just a few werewolves. Not all of them."

"The witches' coven will stand with the warlocks. The warlocks will call for legal action, but that won't be enough. Not when they know that even if October and his accessories are called before the pack's leadership, nothing will be done to them. Nothing that makes up for what they did."

"But they could... make them pay retribution. Bind or imprison them for a length of time. Make sure that they pay for what they have done."

"You cannot keep a werewolf in a cage," Sarah reminded her.

Reg knew that. If they were kept in a cage for the full lunar cycle, it would result in moon madness. The wolf would eventually die.

"Maybe they could be... collared or kept in a compound. The wolf leadership would do something, wouldn't they? They have to do something if they want to protect the rest of the pack from the covens."

"The typical penalty is exile," Marta explained. "But the warlocks are not going to be satisfied with that as an acceptable punishment for a magical attack in the midst of a sacred ritual for the purpose of harming one or more of the warlocks."

Reg had to agree she would not feel that was a severe enough punishment either. Even though she liked October. If he had done something to harm Corvin, and it sounded like he had, then he should have to serve some kind of sentence other than just being exiled from the pack.

"Then what is going to happen?"

"The pack that remains, the members who did not participate in the attack will have to leave. Otherwise, they will be targets. They will have to reestablish the pack somewhere else."

"There is a reason there are no wolves in Florida," Marta told her.

Reg had thought it was cool that the wolves had stayed in Florida after they had been released from Jake's lab. They had actually started to repopulate Florida, something that Jake had been pretending to do but had never actually intended to do. Reg liked the idea of reestablishing a species that had become extinct in that area. Now, they would lose all of that.

"And October? And Corvin?"

"October will be hunted. We have a number of good trackers," Sarah explained. "They won't be limited to Florida. They will go where he goes. No hiding place will be safe, no matter where it is in the world."

Reg felt sick in the pit of her stomach. She did not relish the idea of the werewolves being hunted down all over the world. Of October or the others who had chosen him to be hunted down and... what?

"What will they do? Execute them?"

Sarah shook her head. "Not unless they are unable to secure them any other way. They will be bound, probably in human form. Where and for how long, I don't know. Not in cages but, as you say... with a tracking charm. Forcing them to stay in some designated territory or compound."

It was not quite as barbaric as Reg had feared, but she pictured October being kept under those conditions, and her heart ached. How could anyone do that to another sentient creature? Even if October had harmed Corvin in the attack, he had done it under the belief that Corvin was going to harm Reg or him. That Corvin might put an end to their lives as he had—October believed—put an end to other lives. There had to be some kind of concession made for self-defense or the defense of others, even if October had been mistaken in his judgment. And maybe he hadn't been. Maybe he had been right all along, and this was the only way that he could protect Reg and himself from further attacks.

Harrison and Weston had warned Reg to be aware. That those attacks would be coming. That had to count for something. Didn't all societies allow a plea of self-defense?

"Will there be a hearing? Some kind of court proceeding?"

"No," Sarah shook her head. She was looking tireder and grayer the more they talked about it. "The pack will not approve of it, and there is no provision under the treaty that allows humans to exercise authority over werewolves. It will be done outside the law. Vigilantism."

"What will the pack do if the coven exacts revenge on October and the others?"

"They will consider it an act of war," Marta said flatly. "And they will... retaliate in kind."

Reg took a swig of her tea, but it did not sit well in her stomach. Nothing would now. She was going to keep that uneasy feeling in her stomach forever.

A warlock-werewolf war.

Each side exacting the vengeance they thought appropriate until... what? Until both sides were wiped out? All of the warlocks in the coven and all of the werewolves who had participated in the attack? If a half dozen werewolves had been involved, then they were outnumbered by the warlocks. The coven included thirteen full members as well as the uninitiated. And if they were joined by the witches in Sarah's coven, a similar number of witches, the werewolves were far outnumbered.

The werewolves had the natural advantage of teeth and claws.

But the witches and warlocks had their magical powers, their charms and curses, as well as whatever weapons they chose to arm themselves with.

It would not end until all of the werewolves had been wiped out, and maybe a significant number of the witches and warlocks, too. The wolves had been the aggressors. The human practitioners would not rest until they had all been destroyed.

CHAPTER FORTY-TWO

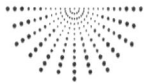

*C*orvin shook his head. "So October decided on his own that I was the one causing the two of you problems in your past lives and that he needed to attack me to prevent me from harming you in this life. Just like a wolf. Hotheaded and not stopping to think about the consequences. He thought this would protect the two of you?"

Reg nodded. Her face was warm. It didn't sound very good when summarized so baldly. It didn't make it sound like October could have reasonably thought that they were in any danger.

Was Corvin the mysterious X? She probed the edges of his mind, trying to get a read on him. But she found the same Corvin there that she had known for two years. Hungry for her powers. Attracted to her. Friendly. He was a predator, even if he did like her, but did he really intend to end her life or October's? She didn't see it.

Corvin pushed back. He couldn't keep her out of his mind completely, not with the bond formed by sharing a psychic connection so many times in the past couple of years. But he nudged back, telling her that she was pushing too far, that he didn't want her there. He grimaced and hunched over slightly.

When he looked back at her, relaxing his muscles again, Reg looked into his glittering dark eyes. His brow furrowed.

"You see?" he challenged. "I have no agenda. No reason to break you and October up or to do anything to harm him. Although," there was a slow burn now, a darkening of his aura, "I can tell you that I do not have kind feelings toward October now. I had nothing against him before this, but he attacked me unprovoked. He needs to pay for that. I won't ignore it and let it go unpunished, no matter what he might have thought about me."

Reg nodded her understanding. She was finding it difficult to catch her breath. She had no reason to doubt Corvin's words. She felt the emotion behind them, the anger and affront that October had dared to do what he had. He would get retribution from October if he were able. His anger wasn't aimed at her, but it was like being trapped in the room with someone who was raging and throwing objects around because he was angry at someone else. It didn't really matter who he was mad at; Reg didn't want to be in the room with that anger or caught in the crossfire.

"He attacked me and my coven when we were at our most vulnerable," Corvin told her, an intense vibrato in his voice. "An attack like this is unprecedented. It is more than just putting his toe across the line. We had no way to defend ourselves. I have never been one to judge an entire species by the action of one, but this is why people like Jake consider werewolves to be animals, inhuman. Do you think a human would ever do something like that? It's monstrous."

"I... I don't know," Reg stammered.

She agreed that October had done something wrong. Even if he were correct and Corvin was the one who had targeted them in past lives, it wasn't right to attack him in this life before he had even done anything wrong. To prejudge him and assume that they knew what he was going to do next... The Corvin in this life might never be a danger to October. He was, of course, a danger to Reg and had already attacked her more than once, but that didn't affect October and was well in the past. Corvin had already been judged by his own coven for his actions against Reg. He'd already paid the price, even if she thought it did not make up for his actions.

"It doesn't seem like…" Reg looked at Corvin's arm. "It doesn't seem like it is such a bad injury. You don't act like you're in a lot of pain, and it doesn't look like it is very extensive. What did he do? I'm not saying it wasn't wrong; I'm just not sure… is it worth starting a war? Innocent people might be hurt or killed. People who had nothing to do with this."

"I'm not the one who started it. We cannot let it go without retribution. Without seeing to it that October is stopped and punished for what he has done. I can't speak for what might happen to anyone else. His pack will undoubtedly protect him, even though they know he was in the wrong."

Corvin looked down at his arm. Reg didn't understand why it was such a big deal. But Sarah had said that it was cursed, which meant that it was worse than Reg could see. It wasn't just the wound in his flesh that was the issue.

"Sarah said it was cursed."

His gaze was hooded. He had not told Sarah the details of the curse. He had kept that to himself.

"Sarah is a wise woman. She recognized the attack for what it was and saw why October attacked when he did."

"But she doesn't know *how* you are cursed."

"I am not required to share that with anyone."

"I know… but I want to know what's going on. I can't really judge what to do if I don't know…"

"You would support the wolves in this war?" he demanded, his voice carrying a hard edge.

"No. Now, I didn't say that. But if there is a way that things can be resolved without anyone else being hurt…"

"It's not your place to broker peace between us. There is no way I will be satisfied with an apology and no retribution.

This was a declaration of war, Reg. I didn't issue it. October did."

Reg nodded. She sipped her drink and didn't try to talk him into telling her about the injury.

Corvin drained his glass and set it down with a loud thump. Not his first drink of the day. Not likely to be his last. But Reg had expected that. She had brought him a bottle to replace the one he was working his way through.

But maybe she shouldn't be encouraging him to drink, especially while she was there. She didn't like dealing with drunks. Especially angry drunks and warlocks with unimaginable powers.

"You think I have powers?" Corvin growled, obviously picking up on this thought. "What good are those powers if I cannot use them?"

Reg looked at him, wondering what he was talking about. She had seen him use his powers many times. She knew that he had been growing in strength and it was getting difficult even for Reg and Sarah together to prevent him from entering the yard. They had a number of wards there to keep unwanted visitors away from the guest cottage so that Reg could feel safe in her own home and enjoy the beauty of the garden without fear that she would be ambushed by Corvin or anyone else with ill feelings toward her. But those wards had failed recently. Corvin had been growing and accessing far more of the power he had gained from the witch doctor.

"Even the smallest exercise of my gifts causes me great pain," Corvin told her. "I cannot so much as try to heal my own injury." He looked down at the bandage covering his arm.

Reg frowned. "You can't use your powers?"

He shook his head. "This is how October hopes to keep me from hurting you or him. By making it impossible for me to access my powers." He shook his head angrily. "How can I lead the coven? How can I continue with any of my work? How am I to…" He didn't finish his sentence, but Reg knew what he had been thinking. How was he to feed if he could not use his charms? How could he satisfy his gnawing hunger for more power if he could not exercise his powers without pain?

He had still been able to read her thoughts or feelings, to tell that she was trying to read him. But she did not know what that had cost him or if he was able to turn it off at will.

"What happens if you try? It just hurts?"

"*Just* hurts?" Corvin shook his head. "You mean like *just* passing a kidney stone? You have no idea of the pain. And the more I try to do, the worse it is. Trying to perform any significant magic would be excruciating."

And that was how October hoped to stop him from doing anything to hurt him or Reg. Corvin would be limited to doing only what a normal, nonmagical human would be able to do.

CHAPTER FORTY-THREE

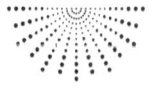

*R*eg frowned at this thought.

"What is it?" Corvin asked, studying her expression.

She didn't feel him probing her mind. He was doing just what any non-practitioner would do. Trying to read her expression and body language without knowing what was in her mind for sure.

"It's just that... stopping you from performing magic doesn't stop you from targeting either of us. You're still intent on punishing him, whether you can use your magic or not. And you could still hurt or betray either of us without any magic. The lives we shared in the past... we were betrayed by words or actions, not magic."

Corvin sat back in his seat, chuckling to himself. "So October has crippled me and started a war and put himself and his people at great risk, all for nothing? To prevent something that could be done by any ordinary person. That's rich. How unbelievably stupid."

Reg bristled at this condemnation, but she kept her thoughts to herself. What October had done *had* been stupid. Brilliant, because she knew no other way to prevent Corvin from using his powers against them, but stupid, because Corvin could still harm them or their relationship through non-magical means. And October had put all of the other wolves at risk. Reg worried about Zora and her cubs. A couple of other wolves in the pack were currently with pup. What would the consequences be for them and their babies?

October might have thought that he was protecting the rest of the pack by only taking a few of them with him to the attack on Corvin, but would Corvin and the warlocks and witches who wanted retribution stop to consider who had been involved and who had not? Or would they just attack without consideration?

It was war, and in a war, there were casualties. Sometimes, innocents were hurt or killed.

"What about the puppies?" she asked Corvin. "What if they get hurt in this war?"

"That's on October, not on me. I am not the one who declared war."

Reg sipped her drink and put it back down. She covered her eyes with both palms. She was still not getting enough sleep, and now she had something else to worry about. Fenris and the other cubs. She would be devastated if one of those precocious young pups was hurt or killed in the crossfire. And Zora... she would be enraged. Reg would not want to be in the path of a wolf mother protecting her puppies or retaliating for their death or injury.

It was all spiraling out of control. Reg felt like she should be able to step in and stop it all. In a way, it was her fault; she was the one who had told October about her memory of Corvin. If she hadn't done that, he would not have done what he had. She felt like she should be able to step into the middle and stop it. To explain to both sides that they were both in the wrong, and if they warred against each other, innocent people and wolves would be hurt.

"How can we stop this?"

Corvin shook his head. "We can't," he said grimly. "Your friend October has started something no one can stop."

*   *   *

Reg looked around, preparing to leave. She had worn out her welcome. Corvin was looking worn and gray. He obviously needed sleep, at the very least. Maybe more than that.

"Is it causing you a lot of pain?" she asked, looking down at his arm.

Corvin wiggled his dusky fingers. "The physical pain is nothing like the agony when trying to perform magic. And I had no idea how much I was using my powers all day long. For little things. It was constantly 'on.' And now…" He shook his head. "I'm doing my best to do nothing but live like someone without any gifts. But even the littlest thing, like reaching out to see how someone is feeling…" He let out a long sigh. "And the pain leaves me very tired."

Reg hovered her hand over Corvin's arm and focused on sending heat into it. She wasn't a great healer, but she could help a little. There wasn't anything she could do about the curse. Corvin would need to consult someone with more experience than Reg. Maybe Letticia could help. Until then, all Reg could do was help his physical healing and strength.

"Ahh," Corvin murmured. "That is good. Thank you."

He leaned back with his eyes closed, and Reg prepared to stand.

"Tell me about this crossing with you and October," Corvin said, his eyes still shut. "I am most interested in hearing about what I did that upset him so much."

Reg considered. "You didn't do anything in the part I remember," she said slowly. "I don't know how that life ended for either of us. It is only speculation that you had anything to do with it. And… I would think you would remember…"

"I do not recall any past lives," Corvin said. "I believe in other lives, of course, but I don't know how many incarnations I might have been through in human form. And I certainly don't remember anything about them."

"Well, it was a previous life for October and me, but I think… you were still you. This life, I mean."

Corvin opened his eyes. "What?"

"Do you remember prohibition? That was this life for you, right?"

"Certainly," Corvin agreed. His brows drew down. "I met your previous incarnation?"

Reg nodded. "Did you ever go by the name Frank?"

"I did." He blinked a couple of times. "I am very curious as to who you were. And how well we knew each other."

"A jazz singer," Reg told him, feeling a little uncomfortable, like she was revealing something embarrassing about herself or assuming someone else's identity. "Lucy May."

He thought back, his eyes distant. Eventually, he sighed and shook his head. "Sorry, no. Doesn't ring a bell. I would have thought that I would remember you."

"Were you a cop? When you went by Frank?"

"More or less," he said obliquely.

"October was a man called Marco." Reg shrugged. "Sorry, I didn't get any last names. It was all pretty…" Casual did not seem like the right word. Everyone had been tense, challenging, passionate. Anything but casual. "Umm… anonymous?"

"There are times when it is best that people not know too much about you. That was a very turbulent time. A lot of… intense people and relationships. Maybe it shouldn't be so surprising that I don't remember you specifically. There were a lot of people to keep an eye on. If you weren't a threat, I can understand the memory lapse."

Reg thought about Frank, how she had felt when he showed up, and how he and Marco had talked to each other and reminded her of dogs circling, sizing each other up. "Do you remember Marco?"

"The name is familiar, but it wouldn't be uncommon for the time or place. He was the owner of an establishment?"

"Yes, I think so. I sang at this 'speakeasy.' I guess I had a relationship with him, though I have no idea if it was exclusive. I think probably not."

"And you and I met." Corvin looked a little smug about this. "And you remembered me. And told October about it."

"Yeah."

He chuckled softly. "Funny how jealousy can stretch across so many years and more than one lifetime. I think I would remember you if we'd had any kind of meaningful relationship. And yet, he goes crazy with just the idea that I knew you both at the time. That may be the only time we met. And that's why he came after me."

Reg shifted uncomfortably. She turned her glass in circles, looking at the ring of moisture left on the coaster she had set it down on.

"It wasn't jealousy."

"Oh, no? You are the two great lovers, joining and rejoining during multiple lives. You are concerned about someone possibly coming around to ruin your life together. My very appearance one time in one memory drives October to attack me and the entire coven in a cowardly sneak attack. A declaration of war because I appear in *one* of your memories." He gave a mocking laugh.

Reg opened her mouth, looking for a way to explain it. To tell him how October's attack had been at least partially justified. But she couldn't.

"I can't explain it. He's... a werewolf. They are more..."

"Passionate? Explosive? Animalistic?"

Reg waved her hand as if fending off his arrows. "I just mean... more impulsive... instinct driven..."

He grunted, nodding. "That's right. And it has certainly landed him in hot water this time."

Reg swallowed. She didn't like to think about what kind of trouble October's impulsive decision had led him into.

"I should be getting on my way. Are you going to have a nap?"

"Yes, I think so. With your healing, it is comfortable as long as I don't move or use any magic."

"Okay. You can... leave me a message if you need something."

"Leave you a message. You plan on being out of touch?"

"Yes... maybe for a while."

CHAPTER FORTY-FOUR

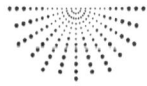

*R*eg had no idea how she was going to find October. He would, of course, be deep under cover. He would not be anywhere a policeman or witch could find him. There would be a lot of people looking for him. It was best to be far away and well hidden.

It was odd leaving Corvin's house knowing he was unlikely to use their psychic connection to spy on her. She had grown accustomed to his calling her at any time with full knowledge of where she was and what she was doing. She used their connection to check in on him, too, to make sure he wasn't anywhere near her when she was coming from or going to the cottage, making sure that he couldn't ambush her.

But now... disabled by October's spell, he couldn't do that without causing himself pain. Severe pain, if she were to believe what he told her. And judging from his pale, tight face, she believed it was the truth.

Could October's spell be reversed? If he said some kind of incantation, could he remove it again? If she explained to him how his actions were going to cause an all-out war and he wanted to stop it before the pups or other members of the pack ended up getting hurt, maybe he would decide that what he had done had been impulsive and ill-advised. He would reverse it and admit his mistake, and take whatever consequences were imposed on him by the pack.

She drove out of Black Sands without a clear idea of where she was going. Maybe she was driving to Davyn's to get his advice or to play with Ember. She hadn't had a firecasting session since the last one, during which she had been so distracted. She should at least talk to Davyn and tell him what was going on in her life.

But he was part of the coven, so he had been there when October and the other members of the pack had attacked. Maybe he had even been one of the injured. She hadn't even asked Sarah who else had been injured; she had been so focused on Corvin. Corvin was October's target. Corvin had been the one who had been cursed. She didn't know how badly any of the others had been slashed. Werewolf scratches and bites were not something to be taken lightly.

A shadow flitted over the car as she drove down the highway. Reg looked up to see what had cast the shadow. A cloud scudding across the sun? A low-flying airplane?

She had a pretty good idea it was not either of those things, and she was rewarded with a glimpse of a certain young dragon she knew.

Rather than drive the rest of the way to Davyn's house, she pulled over at the next crossroad and stopped beside the road.

"Ember!"

Ember dive-bombed her and, even though Reg knew what was coming and tried to stand in place and be unaffected, she still ended up flinching away and gave a little cry of surprise at how close he got to her.

Ember landed beside her and nuzzled up against her face and neck for affection like a big puppy. Reg scratched his ears, jaw, and chin and he purred away, loving it.

"Have you seen any wolves around here?" Reg asked him, and projected a vision of October in his wolf form. Ember and October had met once before while investigating Jake's lab.

Ember flapped his wings enthusiastically, lifting off the ground slightly in his excitement.

"Yeah? Do you know if they are around here? Or if they went somewhere else?"

Ember took to the air and hovered in front of the car. Reg climbed back in and started the engine.

"Take me to the wolves," she told him.

There wasn't much danger of his taking her to the wrong wolves since there weren't any other than October's pack in the state. Though the pack might now be split into two factions. Those who supported October and had participated in the attack on the coven, and those who opposed it. Reg hoped that they didn't all support October simply because he was a werewolf and, therefore, they stood behind him no matter what he did. She needed another voice of reason out there. Someone else telling him that he couldn't be judge, jury, and executioner over Corvin.

At least he *hadn't* executed Corvin.

Had October intended to? Or would Corvin die an excruciatingly slow death, no longer able to slow the aging process with magic, starving due to his inability to feed on the powers of others, and whatever other things Corvin relied upon magic for? He said he hadn't even realized how many things he used magic for. It was probably like when she got a paper cut on one finger, and then discovered that everything she did seemed to involve that one finger, bumping and rubbing it all day long.

Reg tried to quiet the thoughts racing through her brain and simply focus on Ember flying ahead of her. Until she found October or the others in the pack, it didn't matter what she thought. She couldn't do anything until she found them.

They turned off onto smaller and smaller roads. Ember looked back over his shoulder at Reg, encouraging her to go faster. She was already testing the abilities of the car to navigate the bumpier, winding, narrow roads through the green trees. She hoped she would be able to find her way out again. She would need Ember or one of the wolves to guide her back to the highway again.

They reached a clearing, and Ember landed. He sat in the middle of the clearing, looking proud of himself. Reg looked around. There was no sign of any encampment. No indication of any human activity.

But of course, they would find it easier to hide from humans in wolf form. With their enhanced senses, they would be able to hear and smell any approaching humans, and move quietly through the trees and undergrowth to avoid them.

Reg got out of the car and walked around the clearing. She didn't call them or tell them that she was there alone. They could see and hear with their own eyes and ears. She wasn't making them any promises about her intentions, that she wouldn't tell anyone where they were, or that she hadn't brought anybody with her. She was there. Her presence should tell them all they needed to know.

Birds chirped pleasantly in the trees. Leaves rustled. She could smell water from a nearby stream.

It wasn't long before she heard October's voice in her head.

What are you doing here, Reg?

Looking for you.

You shouldn't be here, he told her

Reg looked around. She couldn't see any reason she shouldn't be there. She wasn't doing anything wrong in trying to contact him. He was in trouble and, from what she had discovered of their past lives, they were destined to be intertwined with each other's lives. She was exactly where she was supposed to be.

Are you going to come talk to me? she asked him.

Are you alone?

You have eyes and ears.

She waited. October didn't communicate anything else. Reg sighed and, after a few minutes of silence, went back to her car and sat on the hood and pulled out her phone to entertain herself while she waited.

Her cell signal wasn't good. She needed to download some content while she was at home so she wouldn't end up waiting for hours for someone or something with no entertainment.

Eventually, October walked out of the trees into the clearing. Upright on two legs like any other human.

He looked fine. Definitely in better shape than Corvin. He was handsome and tanned, his green eyes bright with interest. He looked like he had just been out on a hike, no different from any other day. He did not look like Rambo, starting his own private war.

"Reg."

He sat on the hood of the car with her.

"This was really stupid," Reg told him. "I can't believe what you did."

He raised his brows. "Stupid? I just saved you from ever having to worry about what Corvin was going to do to you again."

"If all you're worried about is him performing magic," she pointed out.

He looked confused. Brows drawn down, he gave a little shake of his head.

"What?"

"Was it magic that betrayed you in Egypt?"

He frowned. "No… I don't know. It was the work of a spy or a double agent. Someone who told the enemy our plans."

"So someone could do that even if they didn't have a magical bone in their body."

"Yes."

"And in Greece, we were discovered by a servant who was supposed to keep an eye on me. Where was the magic in that?"

He stared at her.

"You're so worried about Corvin and his powers that you didn't think about all the other ways he could betray us."

"In other lives, he might not have had magic," October conceded. "He might have had to find other ways to get in our way, to do violence or split us up. But in this life… he would use magic. He would use his charms to seduce you, his other powers to bind you and steal your gifts, or maybe to kill me or someone else who is important in my life. An animal uses his claws and teeth. A human uses whatever weapons he has at hand. Corvin is armed with magic; that's what he's going to try to use to defeat us."

"You've started a war. They are going to hunt you."

"I've been hunted before." He looked amused. "In case you haven't noticed, I am an animal. I am used to that."

"You think you're the highest predator on the food chain."

He nodded his agreement with her assessment.

"Well, you aren't. When the witches, warlocks, and other practitioners in Black Sands band together to hunt you and the pack to demand justice, they'll far outnumber you. And if they recruit other humans from other towns and countries…"

"I think you're giving them too much credit. Most humans will not leave their comfortable lives behind to hunt someone who hasn't done them any harm. The only one we did any real harm to was Corvin. And is the town really going to go up in arms over a Hunter? They are safer now. They might make a bunch of noise about it being vigilante justice, but they'll sleep better at night. And we are wolves. We were just doing what wolves do. Following our nature." He shrugged and spread his hands apart. "Exactly how much energy do you think they will put into tracking us down for doing what comes to us naturally?"

"You put the whole pack in danger. What about Zora and the cubs? What about the others who are going to have puppies? They are all in danger."

"No. Maybe I and the others who participated in this... maybe we will be targeted for a while, but it won't last. People will get tired of it. Humans are essentially lazy."

CHAPTER FORTY-FIVE

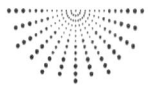

*W*ho else is with you?" Reg asked. She hadn't been told by Sarah or Marta, but they didn't know the pack like Reg did. The other practitioners in Black Sands stayed away from the pack. Or the pack stayed away from everyone else. Reg supposed it was because they were different species. There was, she assumed, a natural suspicion toward creatures who could shift between two different forms. Who appeared to be fully human and yet could also be dangerous wild animals.

October looked toward the trees. Reg didn't hear him call out to the wolves aloud or psychically, but perhaps he had given some prearranged signal. Several other figures stepped out of the woods and walked toward them.

Reg was glad that Zora was not among them. She had assumed that she would not be and would have stayed home to take care of the puppies rather than join the attack on the coven. There were a couple of other women, including Channelle, the woman Reg had met at the coffee shop. She recognized an adolescent boy, remembering how he had curled up to go to sleep after she had rescued him from the lab. Did he remember her, or had he been so sick and exhausted that he hadn't even known she was the one who had broken the binding spell and given him the strength to shift back into his human form before the moon madness could take him, as it had Faolan?

She looked at the wolves, who were waiting to find out what she had to say.

Reg suddenly felt like she should have a prepared speech. Maybe she should have consulted with others before getting there. Maybe Letticia, the leader of the witches, to see if there was some kind of peace that could be brokered between the factions before it did turn into an all-out war. Maybe they could nip it in the bud.

But she hadn't gone to Letticia or talked to Sarah about how the affair could be settled. She didn't have the authority to offer any kind of a deal.

She looked over the small group, and back at October. "I think... you should probably move on. Get out of town for a while and let things cool down."

"We are out of town," October pointed out. "I'm not sure how you tracked us here, but we are being careful to stay out of the way and not attract attention for a while."

"You are still too close. If I could find you, someone else could too."

October folded his arms across his chest and looked at Reg challengingly. "Could they? Unless you are going to lead them here, I don't think anyone else could find us."

Reg looked over at Ember.

It wasn't like he would lead anyone else there. He had imprinted on Reg, the first person he had encountered after hatching.

Except for Davyn. He was a member of the coven that had been attacked. Up until a few months ago, he was the one who had led it. And he was the one who took care of Ember, provided a home for him, a big fireplace, and protection from the outside world. If Davyn asked Ember to track October again, would he? He probably would.

And if the wolves went away? How far would they have to go before Ember would not track them? Would they leave a trail that was easy for Ember to follow no matter how far they went away?

"Ember," October said. "Of course." He reached a hand toward Ember, and the dragon responded by getting close enough to October to get an ear scratch. He purred and nuzzled October. "You can tell him not to follow us again."

"You can try. But I don't know if he will listen. Dragons aren't exactly domestic animals. He will do whatever he likes."

October stared at Ember, and Reg didn't know if he were trying to communicate with him. Human telepathy, werewolf telepathy, and dragon telepathy were all a little different. Dragons communicated best in pictures, not words.

"You don't need to worry about us, Reg," October said, turning back to her. "As I said, we have been hunted before. We knew that this action might trigger an attempt at retaliation. But it had to be done."

"I told you that I didn't know if Corvin was the one who was targeting me."

He shrugged. "Well, we know Corvin *was* targeting you. Maybe he wasn't the one that Harrison was talking about, but he has attacked you in the past, attempted to seduce you and to steal your powers. Whether or not he is the person who has interfered with past lives. So..." October raised his brows. "He needed to be stopped and no one else seemed to be willing to do it. So I did. It was also a warning to his son of what could happen if he did not follow the rules for his kind."

John was, Reg knew, one of the others who had been slashed. But he'd not been cursed as Corvin had. But if John was X, would he take a warning from October seriously? He wasn't exactly stable or reasonable. He might take a warning as a challenge, even if he hadn't been the one who had been targeting Reg initially. Like telling a two-year-old not to do something she thought dangerous, and he had never even thought about it until she put it in his head.

"So you think we're safe," Reg said finally. "You think that you've eliminated the threat."

October rested his hand on Reg's leg. "I have eliminated at least one threat. Maybe there are more. We have no way of knowing all of the hazards and enemies out there. But this was the best way to disable Corvin. Don't ask me why no one ever bothered to do it before."

His hand was warm on her thigh. Reg couldn't decide whether she liked it there or was uncomfortable with it. It made her restless, and she looked at October, wondering what it would be like to be a part of his life.

For the next little while, he would be on the run, and she didn't want to have to leave her life and go into hiding with him. She had run away from enough problems in the past and built up new lives and new names just to have to leave them behind again. She didn't want to do that anymore. She wanted to continue to live her life in Black Sands, with friends and colleagues who knew who she really was and still liked her anyway.

She put her hand over October's briefly, to acknowledge his touch, and then to nudge him away. October curled his hand around her thigh, squeezing. He looked at her with his bright, intense eyes.

"Reg..."

"I have to think about it," Reg told him abruptly. She didn't know whether she was talking about the threat from the unknown entity or the possibility of a relationship with him sometime in the future when he was no longer in hiding. He could take it to mean whatever he liked. She removed his hand from her leg firmly. "I—I don't know."

October pulled back and didn't force the issue. The other members of the pack were all still watching, and Reg felt awkward. She had wanted to know who was involved in the attack, but she didn't want to say too much in front of them. They didn't need any more information about her and October and their relationships in past lives. She didn't want to discuss their future or the impossibility of their future in front of anyone else. She didn't want to discredit him or make him feel like he had lost face in front of his warriors because she disagreed with what they had done. October was more hot-headed than Corvin or the other men in Reg's circle of friends, and she didn't want to cross him or make him feel like she had betrayed their friendship.

The last thing they needed was another betrayal.

She wished she could say that she supported or was grateful for what he had done. She *should* be grateful for it. How many times had she expressed her outrage over the past couple of years that no one had stepped forward to protect her from Corvin? The magical community kept ignoring the predator among them and pretending he was just a regular person who could have commerce with them without consequences. Now October had stepped in and eliminated that threat, and she had mixed feelings about it.

Was cursing Corvin the right decision? Could they have done something else? Given him a warning first?

The other wolves had obviously backed him up, but was that because he was over them in the pack hierarchy and they were simply obeying when he called for help, or was it because they really believed in the mission and believed that it was the only way to deal with Corvin? October wasn't the pack's alpha, but Reg thought he was pretty high up in the power structure. His opinion was definitely sought and respected.

They stood around watching her and October. Maybe having their own discussion telepathically so that she wouldn't know what they were saying. Maybe they were just waiting, watching in respect. The social aspects of werewolf interaction were a little different from human interaction.

Reg did not like Channelle's expression. Maybe she saw

herself as a potential mate for October and did not appreciate his touching Reg and seeming to seek a more intimate relationship.

Reg wanted to tell Channelle she had nothing to worry about, but she couldn't deny her uncertainty about October. Yes, he was hot-headed, but did that mean she wasn't interested in him? It made her stop and seriously consider the options, especially considering her former relationship with Jake. Jake had been controlling and dismissive of Reg and her opinions. Did she want to have anything to do with another man who ignored her ideas or feelings?

Even if she were interested in October, was she ready to commit to a werewolf? Wolves mated for life and, as a non-werewolf, she was doomed never to be a full member of the pack.

She ended up just shrugging at Channelle, uncertain what to think or say. It was too big of an issue for her to decide on the spot.

"Does that mean you're leaving?" October asked. "I assumed if you were coming here, you wanted to stay."

"Umm, no, I wasn't planning to stay here." Reg looked around. Stay where? In the middle of the woods? She had no camping equipment and couldn't just shift into a wolf. "Sorry. I just... I needed to talk to you."

"To try to talk some sense into me," October said with a wolfish grin.

"Well, yes. I hoped... that we could somehow prevent this from escalating into a war between the pack and the coven."

He shrugged. "Too late for that. We'll deal with whatever retaliation they come back with." He drew himself up taller. "We are not looking for trouble, but I'll deal with whatever the consequences are."

CHAPTER FORTY-SIX

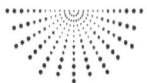

*W*ith a deep feeling of regret, Reg left the clearing, asking Ember to lead her back out of the wilderness.

The wolves probably wouldn't stay in exactly the same place. Now that Reg had been there, they would move to another part of the forest. Not that she would ever be able to find her way back to the same place without help. She was completely turned around and wasn't even sure she would be able to find her way out of the lush green woods without Ember to lead her out.

He floated ahead of the car, flapping lazily now and then. He could easily outpace her going full speed on the highway. It wasn't any effort to keep ahead of her as she slowly bumped over the narrow, rutted roads.

Eventually, they made it out to the highway, and Reg relaxed, knowing she could find her way home by herself. She projected her thanks to Ember, letting him know that he could go on and she would be fine on her own.

He sent her a vision of Davyn's living room, clearly wanting her to go back to the house with him and spend some time together. He loved having his dragon mama there with him. He must not yet be at whatever age was adolescence for dragons, when he would want to separate from any parent figures and go out on his own. Dragon hatchlings didn't normally rely on anyone to take care of them, so it was remarkable to Reg that he would attach to her so strongly.

She didn't know what to do next, so she followed Ember back to Davyn's property. If she'd had something else to do, she might have argued, sent him a picture to make him see why she couldn't stay but, as she was at loose ends, she might as well see if Davyn were home and able to spend a few minutes talking to her.

As luck would have it, Davyn was home and came to the door when he heard a car coming up the gravel road. He smiled at the sight of Ember leading Reg down the drive.

"Reg. I didn't know you were coming."

Reg got out of the car. "Yeah, sorry. I was just out... going for a drive and thinking about things. I didn't really know where I was going."

"No problem. Why don't you come inside for a few minutes?"

She acquiesced. Davyn led the way into the living room and Ember brought up the rear.

Despite the man-sized glass doors leading into the massive fireplace that dominated the architecture of Davyn's house, Ember could barely squeeze into it anymore.

"Only a small fire," Davyn told him. "Julian is home, and we don't want to cook him."

Reg chuckled at the pictures Ember sent her, which suggested Ember wouldn't have minded that result. But he was obedient and only lit a modestly-sized fire. It would make the house pretty warm, keeping off the nighttime chill that still came in the evening, but it wouldn't put Julian in any danger of becoming roast dinner.

"How are you?" Reg asked Davyn, looking him over carefully for any sign of injury from the werewolf attack. But as he was a firecaster, Davyn could heal from minor wounds, and if he had been injured at all in the ambush, there was no sign of it now.

Davyn looked grim. He nodded, acknowledging the question and the seriousness of what had happened.

"I am fine... but this has caused some significant issues."

"Sarah is worried about a warlock/werewolf war and other people being injured."

Davyn nodded and didn't say whether he agreed with Sarah's concern or October's take that humans were too lazy to take it very far, especially when the only one seriously harmed was Corvin. Everyone would be glad, whether they showed it or not, that he had been disabled and would no longer be able to prey upon the unsuspecting or naive residents of Black Sands or the nearby counties.

"Aside from that, the leadership of the coven is now in question again."

"Oh, I hadn't thought about that." Even though she knew that Corvin mainly had been elected because the members of the coven had believed he would be able to give them power and bless them with his gifts, it hadn't occurred to her. She had seen the more immediate problems, such as how Corvin was doing and whether there would be a war in which others would be hurt or killed. The leadership of the coven was not her concern. "So, does that mean you are back to being the leader?"

"There is no automatic succession when the leader of a coven is killed or injured. It is a very rare event. There will need to be a new election if Corvin cannot retake his position. But until then... who will act in the interim?" Davyn shook his head. "I wish there was an easy answer to that question. Many of the coven expect me to step in and take over. But Corvin's heir is also in the coven, and there are those who believe the interim leadership should pass to him."

"Including John himself," Reg guessed.

Davyn nodded. "Of course. It is not a position we are supposed to seek, but that doesn't stop people from coveting it and seeing it as a position of power rather than service."

"Maybe if John gets it in the interim, he'll realize he doesn't want it. That it isn't what he expected. And he can... go on to do something else with his time and energy."

"Perhaps that would be a blessing," Davyn agreed. "But somehow, I don't expect that to be the outcome."

Julian appeared at the top of the stairs and looked over the railing to see who was there visiting with Davyn. He smiled, pleased to find her there. Julian's discovery that Reg was a siren had changed his attitude toward her. He was no longer the bully he had been when she was a child, or the inspector trying to put her behind bars for the unfortunate outcome of an encounter with a goblin in the Everglades. Now, he was excited whenever he saw her, proud of the fact that he had discovered a siren, one of those nearly extinct species, and knew her personally.

"Well, look who's here!"

"I thought you were out of town."

Julian came down the stairs and sat down on the couch with Davyn.

"I was, but now I'm back. And none too soon."

"Oh?" Reg cocked her head. "Why is that?"

"Well, this whole werewolf/warlock war thing. Someone needs to step in and insist that the whole thing be scrapped."

Reg tried to suppress her smile. Julian made it sound like the potential war was simply for their entertainment, and could be settled by one person. Julian could simply come onto the scene and declare the war null and void. No need for it. Things could be settled civilly instead.

"How are you going to get them to scrap it?"

"Well, it obviously must be done," Julian pointed out, sounding pedantic. "Wolves are extinct in Florida. Or at least, they were before October's pack arrived."

"It isn't October's pack. It's Aleph's."

Julian shook his head, frowning. "October is a member of the pack, is he not?"

"Yes."

"Then it is October's pack."

Reg rolled her eyes. "Okay, whatever."

"The point isn't who leads the pack. It is that the pack is here. They are the first wolves to repopulate Florida. There are breeding pairs. Under no circumstances can they be harmed."

Reg looked at him in surprise, then looked at Davyn to make sure that she had understood correctly.

"So the warlocks can't do anything to the wolves in retaliation for the attack?"

"Absolutely not. If there are ongoing problems, we can consider relocating the pack to a less populated area, but there cannot be any retaliation. There cannot be any harm done to the wolves."

Reg laughed. "I've been so worried about them! Especially the puppies. There are at least two other dams who are pregnant right now."

Julian looked delighted at this news. "Wonderful! We must not do anything that could potentially harm the repopulation of wolves in Florida."

"Even if they're werewolves?"

Julian knew that the wolves in question were werewolves, but Reg had to make sure he understood that. He was talking as if they were just regular wolves, living out their lives in one form.

"*Especially* if they are werewolves," Julian said emphatically. "There is an even greater need to protect magical species. It will be a sad day when only standard wolves remain in this country. We must do everything we can to protect the species."

"So nothing can be done to retaliate for the wolf attack."

"You can't expect people to put up with unprovoked attacks on humans without any kind of retribution," Davyn told Julian, "They cannot just attack at will."

Julian shrugged. "Take it up with the department if you want. It may seem unfair to you, but the number of werewolves in this country has declined dramatically due to human-wolf violence just as much as their disappearing habitat. The species must be preserved. Any problems with human-wolf interaction must be dealt with in a way that preserves the species and their reproductive capacity."

He looked from Reg to Davyn, neither of whom knew what to say about this.

"There are other ways to reduce friction between the two species," Julian advised. "There are ways to make the area around a town like Black Sands less hospitable for wolves so that they make their dens in areas farther from civilization."

"Like what?" Reg asked.

"Habitat modification. Lights, music, good fences, and keeping trees and bushes properly pruned. Motion-activated sprinklers."

"You want us to use sprinklers to keep werewolves away from civilization," Davyn demanded.

"It helps to discourage them. In combination with the other measures. They can be quite effective. It takes time and persistence, of course, but if you make things uncomfortable for them and they do not become habituated to humans—"

"What about when they *are* human?" Reg asked. "They can come into town as humans. Unlock gates and open doors. Turn off the music or the sprinklers."

"Don't feed them," Julian insisted. "If they have to hunt outside of town, they don't have any reason to come into town, and—"

"What about to visit? Or shop? Or work or go to school? You're going to tell all the grocery stores and restaurants to stop serving werewolves? How will they know who is or isn't a werewolf?"

"If we don't make it easy for them to do those things, they will have to do them outside of town, in their own areas that we have set aside as preserves. They will learn to stick to their own lands."

Reg shook her head slowly. She had found Julian's patronizing tone and attitudes to be distasteful in the past. She hated how he referred to her species as if she weren't a real person. The way that he assumed humans had the right—and responsibility—to protect and manage all of the other species.

Acting as if the werewolves were nothing more than dumb animals who could be controlled by being squirted or shouted at was the height of arrogance.

"Well, you do that," She told him. "You do all your habitat management things and see how well it works."

"There is no way you are going to be able to prevent all of the members of the coven and their loved ones from retaliating against the wolves who were involved in the attack," Davyn said. "No way."

"They will be fined," Julian pointed out. "And if they permanently harm or kill an endangered species, they will be bound and possibly serve hard time. It is a very serious matter."

Davyn shook his head. "Good luck enforcing that. I don't think you're seeing the big picture here, Julian."

"You're the one who is not seeing the big picture. You think this is just about one little skirmish. It isn't. We're talking about the survival of a species. You don't annihilate a species because of one problem. You learn non-violent ways to prevent further problems."

"Oh, Corvin and John and the others injured in this 'skirmish' will love that."

"They don't have to like it. They only have to obey the law."

"But the wolves don't. They can break the human-werewolf treaty with impunity."

"Breaches of the treaty will be dealt with by their delegations, not ours. They are self-governing. It isn't our place to determine the appropriate penalties. Their own councils will decide the consequences for breaching the treaty. You can give them all of the information you have available. You were there, so you can offer eyewitness testimony. Then they can make a decision based on the evidence."

Reg didn't need to be a psychic to read Davyn's mind. He was less than enthused about Julian's advice.

CHAPTER FORTY-SEVEN

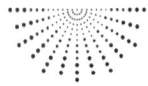

*R*eg went home with a lighter heart. October was convinced that the werewolves could evade any efforts by the warlocks to hunt them, and those efforts would eventually fizzle out. And as much as she hated Julian, he had magical law enforcement behind him, and they would do whatever they could to prevent retaliation against the werewolves.

Corvin, the leader of the coven and most powerful member, was crippled as far as using his magic was concerned. He might be able to whip the others up into a frenzy to go wolf hunting once or twice but, as long as the wolves stayed away from town and out of sight, the warlocks would be unable to wreak their vengeance for the attack.

Disaster would be averted. The wolves would all be fine. Zora and the pups and the pregnant wolves would all be safe from harm.

It had been a long day, and Reg had never caught up with her sleep. She had been on high alert, alarmed by the attack upon the coven and the possibility of an all-out war between the factions, and such emotional stress was exhausting. She had only a couple of clients to see that night and still had enough time for a nap in the afternoon so that she would be awake and alert when they came.

Starlight wanted food but, when Reg lay down on the bed, he decided that the next order of business was for him to take a nap as well, so he cuddled up next to Reg and she closed her eyes, relaxing her body and waiting for sleep to wash over her. It wasn't too far away. She didn't expect it to take more than a few minutes for her to fall asleep.

Reg had only been in bed for a few minutes when she thought she heard a noise in the living room. To begin with, she just ignored it, floating close to dreamland and waiting for sleep to overtake her. But she thought she heard walking. And singing. A low, rhythmic chant.

Soon, all thoughts of sleep fled and she sat up in bed, irritated but also worried about what was going on. Was she going crazy? Encountering a restless spirit? Maybe the lack of sleep was getting to her, and she was hallucinating. In which case, she should just get back in bed and ignore the hallucination.

The hallucination came in the form of Harrison marching back and forth across the cottage, a pink feather boa around his neck, in a very snazzy tuxedo and bowler hat. He smiled at Reg and ended his chant.

"Reg is awake!"

"I'm not sure about that. Are you sure you are not a dream?"

Harrison considered this question and examined the feathers and the fabric of his tux. "Did you dream this?"

"I don't know if I could."

He nodded, apparently satisfied. "Then Reg is awake."

"Great. But I actually want to go to sleep. That's why I was lying down in bed."

"Undoubtedly."

But Harrison did not disappear or make any movement to leave. Not that Reg had expected him to.

"Did you have something to tell me? Is that why you are

here? Did you find something else out about the dark entity you warned me about?"

"Ah," he smiled. "Reg is very intuitive."

Reg sat down on the couch and hugged one of the throw pillows to her. Starlight, of course, didn't jump up on the couch to sit in her lap but rubbed up against Harrison, purring loudly and meowing to be picked up. Harrison picked up the cat and cuddled Starlight to his face making kissy noises and murmuring in his ears.

"What did you want to tell me, Uncle Harrison?"

"I cannot tell you."

"You cannot tell me what you came to tell me?"

"I must take you."

"Take me?" Reg held her hands up defensively. She'd been taken places by Harrison before, and it was rarely a fun occasion. "Take me where?"

"Take me when," Harrison corrected.

"Oh, no." She shook her head. "No time travel."

Harrison ignored her protests. He whispered a few more sweet nothings into Starlight's ears, then put him down on the floor.

"You will see," he told Reg.

In an instant, she was in ancient Egypt. She recognized it immediately. She and Harrison stood unnoticed as the remembered scene of saying goodbye to El-Sayed and blessing him before the battle played out before her. She and Harrison were apparently invisible, as no one noticed their presence. Reg was relieved not to have to interact with her ancient self. She found it very disconcerting to travel to the past and was terrified of changing something by accident.

It was painful watching it all again, knowing what was coming. Watching it unfold in front of her instead of in a dream, Reg was far more aware of the details. The arid heat, the grittiness of the floor beneath her feet, the richness of the costumes and ornamentation around her.

Most of all, there was anxiety in everyone's faces, even though they attempted to put on a brave expression. They faced the possibility that the battle would be lost, and it was the last possible defense.

She had not been aware in her dreams how much time passed between sending the warrior on his way and the news that he had failed. Now, it was excruciating to watch with them, waiting, listening for any sound in the distance that would let them know what direction the battle had gone. Reg's heart pounded. She looked at Harrison, wishing he would hurry things on. He could take her through time, so why didn't he just take her to the resolution of the battle instead of making them wait?

Eventually, the handmaiden brought her the information that they had lost. Their plans had been communicated to the enemy so he had known what to expect and had been ready for them. Betrayal. One of El-Sayed's men must have been a double agent, passing information on to the sorcerer.

But what did that matter now? No matter who it had been, the result was the same.

It was hard for her to stay focused on recognizing and tracking the party who had betrayed them across her previous lives. Watching what happened in Egypt, that was the only life that mattered and she could barely remember her mission to find out the identity of their enemy and stop the repeated betrayals.

She looked out into the street, but the approaching army was too far away for her to identify any of the individuals in it. Her focus returned to the room. She watched the maiden hand the carved, highly polished box of Anubis to her mistress. She wore golden bracelets indicating her elevated position in the temple and had a single ostrich feather hennaed on her arm.

Reg couldn't watch any longer as the priestess handed vials to each of the servants who assembled before her. She didn't want to see the final moments of their mortal lives.

"That's enough," she told Harrison firmly.

He looked at her for a moment, his eyes sad for once instead of laughing. He nodded and took her away.

CHAPTER FORTY-EIGHT

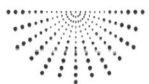

*R*eg had expected Harrison to take her back home but, instead, she found herself in the cool grove in Greece, watching the poetess who had the power of words that Reg did not. She was cuddled too close to Petros, the Olympian wrestler, alone in the darkness, time passing by quickly without her noticing its passage. She was all wrapped up in her discussion, oblivious to everything else.

The night was cool and pleasant. A full moon hung in the sky, casting a silvery light over the trees. An owl hooted in the distance, but the couple seemed oblivious to their surroundings.

What would it be like to be so smitten with someone that she didn't even feel the passage of time? Reg didn't think she had ever felt quite that way about any of the men she had fallen for. She always held something in reserve, wary of being hurt, wary of her devotion not being returned. If she were to get together with October, would that be how she would feel? Would all of their past crossings combine to form a bond between them that was unassailable? From the time they had met, she felt an affinity for him. How much stronger would that become if she nurtured it?

Reg watched the light of Phylakas, the guardian, approaching, making its way through the grove until he stopped before her and spoke.

She saw the poetess move quickly away from the wrestler, but it was too late; they had already been exposed. There was no way to hide the fact that they were sitting alone in the dark with no chaperones, no one to guard their virtue and testify that they had not done anything improper.

Reg stared at the man's arm as he held the lantern up to reveal the lovers. It was feathered with an old burn mark, similar in size and position to the tattoo on the servant in Egypt.

She barely heard the words that passed between the poetess and the guardian, who was supposed to help keep her safe from those who would have taken advantage of her and ensure she did not get into any compromising situations.

Reg had assumed that the situation in Greece had been the fault of the young people involved and not the dark entity Harrison had warned about.

"Is that X?" she asked Harrison. "Is he the one who intends me harm?"

He was her guardian, a man who had served her family for years and volunteered to guard her virtue and safety when she traveled to Olympia for her recitations. How could he be the one who had hurt her?

Harrison nodded, watching the scene unfold in front of them. The poetess's attempts to minimize what had happened, to apologize, to try to explain the compromising position she had been found in. The next day, she would be sent home, and Petros would lose all of his opportunities to make a name for himself, falling from grace.

"Why would he do that?" Reg demanded. "What does he care about their happiness?"

Harrison shrugged. "Many crossings... lives that intertwine and get entangled... it is difficult to unwind and separate them."

"October and me? Or him?" She nodded to the servant, "Phylakas?"

"Yes," Harrison nodded wisely.

All of them. The three of them intertwined across many lifetimes. Was Phylakas always on the outside, looking in at October's and Reg's relationships? Or had he been involved with one or the other of them as well, binding him even more tightly to the repeated cycle? Lovers betrayed, jealousies, death, and destruction of happiness, getting so entangled over time that they could not be separated.

But who was Phylakas in their current life? Surely not Corvin? Was the injury under the bandage he now wore on his arm reminiscent of the marking both the handmaid and Phylakas had worn? Was that why October had slashed him? Was that why the curse was focused there?

October had not told her he knew how to recognize the entity in their lives. But had he? Had he kept it a secret from her while he looked for the feather on the arm of each of the people they came into contact with?

"How do we untangle them?" she asked Harrison. "Can it be done?"

He considered this seriously for some time before answering. "I fear not."

CHAPTER FORTY-NINE

*R*eg was utterly exhausted. How was she supposed to save herself and October? Even with enough knowledge of the past, she could see no way out of the situation they found themselves in. They were bound to go on repeating the same cycle. There was no solution. What was the point of remembering? What was the point of finding out who X was?

"I need to go home," she told Harrison. "Back to my own time and place."

In an instant, she was back in the cottage where she was safe and sound and didn't have to worry about anyone plotting against her.

She leaned against the kitchen counter, weak, too tired to do anything for herself. Even walking across the room to the couch or back to her bedroom seemed impossible.

"Coffee or tea?" Harrison asked her, looking concerned.

"Coffee... chocolate... Jack Daniels..."

Harrison decided that beverages were not sufficient. He bent down and picked her up, cradling her like a child, one arm under her knees and the other around her shoulders. He took her over to the couch and deposited her there, for which Reg was grateful. No more need to stand or walk. She sprawled on the couch, unable to move.

Harrison pressed the button on the coffee maker to start it brewing and, while he waited, poked around in Reg's freezer and cupboards.

Despite the number of times he had acted inept and been unable to operate the coffee machine or other modern conveniences, he now seemed completely competent and, in a few minutes, provided her with a large mug of coffee, a pint of chocolate ice cream, and an unopened bottle of Tennessee whiskey.

Reg struggled to sit upright and started with the coffee.

"Why show me all of that if there isn't anything I can do about it?" she demanded.

"Reg does not like to change the past."

"No. I'm not changing anything in the past. That will just tangle things up even worse. But why can't I change the future? Why can't I change the *now?*"

"There is no need to change what has not happened."

"No... but... how do I prevent the past from repeating itself? How do I protect myself? And even if I protect myself from X in this life, even if I killed him, then what about our future lives? Won't he just be there again the next time? Bound tighter than ever. How do we stop him?"

"These are human affairs," Harrison told her. "Or... mortal affairs," he corrected. Because who knew what form they would come back in the next time. She and October had still been intertwined in other bodily forms, as impossible as that seemed.

"So you don't know?"

He shook his head.

"And you can't do something? You can't just... *poof* him into non-existence?"

Harrison raised his brows. "I do not poof."

"Because you can't or you don't want to?"

"It is the same."

"No, it isn't."

He didn't back down. Reg started in on the ice cream. It was even colder than usual after the hot coffee. Maybe she should have stirred some into her coffee, cooling the coffee down and giving it a creamy mocha flavor. Next time, she would try that. Reg opened the bottle of Jack and took a swig from the bottle without worrying about glasses.

She looked around. "Starlight? Where are you?"

There was no answering meow or thump as Starlight jumped down from his current perch.

"Do you know where he is?" Reg asked Harrison. "Is he in the bedroom?"

Harrison walked over to the bedroom to look in the door. He shook his head.

"He's not there?" Reg asked, looking around. "Well, where is he hiding?"

Harrison took a minute to look around the cottage, calling Starlight softly and making kissy noises.

"Did he get out?" Reg looked toward the door in alarm.

On the one hand, Starlight was strong and wise, probably far more intelligent than Reg, with the wisdom of accumulated lives in much more elevated positions than Reg. But on the other hand, he was a cat, and there were many dangers for an outside cat. Cars, poisons, predators. It wouldn't be the first time Starlight had gotten out, and he had always taken care of himself before, but that didn't mean he was safe.

Harrison went to the door of the cottage, opened it and looked out. He shut the door again.

"He is not here."

"We need to find him."

"He is not here."

"Do you know where he is?"

Harrison was an immortal, he should be able to see Starlight and know what he was doing. But the immortals were not omniscient; she had been told that enough times.

Harrison nodded. "Yes."

"Where, then? Is he close by? Does he need to be rescued?"

"It is not the cat who needs to be rescued."

Reg frowned at his tone and wording. "What? Then who needs to be rescued? What are you talking about?"

Harrison looked at her, lips pursed. "Are you recovered?"

"Yes." Reg sat up straight. She didn't know what kind of trouble they were facing, but if Starlight or some other creature needed to be rescued, she couldn't just lounge about on her couch, paying no attention. "What is it? What's going on?"

Harrison twirled a finger, and before Reg could ask any more questions to figure out what was happening, the cottage had disappeared and, once more, she was whisked away.

It was a place she recognized, where she had previously visited Zora and her cubs or October before the trouble had started.

And they were all there. Zora and the cubs in wolf form, October and Channelle in human form, and several of the other wolves. Reg looked around, trying to sort it out. The scene was rife with tension.

Rather than being with Zora, the pups were with Channelle. Was she babysitting? Maybe Zora wanted to go into town and Channelle had promised to look after them while their mother was away. Maybe October didn't think it was a good idea, with the current trouble between the coven and the pack.

The young wolves were in harnesses, pulling, straining, and biting at them. As far as Reg knew, they had never been leashed before, and they didn't know what to do about it—not that there was anything they could do about it. The harnesses looked sturdy and were fastened tightly.

"What's going on?" Reg asked.

The others turned to look at her. Reg didn't even try to explain how she had gotten there. Sometimes, it was easier not to offer any explanation.

"What are you doing here?" Channelle challenged.

Reg focused on Channelle's sleeve of tattoos on the arm holding the leashes. She took a couple of steps closer, staring at the tattoos. Almost buried in the chaos of other symbols was an ostrich feather.

"It's *you*."

October's brows drew down. He shook his head. "What are you talking about?" He looked back at Channelle, trying to find the thread of the conversation they had been having before Reg had appeared out of thin air. "I don't understand what you are doing with the cubs. Why are they on leashes? We don't bind our own."

"Ask your girlfriend," Channelle sneered, looking at Reg.

"My girlfriend?" October shook his head. "What are you talking about? Reg?"

"It's her," Reg told him, "She's the one who has been sabotaging us. Who has been there across all of these lives, causing trouble, ending our lives. It's her."

"Channelle?" he looked stunned. "That cannot be."

CHAPTER FIFTY

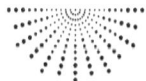

S he is!" Reg insisted. "I have seen her through multiple lives—she has a tattoo of a feather on her arm."

October looked toward Channelle, frowning. "A tattoo of a feather? So what?"

"So I saw her in Egypt with a henna tattoo of a feather, I saw her in Greece with a feather-shaped burn on her—his— arm. And she is here, with a tattoo of a feather in exactly the same place. It is her! She is the one who betrayed our campaign in Egypt. She is the one who broke us up. She's been there every time."

He still didn't believe it. Channelle was doing her best to look confused and outraged but she had not explained what she was doing with the puppies. She clearly meant to take them away, to do some kind of harm, but Reg wasn't sure what.

"Reg... you said that seeing Corvin in one previous life was not enough to convince you that he was the one who was trying to harm you in multiple lives. But you believe that it was Channelle because you saw her in two?"

Reg tried to think of how to explain it. The feather mark on her arm in three different lives was significant, just like October's eyes every time she had seen him. She was sure that if she went back to each life where they had been hurt or betrayed, she would find Channelle there in one form or another, the feather mark on her arm, destined to betray them.

"She is the one," Reg insisted. "Harrison saw her too, he said it was her."

October looked at Channelle, still obviously not believing it. Channelle stared back at him, her expression blank.

Tell her to release the cubs. Zora's voice was in Reg's head.

"Let the puppies go," Reg said immediately. "Why do you have them? Zora says to let them go."

Channelle turned to look at Reg. "You are ruining everything!" she said bitterly. "I knew as soon as I saw you that you were going to ruin it all!"

"Ruin what?" October demanded.

"You and me. She is here to split us up, don't you know that? You see the way she throws herself at you. The minute you laid eyes on her it was 'Reg this' and 'Reg that.' You couldn't stop talking about her. You hardly even knew her, yet you couldn't stop talking about her. When she was with Jake, I thought I could have you back again, but no! She wasn't happy to have just one man. She had Jake, and Corvin, and who knows who else, but she had to have you too. Couldn't leave you alone."

"Reg and I are not seeing each other," October said quietly.

But his soft answer did not help a bit. Especially followed by the apologetic look he gave Reg.

"Look, I don't know what you're so upset about or what you think you are going to accomplish by tying the puppies up. Let's just start over and talk it through calmly."

"She likes them," Channelle hissed. "Yes, it's not enough that she gets you. She has to have everyone's love. She is the great savior. She saves everyone from Jake Bosco. From *her* boyfriend. Everybody owes her. Everybody loves her. Well I don't! And neither will the puppies. Or Zora."

Reg swallowed. Channelle was going to do something to the

puppies in the name of getting her revenge on Reg? She was going to kidnap or torture them and blame it on Reg so that they would hate her? And Zora would know that Channelle would not have hurt them except for Reg, so she would hate Reg too. It wasn't exactly logical, but Channelle wasn't acting based on what Reg had done in this life; she had been conditioned by countless lifetimes where she had resented or been jealous of Reg.

"Channelle... I'm sorry. I didn't mean to... take anything from you. I am not taking October away from you and I didn't mean to... to interfere with your life..."

"You think that you can just walk in and take over. You can take my place and make everyone love you because you could get them out of the lab and break the binding spell. But you weren't the only one involved in that operation. There were a lot of people and wolves involved. They put a lot more effort into it than you. They had been making plans for weeks. You just jumped in at the end and pretended it was all you."

Channelle was yanking on the leashes, and the puppies were yipping and getting more and more agitated. Reg didn't know what Channelle had told them to get them to cooperate with her putting the harnesses and leashes on them. Probably she had told them it was a game. Or maybe that she would take them all into town if they would let her put the leashes on them. They knew that dogs in town had to be on leashes. It would make sense that if they wanted to go into town with her, they would also have to be wearing leashes so as not to attract unwanted attention.

But now they had an inkling that something was wrong, and the four of them were pulling on the leashes, trying to get away from her or nipping at the cuffs of her pants. Fenris had the leash to his harness in his mouth and was grinding away at it, determined to chew through it before Channelle noticed.

Zora paced back and forth, anxious about the puppies, but not daring to get any closer. Reg didn't know whether Channelle had a weapon on her, but whatever threat she had made was obviously keeping Zora and the other wolves back.

"You don't need to do anything to the puppies," Reg said, trying to keep Channelle calm. "I will stay out of your life. I will stay away from the pack. Whatever you want."

"You're lying."

"I have other friends. I don't need to hang out here. October probably isn't even going to be around town, with the coven hunting him. I'm sure he'll want you to stay with him, since you helped him with the attack on Corvin." She swallowed hard, looking for ways to convince Channelle that she would stay out of her life and Channelle should just let the puppies go. "I don't need October, I'm more interested in someone else."

"Corvin Hunter?" Channelle sneered.

"Well, I've always been attracted to him, and now that he can't do any magic to harm me…" Reg forced a smile. "It's the ideal situation, isn't it? I can control him, and be with him as much as I want, without worrying that he is going to steal my powers. He's very handsome, you know. Very sexy."

"You think you're fooling me? I can tell when you're lying."

Reg didn't know if she had made a misstep or if Channelle was just that paranoid.

"I don't want October," Reg said firmly. "And I don't want cubs. I want someone I am compatible with." She did her best to look scathingly at October. "Not someone who won't even enjoy my baking. We don't even like the same foods!"

Channelle perked up a bit at this, maybe remembering how different their tastes had been when they had been at the coffee shop together. Did she really think that Reg would turn someone down because he liked different foods from what she did?

Maybe if she were a baker and he wouldn't eat anything she made, that would be different. But since Reg couldn't cook worth beans, she didn't care what October ate. *If* he'd been her boyfriend, which he wasn't.

Fenris gave a sudden jerk on the leash, leaping away from Channelle, and the section of leash he had been gnawing on gave way and snapped. Channelle gave a cry of alarm. Fenris growled and barked at her. The other cubs tried to pull away as well, but were unsuccessful as they hadn't first chewed on the straps so that they would break with a good yank.

Fenris immediately began teasing the other cubs, oblivious to the danger Channelle presented. Laughing and taunting them that he had escaped and they could not.

Zora tried to get his attention and make him stop, to settle everyone down until the danger was past.

Channelle bared her teeth and growled at Fenris and he growled back.

Reg's heart was in her throat. She didn't want Channelle to do anything to hurt Fenris or the others. Fenris might have turned Jake when he was only a day old, but a nip would have no effect on another werewolf. She didn't want to call and distract him. There were already enough people yelling at him or trying to get his attention. She moved closer, seeing whether she could get her own body between Channelle and the juvenile.

But then what? If Channelle shifted, Reg had little defense against teeth and claws. She could raise a psychic shield to block her, but what would that do for the rest of the puppies Channelle still held? They would be on the other side of the shield with Channelle and Reg would be unable to reach them.

Calm down, she told the puppies in her mind. *If you want to get away from her, you need to calm down.*

They were more interested in Fenris's teasing than what Reg was saying.

I'm free, Fenris taunted, *and you are tied up like pets.*

The other puppies yipped and pulled on the leashes. Channelle growled and yanked on the leashes, jerking them back, and aimed kicks which missed their swiftly moving targets.

"Stop it!" Channelle screamed at them. "You stay still, or you're going to be hanging by your necks!"

The cubs seemed to suddenly realize the seriousness of the situation and stopped tussling, lying down with their chins on the ground, a submissive gesture Reg hoped would calm Channelle.

"Channelle," October said softly, "let them go. This isn't you."

Channelle's eyes flicked to him, then back to Reg. "You don't understand," she hissed. "It's always been about her. Every life, every betrayal. It's always been Reg."

"Harming the pups isn't going to change anything between us."

Except that there was no way October would get together with a woman who had harmed wolf pups. What man could trust a woman like that to raise his offspring?

Reg looked at Harrison, who was still standing next to her, watching the proceedings with polite interest. The affairs of the humans was not his business. It was not something that he would normally get involved in. Other immortals poked their noses where they were not wanted. Weston had seduced Reg's mother, or Norma Jean had seduced him. How many stories were there of Zeus or other gods of Olympus interfering with the affairs of the men—and women—living in the Mediterranean?

"We need to stop her before she hurts one of the puppies," she told Harrison.

He raised his brows and nodded in agreement. He was holding Starlight in his arms, petting him. Where had he come from? Had he been watching over the wolf pack the whole time?

"You can help," Reg pointed out to Harrison. "You could stop her."

"To stop her is *your* choice," Harrison corrected.

"No, I need you to do something. She won't listen to me. She isn't listening to October, and she's in love with him."

In love with him? Or just with the idea of taking him away from Reg?

Harrison looked at Channelle and shrugged. "She has no power over you."

Reg had fought much more powerful entities than Channelle. Why was she balking at taking action herself? She had not hesitated to act when the newborn puppies had been in danger from Jake; what was different now? Despite all of the times that Channelle had interfered with her lives in the past, this time Reg clearly had more power.

Although that had been the case in other lives as well. Channelle had played the parts of servants and spies. She had never been the one with authority over Reg. Instead, she had used deception and ingenuity to drive a wedge between October and Reg.

Even now, Channelle was no threat to Reg, only to the puppies. And what could she really do? Zora, only a few yards away, was in wolf form with savage teeth and claws at her disposal. Reg had other powers. She did not like to use any violence, but there had to be a time and a place, and this seemed to be it.

What did wolves fear?

Fire.

Reg took another step forward and met Channelle's eyes. "You need to let them go."

Channelle shook her head defiantly. "I am not giving in to you. You're not my boss."

Reg held her cupped hands toward each other as if holding a soccer ball. She moved them around, kindling a ball of fire in the space between them..

Channelle's eyes widened, but she stood her ground.

"Nice trick," she spat. "Do you pull rabbits out of a hat too?"

Reg let the fire grow and warm. She knew that Channelle would be able to feel it from where she was.

"It's not a trick. Let the cubs go."

She took another step toward Channelle, and Channelle took a step backward to keep the distance between them. But she still held the leashes.

"I don't have to listen to you."

Reg focused her attention on the leashes. Without them, Channelle would have no more control over the puppies. She would not be able to hit or kick them or hang them by their necks. What kind of a person threatened puppies like that? What kind of a werewolf?

Reg picked a spot a few inches away from the puppies on each of the leashes, focusing her fire on it so that each of the three leashes started to smolder. Reg's nose wrinkled at the acrid smell of the burning leather.

"No!" Channelle protested. "Stop that!" She reached down and tried to smother the fires by patting the leashes against her leg. "Stop! Don't do that!"

But she quickly stopped attempting to smother them as she burned her hands. She pulled on the leashes to try to get the puppies farther away from Reg, but that only had the effect of putting more stress on the places Reg was burning, helping to pull them apart faster.

In a few more seconds, the leashes snapped at the burn points, and the three pups ran back to Zora's side. She licked them and pushed them back, farther away from Channelle. Fenris stayed close to Reg and Channelle rather than running back to his dam, growling and watching Channelle warily.

"You need to go," Reg told Channelle.

Root out this evil, and eliminate it.

Channelle snarled at her. October stepped forward. "She's right," he said tersely. "You are not welcome in the pack any longer. We can't tolerate anyone threatening the young ones."

Channelle's eyes flared with rage and disbelief. "You're choosing her over me?"

October's expression was resolute, though pain flickered in

his eyes. "This isn't about choosing sides. It's about protecting those who are vulnerable. You crossed a line."

Channelle clenched her fists, trembling with anger. "You'll regret this," she spat, backing away slowly. Her gaze shifted to Reg one last time, filled with venomous hatred. She turned and loped into the woods, transforming as she ran and blending with the shadows, quickly disappearing from sight.

CHAPTER FIFTY-ONE

*T*he danger appeared to be past. Reg waited for something else to happen, but everything was quiet. Everyone was watching her, glancing back at the trees to make sure Channelle didn't return, and looking at each other questioningly. But mostly watching her.

"I'm sorry," Reg said, "I didn't mean to cause so much trouble."

"You did not cause this," October said flatly. "This was not your fault in any way. Thank you for freeing the pups and keeping them safe. Channelle is a worthy adversary, a good fighter. None of us wished to attack her and possibly put the pups in harm's way." He gazed toward the woods. "We will be watching, and she will not be allowed near the pack again. If she wishes to challenge me, she may. I would… watch your back. I know you are not a fighter, but you have…" He hesitated, searching for the right words, "With your heritage and your gifts, you have certain instincts. Use them. Don't let yourself get complacent."

Reg looked around the clearing. She reached out with all of her senses, searching for Channelle. The she-wolf was not anywhere in the immediate vicinity. Reg would have to stay on the alert. For how long? Forever? And even beyond that?

Vigilance. Constant attention.

"What about the... uh... cosmic entanglement?" Reg asked tentatively. "I mean... even if she is gone and doesn't come back, even if she decides to give up and do other things, what about the next life? Won't she keep coming back again and again, trying to split us up in future lives? I don't want that..."

Reg didn't want to keep dealing with that threat lifetime after lifetime, never getting the opportunity to live her life to its fullest. She wanted to put an end to the cycle.

October shoved his hands into his pockets and stared up at the sky, thinking. Reg watched Zora and the puppies and let October ponder the problem. She couldn't very well expect him to have the answer on the tip of his tongue, could she? It had taken days to sort out what was going on and to identify Channelle, and Reg had only done so with the assistance of Harrison and his transportation of her across time.

Zora licked the cubs and, although they were too old to be nursing any longer, they lay down and cuddled up with her, seeking the warmth and comfort of her body. Fenris had joined them and was circling the dogpile, still too restless to settle in with them. He would be a good leader in the future, Reg thought —constantly vigilant, a fighter, smart enough to figure out how to get himself out of a tight spot when the other puppies had merely whined and pulled on their leashes. Reg knew what it was like to be different and always be on the alert like that.

"If we want to avoid Channelle's interference in future lives, then we need to break the cycle," October said slowly.

Reg nodded impatiently. That much was obvious. Wasn't that what she had just said?

"I don't mean the cycle of Channelle trying to break us up and change our destinies," October clarified. "I mean... the karmic bond between you and me."

Reg's head whirled, suddenly overcome by memories of countless lives lived together, countless crossings with October in all forms. Not just as man and woman, but sometimes brother and sister or parent and child. Sometimes friends or colleagues. But always together, crossing after crossing. She put out her hand as if to stop the waterfall of memories, and October touched her shoulder, cupping it under his warm palm, steadying her.

"Reg."

"You're right," Reg admitted, though she hated to say it. How could she agree with him? How could she even contemplate breaking the bond between them, a bond that had endured not just in one lifetime but for eons, maybe as long as her soul had existed? "If Channelle is trying to hurt me—hurt us—because we are so close and have established this bond… then the way to stop her in the future is to break that bond."

October nodded soberly. Reg turned to Harrison, who watched the two of them with a slight frown. Starlight was cuddled in his arms, head tucked up under his chin as if they were faces on a totem pole.

"You said that our threads are all entangled, all knotted together. That it is hard to untie it all. But is it possible?"

"Alone?" Harrison shook his head. "It is too much. Fragile mortal psyches…" He shook his head again at the thought. "Too hard."

"With help?"

"With help… perhaps. With a great deal of help." He took a deep breath. "Humans are very, very, very—"

"Okay, we get it," Reg laughed and held up her hand to stop him. "Humans are fragile and stupid."

He cocked his head slightly and shrugged as if that went without saying.

"Will you help us?"

He stroked Starlight's fur. "Of course, I will always help Reg."

Reg reached out to scratch Starlight's jaw. "And will you?" Harrison had told her to remember Starlight's powers. Starlight had known enough to come to the clearing before she or Harrison were aware of the threat Channelle posed to the pups. Starlight had saved her bacon more than once before.

She felt calming, approving feelings from Starlight. His aura was warm and comforting. Reg looked at October and gave a nod. "We will have to try."

CHAPTER FIFTY-TWO

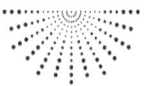

*S*arah unpacked the box of supplies she had brought to the cottage with her, going through the list of the herbs and other items she had brought.

To Reg, it all seemed like unnecessary frippery. Would any of this stuff really have any effect on the entanglement of karmic energy that held her and October together, life after life? What difference could burning candles or herbs make?

Reg supposed she was different from Sarah in that regard. She had to dig down deep into herself to find the gifts and powers she had been forced to suppress for so many years. The memories were inside her, the fire and the psychic power and other gifts were inside her. The physical objects that Sarah sometimes seemed to rely on seemed like they were just ornamentation.

"Reg," Sarah tried to rein in Reg's scattered thoughts and to get her attention.

"Sorry. There's just so much going on... do you really think any of this will help? It seems like... extra work for no reason."

"It can be beneficial to visualize what you are doing. Like when you are meditating with a flame. The fire helps you to focus on something, right?"

Reg nodded.

"And when you and I set wards of protection around the cottage and the garden, we don't actually need to use physical objects to do so, but it makes it easier to be able to imbue an object with power than to just... put it out there."

"I guess," Reg agreed. She had never questioned the need to use an actual object to weave their protection spells, but she supposed what Sarah said was true. They could have just used an incantation or intention to do the same thing, but it would have been a lot harder to get it right and to be sure that it "stuck."

"Well, this may all seem like a lot of unnecessary nonsense. But it will help to focus and guide your thoughts and intentions," Sarah told her. "You and October will be doing a lot of psychic and emotional work. It is helpful to be able to... put that work into action. To see it acted out before you."

"Okay," Reg agreed, acquiescing to Sarah's greater knowledge and experience. She would take whatever help she could get, whatever form it came in. If it was candles and herbs, she would take the old crone's experience and advice.

Sarah nodded. "Good. Now, let's finish getting everything set up before the others arrive."

* * *

October looked around the interior of the cottage when he arrived, green eyes alight with interest. "This is... unexpected."

"Sarah said that it will help. And I figured we needed all the help we can get."

October didn't argue the point. Maybe he, like Reg, felt inadequate to this task.

And not only inadequate but reluctant to do what she knew they had to do. Did she really want to sever ties with October? Not just in this life, but in all future lives as well? She was so comfortable with him and had felt such a connection with him from the first moment they had met. She had not felt that way with anyone else in her recollection. Now, after finding that bond, she was going to intentionally sever it?

October walked by her, looking at all of the magical accouterments and giving her shoulder a little squeeze. She was sure he felt the same way. They were karmically bonded. He wouldn't want to separate any more than Reg did.

But if they were to live free in the next life, and the one after that, without interference from Channelle's soul, they needed to take what action they could. To give themselves a chance to move on and be happy with other partners, other souls.

"Starlight?" Reg looked around and found him sleeping on the couch, waiting for all the arrangements to be made while he had a nap. "I guess it's time to call Harrison."

October nodded.

Reg took a deep breath, but Harrison was already there, standing in front of her.

Only he was Harrison as she had never before seen him. A much more subdued costume than usual, long black robes, long gray hair falling around his shoulders, and a distinctly feminine face despite the long drooping mustache. He had a large pair of menacing-looking scissors in his hand.

"Uncle Harrison?" Reg asked nervously, needing reassurance.

"It is acceptable?" Harrison asked, looking down at his drab robe. He smoothed the worn fabric with one hand.

"One of the fates," October suggested, "the weird sisters."

Harrison brightened a little and nodded. "Fate," he agreed. "Disentangling your future." He hesitated. "Your past?"

It was always difficult for him to understand their view of the timeline, past, present, and future.

"Both, I guess," Reg agreed. "Well… let's get started."

She and Sarah had sprinkled salt in a circle around the table and chairs where they would be sitting. Reg supposed that they should be sitting on the floor or standing, to be grounded or anchored to the earth. But she knew that the process might take a long time, and she didn't want to be too uncomfortable or unable to go on because her legs got tired or cramped.

They each took a chair around the table, including Starlight, who jumped down from the couch and then picked a chair where he sat upright, eyes and ears just above the level of the table.

"First, we light the candles," Reg said nervously, looking from one to the other. She wasn't exactly expecting them to object, but she hadn't ever been in charge of a big spell like this before.

Harrison and October nodded. Starlight gave no sign, just sitting there stock-still with his ears pricked forward.

Reg used her own fire to light the first of the white candles. She handed the other candle to October, and he touched the wick to Reg's candle to light his. They set the candles down in the ornamented candlesticks Sarah had provided.

Cleanse your life.

Fire had purifying powers.

Reg picked up a sprig of sage and passed it through the fire until it started to smolder, then laid it on a salver. She held it up and waved it gently in the direction of each of the four chairs around the table. Cleansing the room. Getting ready for the spell.

"Now... we hold hands," Reg suggested.

She didn't know whether to just hold October's hands as she gazed across the table at him, or if everyone should hold hands. Harrison and Starlight were there to help her through the process, after all. Harrison took her hand on one side. Reg looked at Starlight, wondering how he would feel about her touching his sensitive paw. But instead of the tuxedo cat, a man sat to her left.

Starlight is more than he seems.

She had seen him in this form before only a time or two. Dressed as an Egyptian warrior, like October had been when she had known him in Egypt. He said nothing to her, silent as he always was in this form. Reg swallowed and took his hand as well. October did the same on the other side of the table, completing the circle.

"Now... we need help untangling the threads." Reg swallowed. Each time she thought about the past lives now, the images overwhelmed her. A heavy sadness weighed down on her, knowing that it was her intention to sever these ties, to separate her soul's destiny from October's forever. Could they remain friends after this? Could they even see each other again, or would that muddy the waters and align their fates again?

Harrison squeezed her hand slightly, and the memories started to flow.

Images flashed through Reg's mind. Some that she had already seen, like Egypt and Greece, others in civilizations that she couldn't name, sometimes tiny tribes that didn't even know of the existence of the rest of the world. She piloted a Viking ship. She watched the Salem witch trials with fear, not of being discovered, but of the devil worshipers that were apparently all around her. Man or woman, she participated in wars, going off to battle, unsure she would ever return, protecting her home, family, and country.

And October was at her side in one form or another life after life. Lover, sister, brother in arms. Colleague or opponent.

She knew she wasn't holding his hands directly but, in her mind, the world narrowed, and she wasn't holding hands with Harrison and Starlight, but with October, alone in the room, staring into his eyes at the same time that the visions flashed across her mind.

And Channelle. Reg saw betrayals, heard the insidious words whispered in her ear, felt the shadow creeping along her back trail. How long had this soul been bound to her by love, jealousy, and resentment?

The visions continued to flow for a long time. Reg didn't know how much time had passed before she started to surface.

Her eyes were sticky and swollen. Her cheeks were wet with tears. She had a pounding headache centered in the third eye position on her forehead. She felt dehydrated and disoriented.

"Are you okay?" October asked her hoarsely. Staring across the table at him, Reg saw that his eyes were also swimming in tears.

She slowly released the hands on either side of her. The candles had burned low, with copious drippings hanging from the candlestick holders, a testament to how long the trance had lasted.

Reg moved robotically, following the ritual that Sarah had given her. She looped a red thread around the two candles, winding it in a figure eight. A lemniscate, Sarah had called it. Eternity.

Her life and October's, crossing over and over again, forming an X in the middle. But no more. Now they would be free.

She picked up the scissors Harrison had appeared with. Sarah had brought her sewing scissors, but Reg thought Harrison's scissors of the fates more appropriate.

It is your choice.

She chanted the verse Sarah had helped her to memorize.

> By the light of these flames, we seek to sever,
> The ties that bind us, now and forever.
> Through lifetimes past, we've walked as one,
> Now our journey together is done.

Reg took a deep breath and let it out again. Then, she used the scissors to cut the red thread.

The candles were extinguished.

The heavy sadness that had weighed on Reg's shoulders before the beginning of the ritual was gone, replaced by a void.

She rubbed her face, feeling like she had just woken up. She looked around the cottage, then briefly at the other faces at the table. It was finished. She had completed the ritual. That was all she could do. She didn't know if it would work or what would happen in future lives. But perhaps Reg and October had a chance to progress and enjoy their lives without the threat of Channelle's interference.

At the sacrifice of their future relationship.

But they'd had a good run together. They had shared many different lives together; maybe it was time for them to separate, like a child growing in independence and leaving his mother's side for a life of his own. Like a wolf cub leaving his pack to venture out into the world to learn how to make it on his own.

CHAPTER FIFTY-THREE

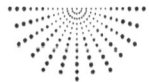

*H*arrison was once again wearing the tuxedo with the pink feather boa. Reg couldn't remember his ever recycling an old outfit again. He must have decided he really liked that one. He lounged on one of the wicker chairs in her living room, long spidery legs stretched out in front of him.

Starlight was back in his familiar feline form, curled up on the couch with Reg, maybe deciding that comforting her was more important than cuddling with his immortal friend today.

"Was it the right choice?" Reg asked. "And will it work? Will it keep Channelle from interfering in our lives in the future? And will it be good for us? I have so many questions and doubts…"

"If Reg did not choose to change it, things would not change," Harrison pointed out.

"And we'd have no chance of things being any different."

He gave a solemn nod.

"You're right," Reg agreed.

She didn't know what else to say. She scratched Starlight's ears.

October had told her quietly after the ceremony that he would likely be leaving town. He had to consider the safety of the pack and, with the attack on Corvin and Channelle's threats toward Zora's cubs, it was safer for them if he were somewhere else.

She didn't know if she would ever see him again. In this life or the next.

It was a daunting thought. But she had gone through most of her current life without knowing him. He had been a bright light in her life for a few months, but that time was past.

She still had her friends in Black Sands. And Harrison. And Starlight.

That would have to be enough.

Did you enjoy this book? Reviews and recommendations are vital to making a book successful.

Please leave a review at your favorite book store or review site and share it with your friends.

Don't miss the following bonus material:
Sign up for mailing list to get a free ebook
Read a sneak preview chapter
Other books by P.D. Workman
Learn more about the author

DON'T MISS A THING! GET THE LATEST NEWS AND A FREE EBOOK

Your First Taste

PDWORKMAN.COM/SIGNUP

PREVIEW CHAPTER 1

$\mathcal{G}$ ideon Darkwood crept through the trees, taking the well-worn pathway to the temple in the orange grove. The moonlight filtered through the dense canopy of orange trees, casting eerie shadows that danced around him as he moved stealthily along the path. The citrusy aroma of oranges lingered in the air, but Gideon's thoughts were far removed from their sweetness.

Though Gideon had traversed this way many times before, it was not he who had worn the path through grass and dirt. That had been formed by the feet of the warlock coven that met there regularly.

It was hard to believe that Corvin now led the coven. Back when they had been young warlocks together, it was unimaginable that a power drinker would ever be allowed to hold such a position in the coven. Back then, Corvin had been barred from even being a member of an established coven. How things had changed since then.

Corvin's leadership of the coven had not been as successful as he had hoped. He had promised the coven members that he would share some of his accumulated powers and gifts with them if elected. And to his credit, he had followed through and tried to do that.

But things had gone awry.

What Corvin had done to merit the attack by the werewolves, Gideon didn't know. And he probably didn't want to know. He'd seen enough of Corvin's nature in the past. They had worked together to maintain the spell of the Temple Orange Grove for decades. Centuries, now. He had seen many of Corvin's highs and lows.

The warlock might have good intentions, but his inborn nature, which he could not change no matter what he willed, always twisted those good intentions into something else.

Since the attack, Corvin had cloistered himself within the walls of his home and would take no visitors. Gideon's attempts to communicate with him had been rebuffed. Corvin said he needed some recovery time and would get back to Gideon when he was feeling better. Many rumors were flying around about the injuries Corvin had received, but Gideon assumed most of the rumors were false. He wouldn't believe any story unless it came from Corvin's own lips, and probably not even then.

He might approach a few of the members of the coven who had been there during the attack to get the whole story. He wasn't sure whether any of them would talk to him. And there might be little they could tell him about the attack. Something like that, an ambush during the spring equinox ritual, must have shocked them. Completely unexpected, as far as he knew. Equinox was supposed to be a time of peace and balance. Most practitioners carefully avoided any offense or conflict that day.

Gideon followed the stones in the ground that had once been the foundations of the temple. It had stood there proudly many years before, but over time, it had fallen into disrepair, and relic hunters had removed many of the stones that had built the walls.

But Gideon was not looking for the stones of the walls.

There was another stone he sought.

Few knew of its existence, but its safety and integrity were vital for the welfare of the people of Black Sands. During the years before the stone had been laid there, life in Black Sands had been chaotic and dangerous. It had not been the sleepy little town it was now, sitting back quietly in contemplation. A place where magical practitioners had free commerce with one another. One of the safest places for psychics and witches to openly practice their craft. It had flourished for many years as the social center for all practitioners for hundreds of miles around.

Yet they were all ignorant of why Black Sands had become the magical mecca it was. That secret was shared by a select few, Gideon among them.

He found the altar stone the warlocks had placed at the central point of the temple. The herbs placed upon it were withered and dry, looking almost as if they had burned in the sunlight.

A faintly familiar smell rose to his nostrils. Pungent and earthy.

He heard a noise and startled, whirled around to look behind him. He pulled his cloak close to him in an effort to blend into the darkness. A cloak of invisibility it was not, but the hood shadowed his face and kept it in darkness and the capacious sleeves covered his white, wrinkled hands.

Had someone followed him here? He had not seen anyone else on the road. He had watched carefully to make sure that no one could follow him. But he was not immune to mistakes.

The leaves of the orange trees rustled in the wind, and the fruit's smell once again covered the subtle scent from the altar a moment earlier.

After standing frozen for several long minutes and seeing no movement around him, Gideon decided he had imagined it. He was being paranoid. Corvin had been injured in a werewolf attack, but that had clearly been planned for when the coven was meeting and was at their most vulnerable. No one knew that Gideon was coming here tonight. The wolves would be far away. They had reportedly left Black Sands and perhaps even Florida. They were not eager to face retribution for what they had done. Cowardly dogs that they were, they hoped that if they just disappeared for a while, people would forget what they had done, and they would not have to pay for it.

Gideon leaned closer to the altar, trying to pick up the scent he had detected a moment earlier. What was it? As old as he was, his sniffer wasn't quite as sensitive or reliable as it had once been. He inhaled deeply, thinking he would only smell the sage and other herbs placed on the altar.

But once again, he detected the pungent smell of another herb—mandrake.

What would they have been using mandrake for in their equinox ritual?

Had Corvin incorporated it into an empowerment ritual? He had promised to share some of his powers with the coven.

Or had it been brought by the wolves? What spell could they have performed? What had they hoped to achieve with the attack on the coven, and on Corvin in particular?

Gideon bent down and brushed the dried herbs from the flat stone of the altar to examine the symbols carved into it. They were rough under his fingertips.

His heart thudded hard in his chest.

The altar stone was broken in half.

He straightened and looked around, the rustling of the leaves again raising goosebumps on his skin. Who was there? Who had followed him? Or had someone already been there, waiting for him? Had someone or something known that he would be coming there?

It was not his first foray there. He had come to the temple grove regularly over the years but had not followed a predictable schedule. He did not want people to know when to expect him there. He came and went quietly without telling anyone of his visits. He would inform Corvin after he was gone, confirming that everything still appeared to be in order and they did not have anything to worry about.

No one could have known he was coming.

"Who's there?" he demanded, his voice cracking and sounding way too tentative for a warlock of his stature. "Show yourself."

No one spoke or moved. Was it all just in his imagination? Paranoia because of the attack and the broken altar? Just the rustling of the wind and night animals?

"*Appare et ostende te!*" he again commanded the intruder to show himself. But there was still no response, and Gideon did not want to use any magic against whoever was there with him.

It was, of course, against his covenants to use magic to harm a creature who had done nothing to him. He had no idea what kind of entity might be there with him. It could be a natural ally or someone who had no intention of interfering with what he was there to do.

Not to mention the possibility of triggering an attack on himself by a more powerful practitioner. As strong as his powers had once been, they were starting to wane. He had used much of his strength over the years in this task, even though the brunt of it was supposed to be borne by Corvin.

And last but not least, he was on sacred ground. The walls of the ancient temple might be long since gone, but its magic was still there. The temple existed there still, even if it had no physical form. Even without the rocks in the foundation that remained. For him to initiate an attack on these grounds might have serious consequences. Just as the wolves now faced the possibility of war with the warlock coven, as well as the witch's coven and several other organizations who had been offended by the attack on the warlocks and sworn retribution.

Gideon did not want to find himself in the same circumstances.

He stood there for a long time, his heart pounding hard in his ears, before he finally decided that the noises he was hearing were just the usual night sounds, like Gideon had heard every time he had come here before. The broken altar had spooked him, that was all.

He held his hands above the altar, beginning his incantation. The gem in the large ring on his finger began to heat and glow. He could feel the power of the words he spoke. He reached out, through the soil beneath his feat, to what he knew lay buried there.

A rumble sounded in the distance. At first, Gideon thought it was thunder, then realized the sky was clear, and it came not from above but from the ground. And it was growing. He could smell sulfur and felt a heaviness in the air. He had never experienced this reaction before. He raised his voice louder, growling out the words. His old hands shook. His breath came in shortened gasps.

The rumble grew into a crescendo, and the glow of the gem in his ring was extinguished.

PREVIEW CHAPTER 2

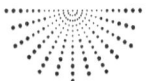

*W*hen Reg wandered out to the kitchen in response to her tuxedo cat Starlight's imperious meows and insistence that he would starve to death if she did not remedy the situation forthwith, she found a note on the coffee machine.

Sarah, the pleasant, gray-haired witch who rented her the guest cottage, knew very well that Reg could not function upon awakening until she'd had at least one cup of coffee. Preferably more. So it was a good place to put a note where Reg would see it as soon as she got up. Reg didn't generally look at the appointment book that lived on the island in the kitchen until later in the day when she was considerably more wide awake.

Come see me and Davyn in the house

Reg yawned and scrubbed at her eyes. She wasn't really ready for company. She needed coffee, a shower, and fresh clothing. And maybe an hour or two to get her engine running.

But she knew she wasn't going to get all of that. Sarah would expect her to be there right away, as soon as she was up. Sarah already thought Reg was a slacker for sleeping so late in the morning, regardless of how late Reg worked into the small hours of the morning.

"What do you think all this is about?" Reg asked Starlight as he noisily chowed down on the stew she'd found in the fridge. The stew that of course Sarah had intended for Reg to eat. "Sarah and Davyn… I hope this isn't anything to do with the werewolf-warlock war."

Starlight didn't even look up from his feast. Reg shook her head. "They aren't going to find October. He and the others knew well enough to get out of town. They won't be sticking around to face whatever the witches and warlocks have in store for them. Do you think that the warlocks and witches would try to track them? Like, into the wilderness?"

Starlight paused in his meal and glared at Reg with one green and one blue eye. She was bothering him with her chatter. He wasn't interested in the wars of humans. Or he already knew the answers to Reg's questions and didn't want to be bothered by her inane chatter.

But it helped Reg to work things out if she could say them out loud. And it helped to say things out loud if she had a cat, so people didn't think she was just crazy.

She had been talking to the voices in her head for years, but there was no need for the general populace to know that.

"It must be something else," Reg concluded. She hit the button on the coffee machine and waited like one of Pavlov's dogs, her mouth-watering, until her coffee cup began to fill.

Maybe she would only need one cup. Sarah would be bound to have coffee on. Or tea. And maybe some muffins or something suitable for breakfast, even if it was Sarah's lunchtime by now.

Starlight had finished eating his breakfast by the time Reg's cup of coffee was ready. He sat on the floor, licking his lips for a few minutes, then his front paws and face, then his back paws, one at a time, with his little bean toes spread wide apart.

Reg watched his ablutions as she took the first few swallows of her piping hot coffee, wincing at the burn. She'd better start her own morning routine if she were going to get over to Sarah's before it was officially afternoon.

* * *

With a fresh, long, colorful skirt and blouse on and her red box braids neatly arranged under a head scarf, Reg was ready to face the day. Or at least ready to face Sarah and Davyn. She gave Starlight a few scratches around his black ears, a quick kiss on the short fur on top of his head, and headed down the stone path across the yard from the guest house to the big house where Sarah was waiting.

Reg raised her hand to knock on the door, even though she knew Sarah always told her to just go right in.

"We're in the living room," Sarah called out before she had the chance to decide. "Come on in."

Sarah must have seen her coming up from the guest cottage. Reg opened the door and let herself in. She crossed through the kitchen and joined Sarah and Davyn at the front of the house.

Reg was relieved to see it was only Sarah and Davyn. She had been worried about finding a whole council or coven waiting for her.

Davyn was not quite as handsome as was Corvin, Reg's nemesis. He was leaner, his features sharper. Dark hair and eyes like Corvin, but clean-shaven. His youthful appearance gave no hint of his actual age, as the magical practitioners tended to look much younger than they really were.

But surely if it had been urgent or there were that many people waiting for her, Sarah would have woken Reg up instead of just leaving a note on the coffee maker.

"Hi," Reg smiled and greeted her mentor and her landlady. "What's going on?"

"Sit down and have some refreshments," Sarah invited.

Reg had been right with her prediction of tea. But with quarter sandwiches rather than muffins. It was apparently too late in the day for muffins. Already past noon, despite Reg's best intentions.

She sat down, chose a tea bag, and poured the steaming hot water from the teapot into her cup. Sarah must have just been in the kitchen pouring boiling water from the kettle. That was how she had seen Reg approaching the house. Reg picked out a couple of sandwiches that she hoped would not bother her stomach so early in the morn— in the day.

"So, are we just having tea? Or is there an occasion?"

"Well… there has been a very unfortunate development," Sarah admitted.

Reg tried to breathe through the immediate tightening of her stomach muscles and the twisting of her intestines. Something unfortunate? She hoped it wasn't something unfortunate to do with the werewolves. Especially not any of the cubs. She was very fond of the little furballs. She was sure that the witches and warlocks would not target puppies, but if they happened to get in the way when they went after October or one of the other wolves who had attacked Corvin's coven…

"What is it? What happened?"

Davyn and Sarah looked at each other as if measuring what to tell Reg. Surely they'd already had enough time to thoroughly discuss what to tell her.

"There was… an attack last night," Davyn said carefully.

"An incident," Sarah corrected.

Davyn looked at her but did not amend his statement.

"We don't know if he was attacked or… if something else happened," Sarah insisted.

"Who?" Reg asked. She didn't really care what they called it. She needed to find out what had happened and see what she was expected to do about it, if anything. She was supposed to be staying out of the way of the war, not taking sides.

"A warlock named Gideon," Davyn told her. "I know that you do not know him. He doesn't live in Black Sands. He has been away for many years. But he is known here."

"Where was he attacked? How did you hear about it?"

"In the Temple Orange Grove."

Reg put her hand over her mouth. The same place as Davyn, Corvin, and the rest of the coven had been when they had been attacked by the wolves.

"What happened?"

"That is a harder question to answer. He has been cursed…"

"Like Corvin?" Reg had seen Corvin several times since he had been attacked, and maybe understood his injury better than anyone else. Her psychic connection with Corvin meant that she could feel it when he tried to use his powers and was afflicted with excruciating pain.

He did not try to use his magic while she was there, but it was like a new paper cut or canker sore that was constantly irritated by incidental movements throughout the day. Corvin was not accustomed to functioning without magic and kept accessing his powers by accident.

Even just charming Reg, something that came to him so naturally he didn't even think of it, was enough to make him jolt and groan, and she could feel both his hunger and his pain.

Corvin was a power drinker, and unlike a regular warlock, he was cursed with a hunger for the powers and gifts of other magical practitioners. He could suck the powers from another person, but was required to abide by certain laws and pacts made by his ancestors, requiring that he only take them in exchange for something else of value, and that the victim had to yield to him voluntarily.

Those practices had been warped and twisted over time until the supposed rules that Corvin followed had become meaningless. He had stolen Reg's powers from her once, supposedly following the rules, but she had no clue that she had been agreeing to give them to him. He had returned them to her, something that was never done, in order to save her life. But he had tried to take them many times since, both by force and by utilizing his magical charms.

"Not like Corvin," Davyn said, recalling Reg to the conversation. "He was... turned into stone."

Reg stared at Davyn. "Turned into stone? Like he was frozen? Paralyzed?"

"More than that. He is actually stone. Like a statue. But no one knows who did this or why."

Sarah shook her head. "It is very strange. Who would do that? And in the Temple Orange Grove. All of these things happening at that sacred site..."

"All of these things? You mean the wolf attack? And now this petrification thing?"

"Yes. It is a special place. Many sacred rites have been performed there. The magic of the ancient temple still exists. That is why the warlock coven often meets there."

"I know," Reg agreed. She had been there only once, when she had been trying to find Davyn. She had been able to see the temple as it had once been, in shining silver and gold light that rose from the ground up into the air in ethereal beauty. It had been breathtaking, but she had been the only one able to see it.

"We are going to go over there to have a look," Davyn said. "See if we can find any clues of who did this terrible thing and why."

"Yeah," Reg nodded. "That makes sense."

They would want to put a stop to whatever was happening in the Temple Orange Grove to make it the center of an apparent outbreak of magical violence. Was it just a coincidence that Gideon had been attacked there after the attack by the werewolves on the coven? Was something attracting them there? Was there a connection between the attacks?

Reg didn't think there was any connection, but it was impossible to know without investigating. Corvin wasn't likely to tell her anything she didn't already know. From what she knew, October and the other wolves had attacked Corvin and the coven to stop Corvin from doing Reg or October any harm, as October had believed that he had harmed them in past lives.

But the person who had been guilty of those attacks had not been Corvin.

That didn't mean Corvin wasn't dangerous. Reg had wished many times that something could be done to make him stop hunting her. The banishment that he had received as a punishment for trying to take her powers from force had not prevented him from pursuing her again. And again, and again. It had proven not to be a deterrent at all.

But October's attack and the curse he had placed on Corvin had stopped Corvin cold, and Reg was grateful to him for that. Confused, because she no longer knew how to view Corvin or whether he would regain his abilities and overcome the curse. Confused because the charms that had drawn her to Corvin so many times in the past were gone, but she still found him attractive.

Sarah leaned forward, meeting Reg's eyes. "We thought you would like to come with us."

* * *

Spellbound Statues, Book #23 of the *Reg Rawlins, Psychic Investigator* series by P.D. Workman can be purchased at pdworkman.com

* * *

ABOUT THE AUTHOR

P.D. Workman is a USA Today Bestselling author and multi-award winner, renowned for her prolific output of over 100 published works that span various genres. With a knack for crafting page-turners, Workman captivates readers with everything from cozy mysteries like the Auntie Clem's Bakery series to gripping young adult and suspense novels.

Her stories resonate deeply as she masterfully weaves sensitive themes—such as childhood trauma, mental illness, and addiction—into compelling narratives that evoke a powerful emotional response. Readers are drawn to her unique voice and empathetic portrayal of complex issues.

With each new release, fans eagerly anticipate another thrilling blend of thought-provoking storytelling and relatable characters that define P.D. Workman's brand as an author of unforgettable page-turners—gripping tales that leave a lasting impact long after the last page is turned.

> P. D. Workman, does not shy from probing the deep psychological scars of childhood trauma, mental illness, and addiction. Also characteristic of this author, these extremely sensitive issues are explored with extensive empathy, described with incredible clarity, and portrayed with profound insight.
>
> — —KIM, GOODREADS REVIEWER

Some of Workman's titles have been translated into Spanish, French, Portuguese, German, and Italian.

Workman began writing at an early age and is a prolific reader as well as writer. She is also passionate about teaching and learning, expresses her creativity through art and cooking, and loves exploring the Calgary parks and green spaces where the Parks Pat Mysteries are set. She was a legal assistant for many years and has done extensive charitable work.

Workman was born and raised in Alberta, Canada, and is married with one adult son.

* * *

Please visit P.D. Workman at pdworkman.com to see what else she is working on, to join her mailing list, and to link to her social networks.

* * *

If you enjoyed this book, please take the time to recommend it to other purchasers with a review or star rating and share it with your friends!

tiktok.com/@pdworkmanauthor

facebook.com/pdworkmanauthor

x.com/pdworkmanauthor

instagram.com/pdworkmanauthor

amazon.com/author/pdworkman

bookbub.com/authors/p-d-workman

goodreads.com/pdworkman

linkedin.com/in/pdworkman

pinterest.com/pdworkmanauthor

youtube.com/pdworkman

patreon.com/pdworkmanauthor

reamstories.com/pdworkmanauthor

Find P.D. Workman's books at

PDWORKMAN.COM

Scan the QR code below